The Heartbreak List

Misti Murphy

Copyright © The Heartbreak List 2023 by Misti Murphy

All rights reserved.

No part of this publication may be reproduced, distributed, or transmitted in any form or by any means, including photocopying, recording, or other electronic or mechanical methods, without the prior written permission of the publisher, except as permitted by U.S. copyright law. For permission requests, contact mistimurphy@mistimurphy.com

The story, all names, characters, and incidents portrayed in this production are fictitious. No identification with actual persons (living or deceased), places, buildings, and products is intended or should be inferred.

Book Cover by Mayhem Cover Creations

Image by WANDER AGUIAR : PHOTOGRAPHY

"Grief is the price we pay for love."

Queen Elizabeth II

Chapter One

Indy

"I can't believe you're getting married in three months," my cousin America screams over the loud music playing in the club where we're celebrating my bachelorette night. "I hate that I'm not going to be here to help you organize everything."

I smile with the straw of my drink between my lips as I sip some incredibly alcoholic cocktail. We graduated college a week ago and all the pieces are falling into place. I landed my dream job and set a date with Gray for our wedding. America is heading to Cambridge. "You have a chance to study under the top linguistics professor in the UK. You have to go. Besides, you organized this party. And you'll be back the week of the wedding."

"Of course I will." She grabs my hand and bounces up and down in her pink heels. "I'm your best friend and maid of honor. You literally can't get married without me."

"Isn't it the groom I can't get married without?" I lift my hand to stare at the ring on my finger. It's a round cut solitaire on a plain gold band. Understated. Sensible. And exactly what I told Gray I wanted when we first started planning our future.

"As if Gray is going anywhere." America touches the gold hoop in her earlobe and turns her attention to our friends on the dance floor. They're easy to spot since they are all wearing pink. She tucks her arm into mine.

"Your perfect fiancé will become your perfect husband and you'll both go on to live your perfect life and have perfect little babies."

"That's the plan." Has been for as long as I can remember. Although my perfect husband-to-be wasn't always Grayson Ford.

It used to be Zac Efron. Actually, I still crush on Zac Efron. He's the kind of infatuation that gets better with age. But Gray has been my number one since I was fifteen-and-a-half, even though my brother's best friend didn't know about my crush on him until I was seventeen, and then waited until after my eighteenth birthday to ask me out on our first date.

"We should join the others." America starts to tug me toward the dance floor. "Let loose. You only celebrate being a bride once."

"I kind of need to pee." I put down my empty glass on the first table we pass then drag my arm free. The headache that I've been trying to shake all day is kicking it up a notch. I could do with a breather. "I'll be back in a few."

"If you're not I'll come looking for you." She continues toward the dance floor, disappearing into the crowd until all I can see is the back of her bouncing mop of corkscrew curls.

I veer off from the main crowd and into the hallway where the bathrooms are located. I massage my temples to ease the throbbing as I locate the right door.

It opens before I can put a hand on it and two girls come racing out in a fit of giggles.

"You might want to wait." One of them tells me over her shoulder before they round the corner.

I jiggle; the alcohol has gone straight through me, and I really need to pee. Maybe someone left the bathroom a mess and they're waiting for one of the employees to clean it up. It wouldn't be the first time some girl puked in a club stall after one too many.

Oh well, I really can't wait. I'm just going to have to hold my breath while I'm in there. Inhaling all the way to my toes, I push the door open an inch to check out what I'm dealing with.

The door moves much further than the inch I planned, and I'm left with my arm out and my hand angled with my fingers up, almost touching the man that fills the empty space. He's tall. Broad across the shoulders, tapering down into cheese grater abs that are… on full display. There are several bruises scattered on his torso. They range from fresh red to dark purple to faded yellow.

A leather jacket wears him well. It drapes like it was made to be worn by a rockstar but ended up on a god. One of war, based on the bruises. Or mischief, by the way his lips curl up. But his smirk has nothing on those eyes.

His eyes are… unique. I've never seen anyone with eyes like his. Except, perhaps on television. And even then… it would have nothing on the way this guy's eyes draw me in. One blue like the sky, the other a yin and yang swirl of chocolate and sapphire.

They're friendly. A little too friendly as his gaze falls over my all-white outfit and pink sash in a way that reminds me of one of those perfume commercials where luxurious silk glides over the woman's skin.

He has thick stubble on his jaw and upper lip like he hasn't bothered to shave for a few days, and dark brown hair falls in waves that almost meet his shoulders. I'm not really into long hair on men, but the strands are so glossy and look so soft that I want to touch it to see if it is that silky. Still, I stumble back to those eyes. Those orbs that must hook many women. Are they natural or—

"You should probably consider breathing at some point." He smiles wider.

His words infiltrate my head, which is fuzzy, from the alcohol and holding my breath for so long. I let out the oxygen I'd been containing, which is more like ninety-eight percent carbon dioxide at this point, and grow lightheaded.

I breathe in the pungent scent of musk and sweat.

A woman appears behind him. Her makeup is on point, and she fluffs her red hair like she wants it to look messy on purpose, so she's probably hiding how it got mussed in the first place. And her tiny black dress is still askew. She pushes it down her hips and thighs until it sits right.

They were having sex in the bathroom. That's what those girls were talking about. Am I surprised? Hardly. Am I curious about what it would be like to be that… spontaneous? Again, no. Gray and I aren't PDA type people. At least not to this degree.

"Wanna come dance?" The girl touches his broad shoulder.

His gaze is still glued to me. "No."

"Seriously?" She opens her purse and takes out a piece of gum that she pops in her mouth. "I thought you said we'd dance."

"That was before my girlfriend showed up." He doesn't miss a beat as he reaches out to tuck a strand of my hair behind my ear. "Sorry I kept you waiting, honey boo."

I roll my eyes at the awful pet name. Does he really think the apology will work, considering, if I were his girlfriend, he clearly thinks I won't care that he was screwing some random?

"Oh my God." She shoves him to the side so she can get by and looks down her nose at me. "You're welcome to him. A big dick isn't everything. Especially when he doesn't know how to use it."

He grins at me, all white teeth, as she totters away on tall black stilettos. "I have a big dick, in case you were wondering."

"I wasn't." I can barely suppress a laugh as the girl spins around and gives him two middle fingers before moving out of sight.

"I'm actually very skilled with it." He leans toward me like we're friends. In cahoots.

"I'm not interested in your dick. Imagined or real." I put my hand up to block his face when he gets too close. I'm not creeped out by him. He seems harmless enough. Truly a friendly drunk, even if he is technically loitering in the women's bathroom. The need to pee has kicked back in and I'm kinda desperate at this point. "Your fly is undone."

"Oh, will you look at that?" He glances down. Adjusting his junk, he pulls the zipper up and latches the button. "I must have been distracted. Don't know what could possibly have stolen my attention. But she must have been fucking pretty."

"Are you trying to flirt with me?" He's no Zac Efron. And while he probably doesn't need to be since he's balls-to-the-wall gorgeous, and genetics kicked it up a notch with those eyes, he's no Gray either. He's just some fuckboy with a few too many drinks under his belt and a more than healthy dose of ego that happens to be making me laugh, and I have better waiting for me. A man who is fully committed to our shared future.

"Yeah. Is it working?"

Not even a little. "I have a fiancé."

"Aw shit." He grins wider. "Of course you do."

"What's that supposed to mean?" I finally just go for it and squeeze between him and the door. It's either that or let pee trickle down my leg.

"You look like a bride." He shakes his head as I choose a cubicle. "This is your bachelorette party?"

Slipping inside, I shimmy my panties down my legs before I sit. The relief is instant. "Yeah."

"When are you getting married?"

"A few months. My best friend is moving to the UK, so we decided to throw the bachelorette party sooner rather than later." Are we really still having a conversation while I'm peeing?

"No strippers?"

"Unless I count you. With your lack of shirt." I smile sweet as pie even though he can't see me while I fix up my panties and flush.

He laughs. "Not a stripper. Though some nights I cut it mighty close. You should come see me, when you're not being a well-behaved bride-to-be. Bring your fiancé. Not here. I work at a different club, it's called Line 'Em Up. Come on a Friday."

"I don't think so." I move to the sink to wash my hands. There's an empty bottle of Jameson on the counter and a couple of small plastic bags with a lime green devil logo on them. Perhaps it's not only alcohol that has him so chatty. "It's not really our scene."

"You're right. Don't bring him." He stretches his arm out to block my path out of the bathroom. "He'll lose his shit when I dance with you. Then I'll have to stop him from hitting me while you burst into tears. After which you'll break up with him, because you're so attracted to me, and then I'll be forced to let you down hard because I'm not that guy. It'll be way too messy."

"Confident much?" I tip my head back and get lost. It's not his piercing stare that makes my skin tingle. It's not attraction that has my breath catching. And it's not his scent either. Perhaps it's this headache that is growing louder. "You don't truly believe that I would show up, do you?"

He licks his lips. "Come on. Live a little."

"I live." I give him my best glare. He doesn't need to hear that this is the first time I've been out dancing or to see a band or to have a drink in the three years I've been legal. I was too busy concentrating on my studies and my career. Getting engaged. Following the plan.

"Hmm." He makes an amused sound in his throat. "Is that so?"

"Yes." I jut out my chin to push my point.

"And yet you have been talking to me for the past five minutes. Even though you can't decide whether you like me, or you're just intrigued. Meanwhile, I bet you have friends waiting on you."

"That's not—" But I'm still standing here, talking to him. Why? What am I getting out of this? A thrill? "We're just talking."

"Is that what you call it? Do you talk to strangers in public toilets often, hmm?" He reaches out and touches my chin before dropping his hand back to his side. "If you ask me, you look bored."

"I didn't ask you."

"No, but may I make a suggestion?"

I side-eye him. He has an opinion. Oh, this is going to be good.

"Stash your panties in your purse and give that fiancé of yours the surprise of his life."

"I'm not going to take advice from you." Even if I'm filled with a sudden need to find out what Gray would do if my panties were in my handbag when he picked me up at the end of the night. "Because I'm not bored or boring. And neither is my relationship."

Talking to this guy certainly isn't the highlight of my night.

"I'd be happy to rescue you."

Is he for real? "I'm getting married."

He shrugs. "From your boredom then. Wanna get out of here? I know a great place to get pancakes."

Even if I wasn't getting married… "It's two in the morning."

"It's never too early for pancakes." He squints, his eyes lit with a twinkle. The kind that would get a girl into trouble if she were into that kind of thing.

"There you are." America grabs my arm and drags me away from the eyes. "I thought you'd gotten sick. You were taking forever."

"Sorry." I touch my engagement ring. It is as solid as ever. Gray is waiting to pick me up from our night out. And some guy who occasionally comes close to being a stripper and spouts motivational quotes like *live a little* is nothing but a cliff note. "I got stuck, talking."

America glances over her shoulder at the guy before raising both eyebrows. "Hmm. I can see why. Those eyes."

"And doesn't he know it?" I chuckle.

"I bet." She giggles as we bump against each other.

"Don't forget," he calls over his shoulder as he finally leaves.

"Don't forget what?" America hustles into the bathroom and checks her hair and makeup in the mirror over the sink. As late as it is, somehow she's still perfect, like a gorgeous Zendaya impersonator.

I glance after him, but he's gone by this point. I rub at my throbbing temples and my vision swims. "He thinks I don't know how to have a good time."

"Because you knocked his advances?" She wrinkles her nose, but then she turns her back to the counter and grins at me. "Or because you told him about how you've had every single part of your life planned out since you were fifteen? Bullet points and all."

"You're a jerk."

"I'm insulted." She presses a hand to her chest but her gaze lights up with amusement. "I'm your best jerk, thank you very much."

"I wish you weren't leaving me." I throw my arms around her.

She clings to me too. "It's only for a year."

"A year is too long when I've been used to you living right next door since we were born."

"You don't even live with your parents anymore. You're all the way across town." She laughs as we leave the bathroom. "I'll be back as often as I can. And we'll talk to each other every day."

"But it isn't the same. Who am I going to hang out with?"

"You could always hang out with that guy." She tips her head in the direction of the bathroom. "I bet Gray would love that."

"Yeah, he'd be thrilled." I laugh, yet I'm antsy. And it isn't entirely because my bestie called me out for being so goal-orientated. Or that some guy thinks he worked out who I am from a few minutes of dialogue. "I'll be right back."

"What are you doing?" America calls after me.

Slipping back into the bathroom, I hold the door closed with my hand while I reach under my dress and tug down my panties. Taking them off, I deposit them in my handbag and then text my fiancé to come and get me.

I can't wait to see how Gray reacts.

Chapter Two

Indy

"There's my beautiful fiancée." Gray spreads his arms and I wobble into them on the pavement outside the club as an old pickup truck roars out of the parking lot.

Head tucked under his chin, I fit perfectly against his sculpted chest. I slip my fingers under the hem of his T-shirt and move them to and fro over the fine trail of hair down the center of his torso. He smells like all of my favorite things. That is to say, he smells like Gray. I inhale the warmth and spice of his body heat. "I missed you."

He chuckles in my hair, his hand grasping and sliding along several locks. "Handsy, how much have you had to drink?"

"A couple." I curl my fingers into his waistband, stretch my fingers inside.

"Three," America says. "At most."

"Do you want a lift?" The vibration of Gray's voice against my head is comforting as he covers my hand with his to stop me from teasing him.

"No, you're in the other direction so I'll catch an Uber with Anna later." America glances back at the entrance to the club. "The other girls are staying, so I'm going to stick around. It's the last time I'll see them all for a while."

"I'll drop by the house tomorrow." I need to get as much time as I can with my bestie and cousin before she leaves. Plus there are still a few boxes of my belongings at my parents' house that I need to move to Gray's condo.

"See you tomorrow." America blows me a kiss on her way back into the club.

"I parked over there." Gray wraps his arm around my shoulders and ushers me toward the blue Tesla at the end of the parking lot.

Once we're inside the car, I relax back into the seat as Gray pulls out of the lot and into traffic. My head is really hurting. Probably because I stopped drinking and I'm dehydrated. *You're a little early, hangover.*

"Did you have a fun night?" Gray glances at me as the car hums along the road in the direction of his condo. "Get your one last hurrah?"

He chuckles at his joke, but I can't muster up the energy to laugh with this heaviness in my gut. Is this really the last time I'll act young and carefree and irresponsible? I snort under my breath. When have I ever been any of those things? I've always been the woman with the plan.

Why is that bothering me so much tonight? It's what I've always wanted. What I've worked for.

"Are you okay, Indy?" Gray glances over at me. "You seem a little quiet. Did you not enjoy yourself?"

"No, I did." I spread my hands out over my skirt and let the conversation drift off.

Gray and I are good like that. There are no awkward pauses. We don't constantly need to talk to be comfortable in each other's presence. He understands me better than anyone. Which is why I can't tell him that I'm weirdly restless tonight. He'll think I have cold feet. But it's not that. I've been planning our wedding since I was fifteen.

Perhaps I am boring.

But would a boring person ditch her panties? And then seduce her fiancé in the front seat of his Tesla? I cross and uncross my legs, letting my dress ride up a little in the process. "Hey, Gray?"

"Yeah, Indy?" He shoots another glance my way.

I press my teeth into my bottom lip. Nerves start in my belly. "I'm not wearing any panties."

His lips part and his pale blues grow hot in the light from the dash. "R-really?"

"Mmhmm." I spread my legs an inch.

"But you were wearing them when you left home." His brow draws lower while he darts glances between me and the road.

"I was." I trail my fingers over my cleavage in what I hope is a seductive move.

He licks his lips as he drops his gaze to my lap. "What happened to them?"

"I took them off." I twist in my seat so that I can lean across the console and plant a kiss on his stubbled jaw while I slide my hand down his chest and cover his growing erection with my hand.

"Jesus, Indy." He breathes quick and hard as he grinds up into my palm. "What are you playing at?"

"I want you." I take his earlobe between my teeth and suck it.

"Indy, I'm driving." His jaw hardens when I pop the button on his slacks so I can feed my hand into his boxer briefs. He takes one hand off the wheel and wraps it around my wrist. "Come on, babe. This is dangerous. We're almost home."

"You don't want me to put it in my mouth?" I ask sweetly.

He groans as his grip on my wrist loosens so that I can circle his cock with my fingers. "Of course I want you to put it in your mouth. But what if the cops..."

I kneel on my seat and bob down to suck on his hard-on.

"Oh, good God."

I smile around his girth as I move up and down the length.

"Indy, where is this coming from?" His fingers curl in my hair and reinforce the motion.

Spontaneous Indy is hitting the ground running. And Gray likes the surprise. A lot.

"Oh fuck." He's moving up and down in his seat as he pumps in and out of my mouth.

I twirl my tongue around the head and down the familiar ridge. Coming up, I push loose tendrils of my hair out of my face. "Touch me, Gray."

"Fucking hell, Indy. What has gotten into you?" His hand finds my knee and starts to glide up.

I stroke his hard length. "Do you like it?"

"It's different." He chuckles as his fingers skim my bare pussy. Then they're gone as he shouts, "Fuck."

Everything happens in slow motion. I lift my head from his cock as the tires squeal on the road a second before a huge bang is followed by the Tesla shuddering and screeching. My whole body is thrown forward, and then dragged back by the seatbelt. My head pinballs between the steering wheel and Gray's chest.

Excruciating pain is followed by a piercing sound in my ears.

"Indy. Oh God, Indy." Gray reaches for my shoulder as I slump on his lap. "Baby, stay with me."

My vision goes black.

I wake up in the hospital. It's pretty obviously a hospital by all the medical equipment everywhere and the IV in my arm. My neck and head hurt worse than anything I've ever felt before. When I reach up to touch my neck, my fingers meet hard plastic.

"Don't move, Indy." Gray rises from somewhere beside me. His blue eyes are full of worry and hurt as he hovers over me. One of his arms is in a sling and there's a wince when he breathes. Locating the button that will call the nurse, he presses it. "We were in a car accident. And they still need to run some tests."

"H-how long was I out?" I touch my temples. The pain is next level. Worse than any migraine I've ever had. Gray is kind of blurry. Like there are two of him.

"A couple of hours." He reaches for the water jug on the table beside the bed and pours some into a cup. "Thirsty?"

"A little." My throat is sore, but then everything is sore.

He adds a straw to the cup and then holds it so that I can sip the cold liquid. "Do you remember what happened?"

It hurts to try and concentrate, but my memory is okay. My stomach pangs and I grow uncomfortably warm. "I do."

Putting the cup down, he sits again. His cheeks hollow as he does. "What were you thinking, Indy?"

"That it might be exciting." I pluck at the blanket covering the lower half of my body. I'm wearing a blue hospital gown. "What happened to my clothes?"

"They needed to remove any metal you were wearing so they could put you in the MRI machine to make sure you hadn't done any real damage." He tsks in the back of his throat. "You've literally studied risk analysis for the past five years, babe. Why would you think it was a smart idea to do… that?"

"You enjoyed it," I whisper.

"Of course I did." He moves closer and sits on the bed. Reaching out, he lifts my chin. "I love everything you do. And everything about you. Including the fact that you don't take risks. Usually. What I don't understand is why?"

I shrug. "Can't I want to do something in the heat of the moment?"

"Yeah, of course." The fine lines around his eyes deepen. "But you don't, Indy. I can't recall the last time you did anything without some kind of plan behind it. One that you've thought through carefully and assessed the consequences."

"Sorry to interrupt." A doctor in scrubs and a white coat enters the room.

"That's okay." Gray straightens. "EJ and your parents are out in the waiting room. I'm going to go tell them that you're awake."

"I'm sorry." I reach for his hand and squeeze it. I didn't mean for us to end up in an accident or in the hospital. I didn't mean to make him worry.

He squeezes my fingertips as he exhales and then lets me go. "I'll be right back."

"How are you feeling?" The doctor approaches. He has kind eyes and a soothing voice.

"My head hurts." I press my fingers to my forehead, but it hurts everywhere. It's like my brain is trying to escape out of my eyes and ears and the base of my skull.

"I'd like to talk to you about that." I'd estimate the man to be in his late fifties, with silver through his black hair and beard. "I'm Doctor Lewis. I specialize in neurosurgery. You were having headaches prior to the accident. Is that right?"

"Sometimes." We were in a car accident. Why am I talking to a neurosurgeon?

"The reason that I ask is we found something on your MRI results that is concerning." His expression does not change as he speaks, but he watches me like he expects me to have a reaction.

"What do you mean, concerning?"

"Well..." He takes a deep breath. "Unfortunately, while we were making sure that there were no injuries from the accident we found a mass in your brain."

"A mass." My pulse starts to race and there's a shake in my hands. What is he talking about? Can't he just spit it out? "Like cancer?"

"A tumor," he corrects with a sympathetic tone. "We'll need to look at whether we can do a biopsy to see if it's malignant."

"You're telling me I have a tumor?" There's an invisible rock on my chest. With every breath the weight grows more and more crushing. Tears sting the back of my eyes. That always happens when I'm overwhelmed. When things don't go the way they're meant to. "And you're not sure if you can perform a biopsy?"

"A biopsy?" Gray stands in the doorway. His face is ashen, and he weaves a little while his gaze darts between my tear-stained face and the doctor's. He rushes to my side. "Indy? What's he talking about?"

"We found a brain tumor," the doctor says when I open my mouth and no words come out.

All of our plans, everything I've worked for... and I have a brain tumor. What the hell, universe? I was antsy about not having any more plans. I didn't need this curveball.

Gray blinks back the shine from his eyes. "So how are you going to treat it? What do we need to do?"

"Tumors in the brain have to be handled very carefully," the doctor says as my parents and brother EJ file into the room. He stops speaking as my mom starts to sob against the back of her hand.

"Go on," I tell him. Gray tightens his hold on my hand. I can barely see my mom through the tears that fill my eyes.

"We have the best neurosurgeon team in the country," the doctor says. "You're in the best hands here. We'll run every test. If it's possible to operate, we will. But if it's not, there are other options."

My breathing grows shallower. This isn't supposed to be happening. It can't be happening. "I didn't plan for this."

"No one does," the doctor says sympathetically.

"What other options?" My dad's voice is gruff as he steps in front of my mom and pulls her protectively to his side.

"There is radiation and chemotherapy," the doctor says. "There are some clinical trials available."

"Oh God." My mom rushes over, wrapping her arms around me and Gray. She sobs into my hair. "My baby."

EJ can barely make eye contact, but when he does he looks like he's going to vomit. "That's if it's cancer, right? What if it's not?"

"They can still be highly effective treatments," the doctor says.

"Gray?" My voice seems to be trying to desert me. "What are we going to do?"

"We're going to get through this, Indy." Gray holds on as tight as ever. "Whatever it takes."

Chapter Three

Theo

The dance music pumping in the nightclub down below fades away as I follow the gorgeous brunette through the stairwell. My skin is slick with sweat and my ribs ache from where I took a mean right hook during the fight, but that's not enough to weigh me down.

The brunette whose name has either escaped me, or I didn't ask for it in the first place, twists to face me with a giddy expression. "You ready?"

"Sure am, sweetheart." I swallow a mouthful of Jameson and pass the two-thirds empty bottle to her as I tug her back down a couple of steps. My lips find her collarbone and I give it a nip. "The question is, are you?"

She whimpers as she threads her hands into my hair and seeks out my lips. "I've always wanted to fuck on the roof of a high-rise. Do you think they'll be able to see it on satellite?"

"I'd count on it." I haul her ass up with one hand and grind against her while I kiss her dirtily. I can't get enough. The first impact. The chase. It's a total high.

She moans as her back hits the cement wall and her legs wrap around me. Her tiny leopard print dress rides up and exposes her ass and thighs. Glued together, we stumble the next few stairs to the roof access.

I have my jacket halfway off as we burst through the doorway and onto the roof. I finish shedding it and drop it on the ground to stop the door from being able to latch when I notice the broken brick. Someone else is already up here.

I drop the brunette to her feet on the concrete as I spot the woman standing on the raised ledge. She has both hands on the railing and strands of her coppery-brown hair fly loose in the wind.

"What did you do that for?" the brunette pouts.

Shit. Is she going to jump? "Hey."

The girl startles.

My stomach pitches. Fuck, I didn't mean to frighten her. That was so stupid.

"Oh my God." The brunette gasps behind me.

I gesture at her to stay where she is as I take deliberate strides across the rooftop toward the woman on the ledge. Not so slow I don't have a hope of reaching her, but not so fast it scares her into action.

"Hey." My heart is booming like a drum at how close to the edge she truly is, but I've already spooked her. I work to keep my voice as even and measured as possible. "You should get down from there."

She moves forward one bare-footed inch. Her legs are bare too, under a black suit jacket that is way too big and masculine for her slight frame. The railing isn't high enough to keep her from climbing it if she's determined enough.

I can't let that happen.

"Oh God, you have to help her," the brunette yells at me, her voice strained.

"I'm trying," I snap over my shoulder before focusing on the girl. I was having such a sweet night, riding the high of winning my match coupled with whisky and lust. Rescuing some chick with a death wish wasn't on my dance card for this evening. "Hey, what's your name?"

Her shoes have been discarded at the base of the ledge. Her knuckles are white from her grip on the railing. "Go away."

"I can't do that." I scratch the back of my head. I'm not sure what I'm supposed to do here. How I'm supposed to convince her to get down when things must be terrible for her to be up there in the first place. I'm the last person to say that things can get better when you hit that low point.

But things don't get worse once you're at rock bottom either. It's one consistent level of misery and shit.

"It's Indy." Her voice is thready and evaporates in the wind.

"Indy? That's a beautiful name." It's pretty and unusual and makes me think of blue summer skies. The kind that makes even the grumpiest person want to smile. "I'm Theo. Do you think you could come down from there?"

She sobs, shaking her head agitatedly. "I'm not going to jump."

"Well, Indy, that would be a lot easier to believe if you'd come down from there." I reach out and wrap a hand around her upper arm, but she has such a hold on the railing that she doesn't budge. Ripping her away from it would hurt her, but I'm inclined to do it anyway. If it becomes necessary. At least I have a grip on her. I'm not so freaked out that she could easily disappear from my sight and over the edge.

"You don't need to hold onto me." She turns her head enough that I can see the angle of her profile and the tears staining her cheek. "I needed to be alone. To think."

It's been a couple of weeks, but I haven't forgotten her face. Even if I was high on winning and E at the time. I'd been as close to at peace as I could get when she set her whisky colored gaze on me. When she'd held her breath for far longer than most people can. She'd been sexy in white too. Getting married. What happened between then and now for her to end up on this rooftop?

I swallow around the sudden burst of emotion that fills my throat. It's like a clog that grows and grows and grows around me, changing into quicksand that will drag me under if I let it. The urge to swig from the bottle of Jameson I handed off to the groupie is almost enough for me to leave the girl on the ledge. And I can't do that, so I shove my own issues aside. There'll be plenty of time to numb them later since they're never fucking far from the surface.

"You should leave," I tell the brunette who continues to hover.

The groupie tilts her head to the side. "What?"

"You heard my new friend. She wants to be alone. That means you gotta go." I can only focus on the girl on the ledge. She can yell at me or hit me. Whatever she needs to do. Until I'm sure she's safe.

The brunette pouts. "But I thought we were going to—"

"Fuck off," I growl at her.

"Fuck you," she screams back and then marches into the building, taking my Jameson with her.

"Yeah. Whatever." Damn it, she could have left the booze. I honestly don't give a fuck about some groupie who wants to fuck because she gets off on the fact that I flattened some guy earlier. Watching us beat the crap out of each other in the cage is an aphrodisiac to girls like her. And they're a dime a dozen. All it would take is marching back inside to find the next one.

I exhale to clear the tension that's settled in my muscles. The girl on the ledge is nothing like those girls. She's the kind of girl who needs more. She's the kind of girl who takes a guy's entire fucking heart and becomes his entire fucking world, so much so that he slides a rock on her finger and promises her forever. Only to find out that loving her forever doesn't include having her in his life. "If you're not planning on jumping, perhaps you could put me at ease and step down from there?"

"I told you I wanted to be alone," she says.

"Okay, time to get down." I wrap my hands around her waist and lift her off her feet.

"Put me down." She struggles against my grip as I haul her a few feet from the edge before letting her toes touch the roof proper. Bursting out of my arms, she whirls on me. Her finger jabs my chest before her eyes widen. "It's you."

"It's me." I stay still now that she's down. I don't need to hold onto her. I could tackle her before she made it to the railing again.

"You're the guy from the bathroom. The eyes."

"And you're the bride." Is she still the bride? Or are we on the rooftop because some asshole broke her heart? Point me at the guy; he and I need to have a few words about how the hell she ended up here alone. I push my hands into the pockets of my jeans to stop from making fists. "Or did he hurt you?"

"Gray could never hurt me." Her face slackens and her hand drops to her side. She shoots another longing glance at the skyline. "I wanted to imagine what it would be like."

"Okay, that's—"

"I wanted to pretend that I was in control. I wasn't going to jump." She turns those dark amber eyes on me again.

She seems so tiny in the suit jacket she holds tightly around her body. Her cheeks are hollowed. She's lost more weight than is healthy in the time since we last collided. The sparkle of happiness that had surrounded her that night is gone.

"I'm still getting married." She reaches up to push her hair out of her face and the jacket sleeve falls, revealing that ring still on her finger. It's simple and delicate.

"Good... right?" That means she's not heartbroken, at least. Not wondering how to go on without the love of her life, knowing that every single day is going to be spent pointlessly trying to keep from suffocating in quicksand. And then drowning in booze and pills and adrenaline to keep the ache at bay.

"It's supposed to be." She moves toward the edge again, and I grab her arm before she gets too far. Looking up at me, she sighs. "I'm going to collect my shoes."

"I'll get them." I leave her standing there while I snag her shoes, then draw her over to a picnic table someone brought up here. "Sit."

She takes a seat on the tabletop. I hand her the shoes before collecting my jacket from the doorway and making sure the brick is still stopping it from latching. Shrugging on the leather, I go back to her. "It isn't good?"

"Gray loves me." She bows her head and stares down at her lap. "If that's what you're asking."

"I..." scratch my jaw. A few days' growth pricks my fingers. I need to shave. "And you love... Gray?"

"Since I was eighteen." She adjusts the lapels of the jacket over her lap. "That's not... it's not about him. Or us. Or the wedding."

"Okay." I take a seat beside her and wait. Whatever she needs to say, whatever she needs to get out... I can sit here and wait and listen. Sometimes the only thing that helps is having someone who has an inkling of what you're going through to confide in when you're staring into that abyss.

She picks at the quick around short, oval nails but eventually wrings both hands together and places them in her lap. Her chest rises slowly and falls even slower. "I have a brain tumor. It's inoperable."

"Oh." There are no words. There is nothing that she would want to hear or that could help. A familiar ache swells in my chest. I shouldn't be on this roof. I shouldn't be the one she's talking to. But if I have to be here... if I have to be the one... then all I can do is listen.

"The doctors..." She sniffles. "They're putting me on radiation and chemotherapy. They keep using words like *staying optimistic* and *positive outcomes*."

"That's encouraging, right?" I hunker into my shoulders. "That means they have hope."

"It means they want me to have hope." She snorts softly under her breath as she shakes her head.

"Perhaps it's not as bad as it seems." I'm grasping at straws. She was on the ledge. Considering jumping. Of course it's bad. Her fiancé must be devastated. My jaw tightens at the hinge. He must be worried sick. Must be beside himself.

She giggles but it's strained.

Two weeks ago, she was so carefree. She'd smiled and laughed and talked absolute shit with me during our weird bathroom stare down. She's more reserved tonight.

"We're strangers." She wraps her hands around her ankles and hugs herself into a ball. "So you don't know that I graduated with a Master's degree in finance. That I'm supposed to start working at the biggest risk management firm in Chicago."

I stare at my hands. Rub one thumb over the joint of the other. "Sounds... interesting."

She sniffles as she wipes her cheeks. "I'm aware of what people think about my chosen profession. That calculating risk is boring."

"Well, I wasn't going to say anything." I cup the back of my neck and squeeze. "I'm a bartender five nights a week. There are people out there who think serving drinks isn't a career at all."

"Yeah." She expels an emotionally laden breath.

We fall silent and I consider trying to talk her into calling her fiancé. It's the least I should do. Make sure she gets off this roof. Gets home safe. And I'll pick up another groupie and another bottle of Jameson on my way out. But I don't do any of it. I don't even bring it up. "So you calculated the risk, huh? On the tumor?"

"I'm not the kind of person who likes not knowing." She drags the tendril of hair that's fallen over her face back behind her ear. "I've spent my life planning my dream future. From the career in risk management to getting engaged to the right guy and planning a picture-perfect wedding. I've even picked out the neighborhood we'll live in. The school our two children will go to. What kind of dog we'll have."

"And your fiancé... he's on board?" I nudge her gently.

"Of course he is." Her tone is sharp, but then she puts her head in her hand and groans. "Does it even matter that we're on the same page when there is no future? I planned my entire freaking life, but I didn't factor in dying at twenty-five. And there is nothing I can do. Everything is... out of my hands. I have six months, maybe. I've spent my whole life preparing for a future that I won't ever get to experience."

"Hey. Hang on." I gingerly put my hand on her back in an attempt to comfort. I don't want to scare her if she doesn't like touch, though. "You know the statistics. And that's smart."

"It's scary."

"That too. But it's not everything, Indy. Sometimes statistics don't matter half as much as we think they do." Sometimes we're the outlier. "Otherwise, my life would be completely different."

"W-what do you mean?"

"Nothing." I grit my teeth. "All I'm saying it that perhaps you're the statistical exception."

"I want to believe that." She wraps her arms around herself and starts to rock. "I have so many things that I want to do that I haven't accomplished. Some of them didn't even matter until I realized I would never…" She starts to cry.

We sit on that picnic table for a long time, side-by-side, while she cries. Grief never gets easier. I don't think it matters whether you're grieving for yourself or someone else. It hurts everyone it touches.

Eventually she wipes the wetness from her cheeks. Sniffs. "I'm sorry. I ruined your night."

Oh God. She thinks she ruined my night? I haven't had a decent night in three years. It's all a distraction at this point. "Don't even worry about it."

"But I did ruin it."

"Nah." I stand and then step down from the seat while I card a hand through my hair. "Besides, rescuing a damsel in distress was on my bucket list."

"Your bucket list?" She tips her head to one side.

"It doesn't matter." I hold out a hand to her. "Let's get you home."

With her hand tucked into mine, I lead her back inside the building. We bypass the club where the music is still pumping, and step over a drunk on our way down to the ground floor. Shoving open the exit door, I draw her onto the pavement and start looking for a cab.

It takes a few minutes until one crosses our path, and I step out and hail the driver. When it pulls up to the curb, I open the door and safely stow her inside. I don't follow her in, though the urge to see her to her door is strong. Her fiancé probably wouldn't appreciate that, despite my best intentions and her adventure tonight. Still… it makes me fidgety to walk away. "Are you going to be okay from here?"

She rearranges the sides of the jacket over her lap. "Yeah. I really wasn't going to jump. I just…"

"I get it."

She smiles softly. "Thanks for listening to me. Thanks… for everything."

"You're welcome." I step back and close the door. Tap the roof once I'm clear and shove my hands in my pockets as the car departs. I get the strong sense that I'll never see Indy again, and while that's probably for the best, I can't help feeling like she'll stick in my thoughts for a long time to come.

Chapter Four

Indy

Heels in one hand, I shut the door to the condo as slowly and as quietly as I can. It's way past midnight, and my phone was dead when I pulled it out in the cab. It shouldn't have been, but I ignored a lot of calls while I was up on that ledge.

The latch clicks into place with the volume of a child tattling in the otherwise silent room. It makes me jump and my shoulders climb to my ears. My heels fall to the floor with a *thud, thud*. Damn it, there's no way I didn't wake up Gray.

The light overhead switches on. "Indy?"

I grimace as my eyes adjust to the light. "Sorry, Gray. I didn't mean to wake you."

"Wake me?" He's gorgeous in black sweatpants and not a stitch else. His blond hair looks like he's put his fingers through it a lot. It's furrowed back and forth into clumps that stand on end. He drinks me in before he drags a hand up over his face. "Wake me? I haven't slept. Do you have any clue what time it is?"

"Uh, well..." I glance at the clock on the wall. It's nearly four. In the morning. Shit. "I didn't realize."

"Where were you?" He marches across the room and wraps his hands around my upper arms. He's not rough, but there's tension in his muscles.

In his jaw. His palms slide down my arms. "Do you have any idea how worried I was? How worried we all were?"

"I'm sorry." I reach up to shove my hair back. I am sorry, and that's not enough, but it's all I have. I've never walked out on family dinner before. Never not answered my phone for hours. But everyone was looking at me with those long faces.

Gray and my mom were talking about the new treatments that she's been researching on Google. And EJ was so quiet and wouldn't look at me at all. My dad kept having to leave the room to pull himself together.

I couldn't breathe. It hurt too much. And when my mom started telling Gray about how much success one of the trials had been having and that I could be well on my way to recovery in time for our wedding, I couldn't stand it anymore.

We were all in that hospital room when they gave me my prognosis. The chances of anything working for me are too slim to grasp onto. Gray is going to lose me. My family is going to have to say goodbye. Everything is crumbling around me, and I can't even confide in my best friend because America is in the UK. I didn't have the heart to tell her about the tumor. She would have stayed, and I couldn't let her lose her future alone with mine.

So I made my parents promise not to tell anyone. Not America or my aunt and uncle. Not yet. Not until I work out how to keep her from feeling guilty about being away.

I have never felt so out of control.

"You're sick, baby. What if something had happened to you?" His posture is rigid and his neck cords when he bunches his jaw. "What if you took a turn?"

"I didn't." I take his jaw in my fingertips. "I needed to be alone. I needed time to think. Nothing happened."

I don't tell him that I stood on top of the building where my dad used to have his office, where when I was a kid I used to daydream about what my life would be, wondering what it would be like to take my fate in my own hands. Like deciding the time and the destination is a choice I have the power to make.

I don't tell him because he'll think I was going to jump the way Theo did when he stumbled upon me tonight. Not that it was ever an option. I don't want my life to end in six months let alone now.

Gray will worry even more, if I try to explain. Become that much more protective. He'll want to hear all about Theo too, and I have no explanation for why I spent my night opening up to a stranger instead of him.

"But something could have happened." He draws breath and releases it. "You could have been hurt, Indy. And I can't bear it."

His shoulders start to shake with tiny tremors as he drags me into his embrace. He engulfs me, his body collapsing around mine. He's trying so hard to convince us both that things aren't as bad as they are, but deep down he knows that he's going to lose me. At some point he'll have to accept it. And so will I. Somehow.

Tears fill my eyes. They do that a lot these days. No matter how much I tell myself that I won't cry again… or that I'm stronger than that… they spring up more times a day than can possibly be healthy.

It's grief and loss and pain. It's everything we'll never get to be, and I'm not yet to the point where anger has overtaken the ache, though I feel that multiple times a day also. I want to rage at the unfairness. Instead I cry for the love that will be lost and the future we were supposed to have.

He'll be a widow within months of our marriage. Alone and trying to pick up the pieces.

I'm not sure at this point it's even fair to go through with it, but every time I start to bring it up, he moves the conversation to the venue, or the guest list, or the officiant, or the menu. So that we're still steadily progressing toward a day that should be the happiest of our lives. And I can't find the words to tear it all down. How many times will I break his heart before I'm gone?

"I'm here, Gray." I can barely get the words out through the thickness in my throat. I'm here for as long as I have left. I seek out his lips and he claims my mouth with a desperation that wraps like a string around my heart, drawing more pain to the surface.

His fingers dig into my hair as his tongue sweeps wetly over mine, and all I can taste is the salt of our sadness. In the way our mouths move and then on his skin as his lips press to my collarbone and mine glaze his shoulder.

He shoves his suit jacket from my shoulders. It's the same one he was wearing when we went to dinner tonight. The one I tossed on in a hurry right before I raced out the front door of my parents' house and into the back seat of an Uber. It pools around my elbows while he kisses me, while he slides his big hands over my hips and down to my ass to lift me up and press me against him. "Indy, I need you."

"I need you too." It's been weeks since he's touched me. Weeks since the ill-handled blow job and the car crash that turned out to be the tip of this fucked up iceberg we've hurtled into.

Weeks since he planted me on any flat surface—this side table for instance—parted my thighs and stepped between them to kiss me like he'll never get enough. That certain something curls in my belly and soaks my panties.

Every word, every look, every touch has been loaded with fear. Until I felt like I would scream if I spent one more moment with him treating me like I'm breakable. I am breakable. I am dying. But God, I don't want to live that way for however long I have left. I don't want that to be who he remembers. I don't want that to be who anyone remembers.

He has me out of that jacket in a matter of seconds. I have the tie on his sweatpants unraveled too. Digging my hand past the waistband, I wrap it around the hardness I find there. He groans against my mouth as he tenses all over.

"Indy, fuck." He reaches between us to grasp my wrist. "That feels nice, but there's something I need more. You in my mouth. On my tongue. It's been weeks and—"

"I need that too." My heart thuds and my pulse races as I hold onto Gray's shoulders while he helps me out of my underwear. Then he drops to his knees in front of me. His gray-blue gaze is hazy. His pupils are heavy and make the blue dark.

I jolt as my mind throws up an image of Theo. Of him looking up at me tonight on the ledge. His irises dark with the lack of light. One blue eye. One a swirl of brown and blue.

"Indy, you okay?" One of Gray's hands covers my knee, the other is on my thigh. He can tell I went somewhere.

He'd never suspect that it was to thinking of another man. A man who listened to me and didn't attempt to make it all better. A man who somehow got that what I needed was the quiet companionship of a stranger while my world falls apart. There's nothing sexual or sensual about my thoughts. Even if the timing is terrible.

I shove Theo out of my head. I'll never see him again. It was pure coincidence that we ended up crossing paths tonight. I spread my thighs wider for Gray. "Yeah."

"You sure?" He studies me like he's preparing for the worst. He starts to withdraw the hand on my thigh.

"I'm sure." I catch his hand and slide it higher. Press it to the spot where I'm wet and aching for him. "Gray, make me come."

His finger traces my seam lightly before digging in. His lips form a seal around my clit, and I incline back to get the angle better. The back of my skull bumps the wall as he loves me with his tongue. Burrowing my fingers into his hair, I lean into the sweet torture and embrace the feeling of being alive as he gives me an orgasm.

When it's over, when he's done bringing me down the same way he took me up and over the edge, he rises to his feet and carries me into the bedroom. He lowers me until my toes sink into the plush carpet, and then pulls down the zipper on the back of my dress before helping me out of it and my bra.

He sheds his sweatpants as I lie on the bed. Climbs onto the mattress beside me, and switches off the lamp, plunging the room into darkness.

"Gray?" I reach out for him.

"You're tired." He turns me onto my side in his arms.

"I thought we were going to have sex." I want to have sex. I need him. Need the connection.

"You're tired and you need all of your strength to fight for me, baby." He kisses my cheek. Kisses my hair. "We're starting chemo tomorrow, remember? Radiation next week?"

"Oh." But won't that make me feel worse? The doctor ran us through the side effects after he dashed any hope that I would be suitable for surgery. Nausea and tiredness and my hair might fall out. Vomiting and headaches too. Like I don't have enough headaches as it is. Wouldn't it make sense to have sex while I still have the energy? "I'm not that tired."

"It's four in the morning, Indy," he reminds me as he wraps my arms to my chest with his own. "And I need you at your best. I need you..."

His pain rolls down the strong lines of his nose and jaw and drips slickly onto my skin.

What can I possibly say to him to stop him from hurting? Everything is such a fucking mess.

He swallows thickly. Presses his lips to the spot where his tears dry on my shoulder. "I love you, baby. Let's get some sleep."

Neither of us falls asleep. Not until the sky goes from inky to charcoal and the sun is almost breaking the horizon. But we don't talk either. It's too much. Too hard.

Gray's breath finally grows soft and deep and slow. It's rhythmic and comforting. How many times have I fallen asleep in his arms believing we would have forever? That we'd get married and move close to my parents. He'd continue to rep his clients from his home office in between trips out of state while I'd work my way up at RAM. And then we'd have our first child. A little boy with my eyes and his nose.

My heart cracks down the middle all over again. That isn't my future anymore. I'll never be a mother, and we won't buy that house with the home office.

I climb out of bed when Gray rolls onto his back. Grab one of his T-shirts and slip it on as I leave the bedroom. How can I sleep when I'm running on limited time? How can I dwell on a future I will never see? Gray wants to pretend that this is only a speed bump because it hurts too much to be realistic, but I can't do that. I don't have the luxury of time anymore.

In the kitchen I fill a glass with OJ and grab the chunky knitted throw from the couch on my way out onto the balcony. It's cold and quiet, and I wrap the shawl around my shoulders.

A few cars move down below. People on the early shift or perhaps they're coming home late. Are they moving on autopilot? Do they have any idea how quickly everything can change? I hope not.

I tuck my feet up under me on the padded cocoon chair with the fern wall at my back. The sun is sliding over the horizon, pushing back the gray as it rises. It has those soft wavy edges as it kisses everything with a promising glow.

Standing on that ledge tonight...I wanted...to feel alive. If I have a finite amount of time, I want every minute to count. I'll do the therapies and the medicines like Gray and my family want me to do. I'll try to get better. But I need to live too. Experience things. Enough for a lifetime.

What was it that Theo said last night? That rescuing a damsel in distress was on his bucket list.

I put my empty glass on the small table beside me and pick up the notepad and pencil Gray keeps there. Flipping through to a fresh page, I write down three words...

My Bucket List.

Chapter Five

Theo

Standing behind the barriers at the bottom of the rock wall, I crane my neck. Pez crawls up the face with nothing but climbing shoes, shorts, and extreme confidence. He barely pauses to dig his hands into the chalk bag slung from the belt around his waist as he focuses on beating the previous competitor's time.

My friend acts like he has a death wish, but he climbs like he's Spider-man. A few months ago he had a serious accident and that didn't stop him. It didn't even slow him down. Once he was cleared to climb, he was back at it. Without ropes or harnesses or any sense of caution. But he has this intuitive ability to read the veins and cracks and grit in front of him before he ever lays a hand on it.

Indoor climbing is practically a walk in the park for him, and he makes speed climbing look like an artform as he moves fluidly up the face without fear or apparent thought.

My sister Shae would call it an ADHD skill. That Pez has the data sets from hundreds of climbs under his belt and can use each and every one of them to analyze which path will take him to the top with ease and which will lead to certain death. And he can do it far faster than most people.

His girlfriend Ramzi watches from close by. As usual her gaze is glued to him, and she looks like her heart is in her mouth. She's seen him fall before. Seen him break bones. I can imagine each time he climbs un-roped she freaks out a little. Wonders if it will be the last time.

Pez doesn't have those data sets when it comes to Ramzi, and that girl has a lot of issues. It took them a long time to get together, and it almost ended before it could really begin. They're both seeing a therapist to help them find their path together.

Sometimes I wonder whether I should talk to a therapist about what the hell is wrong with me. But I don't think some shrink in an office with a couch and notepad is ready for the level of fucked up I have going on.

I couldn't be in love like Pez and Ramzi. Not even with therapy. I was once, and that was enough. I learned who I am and what I'm capable of. And love—perfect, white dresses and picket fences love—isn't on that list. Life is too short for monotony and monogamy.

Life is simply too fucking short.

I picture Indy on that rooftop. I picture the bad fit of her jacket swamping her, and the copper tones in her hair. She'd felt brittle when I put my hands around her waist to lift her off the ledge.

I shouldn't be thinking about her. It's pointless. Even if she wasn't dying, she has a fiancé. Even if she didn't have a fiancé she'd still be dying. And if neither of those things were true, she'd still be the type of girl who wants more than I ever was willing to offer her that night in the club restroom. But she's been in my thoughts more than I care to admit to. Is she in good spirits? Is the radiation helping? Is she sleeping at all? Or does she replay our conversation on the rooftop to herself in the middle of the night like I do?

Because honestly, I can't stop thinking about her belief in statistics. If they're truly the big picture, then I should have syphilis. I should be in jail. I should be dead. I am neither dead nor in jail, and thanks to routine bloodwork I know I don't have syphilis. Or any other nasties.

But she's certain she's dying. Six months. No future. And what did I say? Something stupidly vague about statistics not meaning much.

Lucas, one of the other bartenders at Line 'Em Up, joins me. He has his neck craned all the way back and he's following Pez's path the same as I am. "He has some balls on him, that's for sure."

"Giant, hairy ones." I grin as Pez reaches the top. I push away thoughts of Indy. All that's left is for Pez to come back down, and he attacks that with the same vigor as his ascension.

"Want to grab a burger on the way to the bar?" Lucas rubs a hand over his taut stomach. "I'm famished."

"I could do with something juicy and pink between my teeth." I smirk when he makes that face. The one that says he thinks I'm a manwhore.

He isn't wrong, but sometimes I like to lay it on a little thick to offend his sensibilities. The guy has a white picket fence and a St. Bernard, for fuck's sake, but hasn't dated a single woman, or man, in the time that we've been working together. Hasn't even had a one-nighter as far as I'm aware. "I'll find out if Pez and Ramzi want to join us."

Pez is almost on the ground already, and Ramzi is moving through the crowd toward him. As his feet hit the mat, she throws both arms around him. He takes her face in his hands and kisses her before they walk toward me together, both sporting big goofy grins. Pez has his arm slung around her shoulder and she holds onto his hand as though keeping it in place.

"We're going to grab burgers on the way to work." I point at Lucas over my shoulder. "You want to join us?"

Pez glances down at Ramzi and shakes his head. "Sorry, man. We need to go home and check on the cat. The little shithead likes to break our things when we're not around."

"Plus, you stink." Ramzi lays a hand on his chest and leans in to inhale. "You should really shower before you go to work."

She doesn't give one single fuck that he's sweaty. Well, actually... "Fine. You two go home and have sex."

I chuckle inwardly as I walk away, and they half-heartedly attempt to deny the obvious. They can't keep their hands to themselves, which is exactly how it should be.

Lucas raises an eyebrow as I get to him.

"They have better things to do." I drag my keys from my pocket. "I've got my truck."

Thirty-five minutes later we've parked the truck in the parking lot at the bar and walked the few blocks to Burgasms to pick up lunch.

We're walking back when I spot a familiar profile through the storefront window of a narrow bookshop. Her head is bowed over the book in her hands. Her brown hair is tied up in a ponytail and her denim shorts are too big for her, held up with a navy scarf she's knotted in a bow. She looks tired as she pulls the side of the striped cardigan around her with a shiver.

"Do you know her?" Lucas's gruff voice reminds me that he's there.

"We've met." I step back from the building. I didn't realize I'd gotten so close. Like a kid with his nose up against the window of a candy shop. Seeing her takes the edge off my thoughts.

"Do you want to say hello? I'll open the bar."

"No." I spin away from the window as she moves between tables. I'm already thinking too much about her. Already too invested in her future. What comes next? Making friends? Hanging out? Giving a fuck? "We should go."

I barely make it three steps before she walks out onto the pavement in front of me. Karma might as well be waving a giant middle finger at me.

Her smoke and honey eyes widen. "Theo?"

"This one knows your name?" Lucas snorts behind me like he almost can't believe it.

It's easy to ignore Lucas when Indy laughs. She beams at him over my shoulder and her face lights up. "That's because he isn't trying to fuck me."

Lucas chokes and then covers it up with a cough. When he can get himself under control, he holds out a hand. "I'm Lucas."

She places her hand in his. "Indy. It's nice to meet you."

I'm happy to be the butt of their joke. I'm glad to see her looking more cheerful. Even if she's lost more weight and those shadows under her eyes are darker. Even if the light fades too quickly, softens into something duller that Lucas either politely ignores or doesn't catch.

"Is that an engagement ring?" Lucas narrows in on the diamond on her finger.

She steals her hand back and pushes that one stubborn strand back from her face while the sun glints on the threads of copper in her hair. She smiles softly. "It is."

"Your fiancé must be one lucky man." Lucas straightens and smiles right back at her.

Now he can talk to a woman? When she's not a threat to his solitary existence?

She darts a pleading glance my way as she brings the book to her abdomen and holds it there like a shield. *1001 Things To Do Before You Die.* Her eyes brighten. "H-he—"

"Can you open the bar?" I shove the sack with my food in it at Lucas's chest. Indy doesn't need to get stuck in an awkward conversation about whether her fiancé is lucky that his soon-to-be-wife is dying. "Do you have time for a coffee?"

"I..." She digs in her purse for her phone and lights up the screen. "I have time."

We leave Lucas to go to the bar and head off in the opposite direction. She keeps her book close while we walk.

"There's a bakery up here." I indicate the direction we should go. "One that serves baked treats in the shape of naughty body parts, but that's not why we're going there."

"It isn't?" She raises an eyebrow at me and then she laughs. And it's almost as carefree as that first night at the club. Like we're friends. Like we've known each other a long time and this is who we have always been.

"The coffee is the best around. And you look like you could use a break. Was it Lucas's dumb question or are you not feeling well?"

"A little of both," she says as I usher her into a building where all the bricks have been painted a deep, bright blue.

Inside, the walls are striped white and pink along the top half, while the bottom half is a deep raspberry color. White tables and chairs fill most of the space and cases full of exquisitely pornographic cupcakes are on display behind them.

A guy in his early twenties leans against the counter beside the coffee machine. He's reading a magazine but looks up when we enter.

"Okay, why don't you take a seat and I'll order the drinks?" I gesture at the closest table then pull out a chair so that she can sit. "How do you like your coffee?"

"Actually." She puts the book on the table but goes straight back to touching her belly. "I'll have water. With ice if possible."

"Do you want anything else? A boob cupcake? A dick cake pop? I hear cock and carbs are a girl's best friend."

She laughs and eyes the display case like she's considering. But then she sinks back in the chair. "I can't. Gray found all these articles about how fasting while doing chemo can help tumors shrink faster and protect healthy cells... He brought it up with the doctor and he figured it couldn't hurt to try... so we're doing that. I'm starving and I miss food, but Gray will miss me more, so I don't have the heart to tell him that I want a damn pastry."

I order a coffee for me and an ice water for Indy, then pick out a few cupcakes for the guys at the bar. And then I pick out one for Indy to take home with her because she has to eat some time. And surely her fiancé wouldn't begrudge her the creamy sweetness of a chocolate dick pop.

Taking the boxes back to the table I hand her the single cake. "Taste test for your wedding cake."

"We've ordered with St. Pierre." She flips open the box and blushes when she sees what is inside. "But thank you."

"St. Pierre, huh? The man is a legend."

"He's talented," she says.

"He's a pastry chef god. Sometimes when I can't sleep, I binge his show on TV. But he's no Dolly and her *pink bits* cakes." I stretch out one finger and push the box another inch toward her. "You only get to lick the cream out of a dick pop once."

"I'll take it home." She stows the box in her bag. "Thank you."

I settle back in my chair. Link my hands together in my lap and stretch out my legs. "So how are you going with treatment?"

"Uh... not great." Her face grows pinched. "I'm on chemo pills. Then there's the drugs to suppress the tumor's growth, and the drugs that will hopefully shrink it. The drugs to help with the nausea, and the ones that help with the pain. I practically rattle when I walk, and I'm exhausted all the time. I'm so sick most of the time that I don't even care that I don't eat."

Her interest swings to the other pink box still on the table between us, and I can't quite believe, even with the constant unsettled stomach, that she wants to ditch food to make her fiancé happy.

"You're not wearing your leather jacket." She runs her gaze over my torso and heat creeps up my neck. "But you are wearing a shirt. I honestly suspected you didn't own any."

I pluck at the lightweight cotton, stretching it in the process. It has the logo of the bar on it. "Work uniform. No doubt, I'll lose it later."

"Another night of debauchery?" Her eyes light up with amusement.

Our drinks come. Mine scalding, bitter, and extra strong because I have a long shift ahead of me. Hers, tinkling in the glass when she stirs it with a straw.

I frown at my cup. "Distracting myself."

"I'm sorry." She plays with that ring on her finger. It twirls, it's so loose. Does she worry that she'll lose her engagement ring? That it will slip off when she isn't paying attention? "I shouldn't have asked. It's none of my business."

I could explain to her how I stumbled into underground fighting when I first moved to the city. I could tell her that I couldn't sleep, or eat, or breathe and that I was in constant fucking agony. That I found getting in the cage and lashing out was the one thing that curbed my anger and my pain. That it numbed me enough to function like a robot.

I could tell her that the girls that came with it became a drug. That for a little while each night I get lost in the chase. That coupled with the booze and the drugs, I can pretend that I'm somewhere else until the past all comes crushing down on me.

But then she'd worry about Gray, and what he'll do when she's gone, and he can't bear the pain. She thinks I have no regrets, when all I have are regrets. "What does Gray do?"

"He's a sports agent. He reps a couple of the Rockets."

"Fucking hockey players?" I sit up straighter. "Are you serious? That's what he does for a living? Dream job, right there."

She nods. "It's definitely his. Is that what you'd want to do if you weren't tending bar?"

"I actually love tending bar. It's therapy and a party rolled into one. Well, for the people who come into the bar it can be like therapy. I've heard some amazing stories and sent many a poor man home to make up with his girl." I rest my elbows on the table and lean closer.

"You're certainly a good listener." She glances down at her lap and her pale cheeks gain some color. "Thank you for the other night."

"You don't need to blush." I pick up my coffee, which is no longer so hot it could burn the hairs out of a Yeti's nostril. "All I did was listen."

"It's embarrassing." She rubs at her nose and moans low in her throat. "I was a mess."

I reach across the table and tip her chin up so that our gazes lock. I'm uncomfortably aware that I'm touching her, and I shouldn't be. It prickles in my ribcage with every breath. "You were going through your darkest hour, and you needed a friend. I was there."

Her eyes grow bright as I sit back. She blinks back the emotions and rubs her lips together. "Are we friends, Theo? Is that what we are?"

"Do you want us to be friends, Indy?" I brush my thumb over a nick in the table. If I do it enough times, perhaps I'll be able to rub it out of existence. And perhaps if I agree to be friends with the dying girl, I won't wonder how she's doing all the time.

"I'd like that." She smiles. "But I'm afraid you'll be the one getting the bum end of this friendship."

"What? Because you're more than likely going to die soon?" I could try to sugar coat things, but I don't believe Indy would appreciate it.

"I probably only have six months. Maybe less."

"I'm aware."

"You'll miss me when I'm gone." Her gaze is playful but brittle.

"There's a chance that I'll think about you from time to time." But I'm already doing that, and this isn't my first foray into losing someone. I can handle it if all the radiation and drugs doesn't change her prognosis. It's not like it'll destroy my entire world.

Her phone rings and she digs through her bag in search of it. She dumps the cupcake, and the book she bought, and a notepad on the table before she finally finds her phone. She manages to answer it before whoever is on the other end hangs up. "Hey, Mom."

She turns in her chair so that she's angled away from me as she speaks to the other woman. "I'm sorry. I didn't mean to make you worry."

I pick up the notepad she tossed out on the table. The top page is titled "My Bucket List" and has been numbered. So far there isn't much on it.

1. *Get a tattoo.*

2. *Dye my hair a crazy color.*

3. *Visit an adult store.*

"I ran into a friend," she tells her mom. "I'm on my way now."

"What's this?" I hold the notepad out of reach as she stands and starts gathering her stuff.

"It was what you said the other night. About how rescuing a damsel in distress was on your bucket list..." She snatches it out of my hand and tosses it into her bag.

"Shit, I didn't mean that." There's no way I would ever willingly go out of my way to find a woman in need of a rescue to check it off like an accomplishment. "It's one of those things people say..."

"Yes, I understand that." She pulls the strap of her bag over her shoulder as I rise to my feet. "The future that I thought I would have is... over. But there are still things that I want to do. Experiences I want to have. So I started a bucket list. I spent so long living for my future, I need to spend whatever time I have left living in the now. Doing everything I put off or thought didn't fit."

"When do we start?" I ask.

Her expression slackens. "Start?"

"Marking things off your list. You're going to need a friend to help you come up with awesome once in a lifetime experiences, and to be there while you get that tattoo, right?"

"You'd go with me?"

"Yeah, of course. Let me give you my number." I hold out my hand for her device and she unlocks it and gives it over. I hand it back once I've finished entering my digits and called my phone, so I have her number too.

"I have to go. I'm running so late." She's already backing away from the table as I scoop up the carton of cupcakes for the crew. She waves her phone in the air. "I'll talk to you soon."

"Any time." I raise a hand and wiggle my fingers as she disappears out the door. Possibly sooner than later if I can call in a favor on that tattoo she wants.

Chapter Six

Indy

When I was six, I fell off the monkey bars and broke my arm. It was an open fracture and the bone sawed through my skin, leaving me with a decent—to this day—scar. I remember that it hurt a lot, but it's my mother's ashen face and teary eyes that I think about most when I recall that incident.

Even after all this time my heart still pounds and my hands grow clammy thinking about it. Seated in one of the Cape Cod Adirondacks, I wipe the dampness on my shorts and then rub my thumb to and fro over the raised scar on my upper arm, while I watch my dad grilling.

He doesn't say much as he flips steaks coated in his secret sauce recipe. But what does one say when one is faced with losing their only daughter?

I can't imagine what it must feel like for them to be aware that they're losing a child. Every time she thinks I'm not paying attention, I see that same frantic look in my mom's eyes that she had the day I broke my arm. They're pretending everything will be fine, but they're terrified.

It's the reason that I walked out of our last family dinner. The reason why I'm contemplating how difficult it would be to jump the back fence and outrun the next-door neighbor's pit bull, instead of sitting through another one.

"Mom said to make sure that you're warm enough." EJ drapes one of Mom's homemade quilts around my shoulders before he takes a seat on the lounger next to mine. He's still dressed for the office in charcoal slacks and a pale blue business shirt.

"Thanks." I pull the comforting weight around me and inhale. It smells like rainy Sundays playing board games in the family room. Often Gray would join us because he didn't much enjoy being at his own home. His parents fought a lot before they got divorced.

Hooking a finger through the knot in his tie, EJ tugs it loose while he takes a swig from the neck of a Miller Lite. "She thinks you'll die of chill before we ever have to worry about your brain liquefying and bleeding out your ears."

I snort against the back of my hand. "I should hope so. That would be a terrible way to go."

"Yeah." His mouth curves down in the corners and he runs his thumb over the label on the bottle, his joke giving way to reality.

It's more likely that my brain will herniate and touch my brain stem, causing important organs to stop working completely. Or that I'll lose the ability to swallow and aspirate on my own saliva and choke to death. Or that I'll have a seizure that I won't recover from. There's also the possibility that I'll simply fall asleep at some point and not wake up. I hope for that one the most. It sounds peaceful. "At least you'll be the golden child for the first time in your life."

"Indy." His pained gaze meets mine.

"Come on, EJ, I need someone to act normally around me." My phone chirps with a text notification, and I swipe the screen to bring it up.

> ***Theo: Have you decided what kind of tattoo you want to get?***

"Gray?" EJ settles back on the lounger with a hand behind his head.

"Uh, no." I press my lips together as I consider my reply to Theo's question. I've only managed to decide I want a tattoo, but not what or where. Should it be thoughtful or daring? Small and hidden? Or out there for everyone to see? "A friend."

"You have friends?" He smirks.

"You're a jerk." I roll my eyes at my big brother. It's the type of normalcy I crave. Where I'm not the girl everyone needs to be extra cautious and vigilant around. I smile as I type out a text. "That was weak, even for you, bro."

Indy: I'm not sure. A butterfly or flowers maybe. Until recently I didn't expect I'd ever give into this whim.

"Is Gray on his way?" EJ's mouth bunches and the lines in his forehead deepen. "I thought he'd be here already."

"He's running late. He had to meet Patton on the way over. His renegotiated contract was finally ready to sign."

Theo: Ahh, so cutesy then?

Indy: I guess.

"There's my bro. Were your ears burning?" EJ jumps up and stalks toward the house where I suspect his best friend has appeared.

Theo: I've got the perfect thing.

He asks me to meet him in a couple of days. My chest grows light. Am I really going to get a tattoo? Cross a thing of my bucket list? I've secretly wanted ink for as long as I can remember. I almost got a butterfly when I went with America to get her tattoo a year ago. But I chickened out.

Indy: Where?

"Hey, babe." Gray leans around the back of the chair to kiss my cheek as I put my phone down beside me. He squeezes my arm. "How are you feeling?"

"Tired." I eye the beef that dad's currently prodding with a pair of tongs. I have that cake in my bag still too. The one I was tempted to eat on my way over here but didn't. My stomach gurgles and I flatten a palm over it. "A little hungry."

"We'll eat soon. You remember why we're doing it?" He sheds his jacket and takes off his tie before he drops them both over a seat at the table.

"So we can look svelte in the wedding pictures?" I stick my tongue in my cheek.

His face crumples. "Indy, that's—"

"I was joking. It's for the chemo." How could I possibly forget that the reason my fiancé and my brother and my parents are all on this fasting bandwagon is to support me while I go through treatment? Tonight's family dinner will be the first time any of us have eaten in two days. "It's supposed to help my healthy cells stay strong. I agreed to try everything. I'm on board with it, Gray."

"Fuck." He runs a hand through his ashy strands while he gulps air. He scoops me up from the Adirondack then straddles it so that I'm sitting between his thighs.

His body is hard and warm and in his arms is one of my favorite places to find myself. Is it wrong that I'm glad I'm the one who's journey will come to an end and not the other way around? I wouldn't survive without his love. His embrace. Or his lips against my neck. Thinking about it creates a fissure in my chest that I can barely stand.

"I didn't mean to be critical, babe. I want the best for you."

"Beer," my brother's gruff voice interrupts as he taps Gray on the shoulder with a bottle. He doesn't look at me, which seems to be his way of keeping his emotions to himself. "Careful, they go down a little too easy."

"Thanks." Gray takes the Miller Lite and puts it down next to my bag so that he can wrap both arms around me.

I rest my head on his shoulder, ignoring the way my eyes burn.

"It's hard, Indy." He presses his lips to my forehead and leaves them there. "But it'll be worth it when you're better. You'll see."

"How are the steaks coming, Oz?" Mom carries a platter out to the table. She's made caprese, with both red and yellow tomatoes and the tiny mozzarella balls.

It's my favorite vegetable dish. Has been since I was little. I wipe the corners of my mouth for any drool.

"You're not the golden child. They pity you is all." EJ grins at me.

"Edward James," Mom shrills.

"That means when I die, I'll still be their favorite. There's no way you can win at this point." I smirk at EJ as I push away from Gray's embrace to take a seat at the table. "I'm so ready to eat."

"You two are so morbid." My mother presses a hand to her chest. She has that stony expression she gets when she disapproves of our actions. "I can't believe this is how you behave."

"Steaks are perfect," Dad announces as he places them on a platter while EJ and Gray join me and Mom at the table.

Dinners with my family have always been the highlight of my week, but now they're awkward. My dad swallows a lot, probably avoiding speaking in that way. My mom keeps shooting fearful glances at me when she thinks I'm distracted.

And even when we manage to act like we're normal... even when we manage to forget for a little while that I'm sick... it all comes crushing down on us in the very next breath.

My mom cries and my dad holds onto me for an extra-long time while we say our goodbyes.

By the time Gray helps me into the car to go home, I'm physically and emotionally exhausted. And so is he.

"I don't know how I'm supposed to do that next week." And the week after that. And the one after that. And for however many more I have after that. The tears start and they don't stop coming no matter how many times I wipe them away. I never in a million years thought it would be this hard to be around my family.

"They love you, Indy." Gray rests his hand on my knee while he concentrates on the road. "They love you so much. That's all. We all love you so much."

I'm failing them. I feel like I didn't try hard enough or be careful enough. Like I could have stopped this from happening if I'd been more cautious. If I'd worn more sunscreen or drank less wine or practiced meditation or yoga. I'm hurting them and I can't do anything to stop their pain.

I curl my hand around Gray's and hold on tight. Turning my watery stare to the window, I let my tears track down my cheeks. I don't bother dashing them away.

My heart is cracking down the middle and there's nothing I can do to stop the ache that fills its place. I cry for all the pain that my family are in. I cry for Gray who is trying so very hard to save my life.

I must fall asleep because the next thing I know, Gray is leaning over me and unbuckling my seatbelt. We're in the parking structure under our building. I rub the grit from my eyes. They're still blurry when I take my hands away. My heart climbs into my throat. The doctor warned me that I could lose my sight. That the tumor could make me blind. But I blink and it's not as bad. It's only my webbed lashes.

Gray scoops me out of the car with both arms.

"I can walk." My head is pounding. I rest my cheek against his chest and yawn.

"You can let me look after you, babe." He shuts the door of the rental car with his hip.

The sway of his walk as he carries me into the elevator and then into the condo is comforting. He tugs my boots off my feet, and they drop with a *thud, thud* near the front door before he carries me into the bedroom and lays me down on the bed.

"I'm going to go back down and collect my briefcase and jacket. I'll grab your bag too." The weight of the fuzzy throw settles over me before he presses his lips to my temple. "Get some sleep. I'll wake you when it's time to take your meds."

"Thanks." I'm already sliding back into sleep as he leaves the room.

When I wake a few hours have passed. I draw the blanket tight around me as I wander out to find him set up with his laptop in the kitchen.

He glances at his Oris watch while I fill a glass from the dispenser on the fridge. "I was going to let you sleep a bit longer."

"It's okay." I rest a hip against the cupboard while I sip my chilled water and eyeball the pill bottles all lined up in a row. "I slept long enough. I doubt I'll sleep anymore tonight."

"Well, I'm almost done here then we can watch a movie. I need to finish this email first."

His brow troughs and he tugs the side of his bottom lip between his teeth. He's so cute when he does that. He gets so lost in thought.

His gaze finds mine over the lid of his laptop. He rubs a hand over his jaw. "Indy, why was there an obscene cupcake in your bag?"

"You went through my bag?" I raise a brow at him. We're not the kind of people to have secrets. I've never felt the need to keep anything from him. He knows my family, my friends, my deepest dreams and desires.

Or, at least, what I thought were my dreams and desires.

"Your phone was ringing."

"Oh." I lower my gaze. Of course he isn't going through my bag like he doesn't trust me. My phone rang and he wanted to answer it. Something we've always done for each other. I can understand why he's questioning the cupcake. "I ran into a friend this afternoon and we ended up at this cute bakery."

"And you decided to hell with the science and giving your body the best chance of recovery?"

"No." I shove away from the counter to walk around the island to where he sits. "It was in case I felt like trying it after dinner. They're supposed to be really great cakes. The best in the city. Better than St. Pierre."

"That's a tall order." He swivels the stool away from the island so that he's facing me.

"It is." I sway into his arms. "I swear, I didn't even have a nibble. I know how important it is to you that I look after myself."

"It should be important to you, too." He engulfs me.

"It is." I smooth my hands up and down his back. "And I promise that I'm not eating cupcakes while no one is looking."

"I'm so damn scared of losing you. It's all I can think about." He kisses my cheek and my jaw and my throat. "You're my world. How am I supposed to not take your life seriously when it's so precious to me?"

There's a lump in my throat, and swallowing doesn't budge it. Gray is a fixer. When there's a problem, he works it until he finds the solution. I love that about him, but I'm not sure that skill isn't setting him up for more pain than he can handle. "You can't make me better, Gray."

Gray doesn't respond, except to hold me tighter. Eventually he clears his throat. "So these cakes... better than St. Pierre? Really?"

"Or so I've been told." I smile as he brings about an end to our argument.

"Well, then we better try it, huh? Make sure we're ordering our wedding cake from the right vendor?"

"Gray, maybe we should—"

He takes my jaw in his hand and stares into my eyes. "I love you, Indy. And I want to marry you. However long we have...whether it's decades...or a few months...I want to call you my wife. In sickness or health. I know how much it means to you."

I clasp my hand over his and rub my cheek against his palm. It does mean a lot to me. That's why it's still on my bucket list. Because my values haven't changed all that much. My childhood was happy, and I had great role models in my parents. A relationship like theirs is something I've always wanted for myself. It's what I've found with Gray. I want to marry him, even if our lives together have almost run their course. I wish we could have babies together too. "Of course, I want that too."

He claims my mouth in a bittersweet kiss as he stands. His hands on my waist, he lifts me to sit on the counter before he inches back. "I'll grab the cake."

He collects the pink box from the top shelf in the fridge and two forks from the cutlery drawer before sitting beside me.

When he flips open the box, I dig into the moist, springy cake and tear off a forkful. Thick white chocolate icing oozes from inside the rectangular treat.

Gray makes a choking noise as I pop it in my mouth. He's more restrained as he takes his own bite. But then he takes another forkful. "Do you know what this reminds me of?"

I raise a solitary brow. "Other than eating dick?"

"I'm scared for my manhood if this reminds you of blow jobs, babe." He chuckles as he reaches under the counter to cup himself. "No. That bakery we found in Michigan when we were looking at schools."

"You told me it didn't matter where I went to school." The memory is a warm bubble in my chest. We'd stood under the awning, and the whole world could have passed us by. We were so into each other. "You'd come visit me every weekend."

"Because I knew I couldn't get through a week without seeing you." He takes my hand and rubs soothing circles over my knuckles with his thumb. "I was already completely smitten."

We fall into reminiscing about the early days while we eat cock cake from a pink box. There are so many emotions—good and bad—tied up in our memories. We cry and we laugh, and we smile, and we kiss. And then we cry some more because in the end that's all I'll leave him with.

Memories of what we were. Dreams of what we could have been.

Chapter Seven

Indy

I race off the train and through the heavy foot traffic. My bag bumps against my hip as I power walk down the sidewalk.

I asked Theo to come with me to get a tattoo and he went out of his way to set it up for me. But I didn't consider the role chemo would play in what I can and can't do. I didn't google that shit until I was sitting on the train.

The hard candy I'm sucking on to help with the nausea is almost a puddle of apple flavoring on my tongue as I turn the corner.

He's waiting up ahead, leaning against the tattoo shop with his hands in the pockets of his leather jacket and one foot resting on the brickwork behind him. He's wearing a shirt again. And he's so chill. Like he has nothing better in the world to do than hang out with a dying girl.

I can't imagine that's true though.

"Sorry I'm late." I press my hands to my knees as I try to catch my breath.

"Hey." He shoves away from the wall. "Are you okay?"

"Mmhmm." I nod, but it takes much longer than it should to recover. Being sick has done a number on my strength and stamina. When I finally manage to breathe at a normal rate and stand up straight, I check out the parlor through the big windows.

It's all open space from this angle. There are several dark leather couches in the waiting area and the walls are covered in tattoo designs and art. A long wooden counter separates us from a man with a turquoise mohawk who is tattooing a woman's arm.

It's scary and thrilling and I wish these nerves in my belly were because I'm about to walk in there and get my first piece of ink. "I'm sorry, Theo. I can't do this."

Because chemo and tattoos don't mix. I can't even dye my hair as long as I'm on treatment. Not that it matters. I'll probably lose my locks anyway. But the tattoo... I was ready. I'd stood in front of the mirror after my shower this morning, imagining ink on different body parts. I'd finally settled on an arm piece. Not too big, not too small.

"It's the chemo, right?" Theo bumps my shoulder gently with his own. "You can't risk infection."

"Yeah." I turn away from the window. "How did you—"

"Google." He rubs the bottom of his nose with his thumb. "My grandma had cancer a million years ago, and I remembered my parents rattling off a list of things they didn't want her doing. Mainly drinking and smoking. Which were two of her four favorite vices. The other two were Sudoku and cussing up a storm."

"Your grandma sounds fun." I glance at him out of the corner of my eye.

"She was." His smile is indulgent and sad at the same time. He and his grandma must have been close. He must miss her a lot. "Anyway, I was thinking about Grandma last night and it occurred to me that I should google what you could and can't do in your current situation."

"No tattoo." I sigh. "No dying my hair."

"No drinking, smoking, fighting or..." His mouth curls up on one side. "Fucking strangers."

"Well, that last one isn't a problem." I can't even get Gray to have sex with me these days. Not that I have the energy for it all that often. I have no interest in sleeping with anyone else. "And actually, none of them are a problem."

"Perhaps not for you." Theo snorts to himself while he rocks on the balls of his feet.

I stick my tongue in my cheek. "I guess we should both be glad I'm the one dying, huh?"

He turns so that we're facing each other. There's a boyishness to his smile. It's replaced the sadness and a flash of seriousness. "So here is what we're going to do."

Butterflies start in my belly.

"We're going to go inside and meet Harlan. I asked him to draw up something special for you."

"But—"

"It's a temporary tattoo. It'll last a few weeks and won't be a problem with the chemo." He leans in and takes my elbow. "I made sure."

"Seriously?" He went above and beyond so I'd be able to cross this off my bucket list. I'm suddenly awake and practically bouncing on my toes as warmth radiates through me.

"Yes, seriously." He ushers me into the shop, grinning. "And once we're done here you can come to the bar while I open, and we'll work on what should really be on that list of yours."

The man with the turquoise mohawk looks up from the arm piece he's working on.

Theo approaches the counter. "We're here to see Harlan."

The guy nods and calls out to someone who must be in the back.

A few minutes later another man saunters into the main room. He has shoulder length, finger combed blond waves, and an incredible jawline. His body has been melted down and poured into jeans and a white muscle top that is so fitted it looks like if he flexed, he would rip through it like a werewolf under a full moon. And the tattoos are so... prolific, artistic, delicious. They give him that wild boy vibe.

America would love him. My chest tightens. She would want to be here, doing this.

Theo chuckles as he steps forward to clasp arms and bro hug with the guy. "This is my friend I was telling you about. Indy."

"Hello, Indy. I'm Harlan." He has these pale green eyes that seem to see everything as he sweeps them over me from head to toe and back again. They brighten when he smiles. Lines crinkle his cheek as he takes my hand and covers it with his. "What are you doing with this asshole? You're not his sister, and you don't seem like one of those fight groupies."

"Fight groupies?" The first time I saw him he was covered in bruises, the next time... well, I was pre-occupied. Since then he's worn a T-shirt that's barely more than a second skin. I assumed... I don't know what I assumed the bruising was from. Fighting makes sense though. That must be why he said it was one of his vices.

Harlan looks to Theo. "She doesn't know?"

"What?" I glance between the two men, both with their lips pressed together into tight lines. It seems whatever the secret is, it's a bone of contention between them.

"She's a friend." Theo crosses his arms. "That's all. How about we stop asking stupid questions and concentrate on the tattoo?"

"You'll love it." Harlan walks over to a station, where he gestures for me to sit. "Theo told me that you wanted cutesy and that it should be symbolic, to represent the bucket list."

"You put that much effort into this?" Why?

Theo still has his arms crossed over his chest as he leans against a cupboard, but he also has a good vantage point to supervise from. "Tattoos should mean something."

"Have you decided where you want to put it?" Harlan asks me.

"On my arm." I pull up the sleeve of the loose peasant top that I'm wearing and cover the top half of my forearm with my hand to indicate the placement.

"Oh, yeah. It'll be perfect." His smile widens. "I'll go grab the decal off the printer and we'll put it on."

"What does your tattoo mean?" I glance at the waistband of his jeans. While his arms are bare, I noticed the hint of a tattoo above that hard line where his torso meets his hip. He has at least one that he doesn't show off.

"You noticed that, huh?" He jacks up a brow.

I glance away. Check out the artwork on the wall. Chew on my thumbnail. "You were half-naked. Slightly more than half. It wasn't like it was hidden."

He makes a huffing noise. "Yeah, it means something."

"What?"

He bunches his jaw. "It's personal."

Perhaps, it's embarrassing. Like its meaning is don't get a tattoo after losing a drunken bet.

"Here we are." Harlan comes back into the room with my temporary tattoo. He holds it up for us to see.

It's a black and white kitten wearing huge and colorful glasses. It's sitting in a teacup, and is impossibly adorable, but I can't imagine why Theo chose it. "What does it mean?"

"Why don't you tell her?" Theo tells Harlan.

"Well, cats symbolize femininity and gracefulness." He grabs a spinning stool and sits in front of me. "Two things that I can tell you have in spades."

I smile at Harlan and then I smile at Theo. "You two thought it was cute. Admit it."

"It's going to be very cute on you." Harlan winks as he helps me arrange my arm so that it will be easy to put the tattoo on, and then he cleans the area with a swab. Pulling off the clear layer, he positions the paper on my skin and holds it in place with his hand until he has it taped down.

"Stop flirting with her," Theo grumbles. "She has a fiancé."

"I do." I lift my hand and flash him my ring. It's getting loose. I'm going to have to get it resized soon. Or put it away so I don't lose it.

"That's too bad." Harlan shakes his head. "But of course a pretty girl like you would be off the market."

"Cats have nine lives." Theo clears his throat.

"Sorry?" I glance up at him as he moves nearer to observe over Harlan's shoulder while he finishes transferring the tattoo to my skin.

Theo shrugs. "Cats have nine lives. They symbolize rebirth. And luck."

Harlan tosses the backing in the trash. "And they look really sweet on you."

I stare at the image on my arm with a big smile on my face. I always wanted a tattoo and even though it's only temporary, it looks real.

"The level of detail in your artwork always amazes me, Harlan." Theo grabs my hand and bends over my arm to check the tattoo out up close. He smiles as our eyes lock. "Do you like it?"

"I think I want to come back and tattoo it on my skin forever." I beam at him, and then at Harlan.

"She loves it." Harlan dusts his hands together as he and Theo exchange smirks.

"Can you take a photo?" America should have been here for this. I have to show her. "I want to document it."

"Sure." Theo takes out his phone and snaps a handful of photos. He thumbs through them and a shadow flickers across his face, but it's gone when he lifts his gaze. "I'll text them to you."

"Thank you." Maybe I imagined the emotion I glimpsed. It's possible that I'm projecting my own less than positive emotions onto other people. Like buying a particular car, then seeing that car everywhere.

"Hey, Harlan, take one of the two of us." Theo offers his phone to the tattoo artist. "Is that okay with you, Indy?"

I pat the padded surface next to me. I wouldn't have gotten a tattoo, no matter how temporary, without him. And I certainly wouldn't have gotten it today. I would have let chemo derail me completely. "I couldn't have done this without you."

Theo sits on the end of the seat, our thighs touching, because there's not really enough room for two people. His hands are linked in his lap, and I am smiling so hard. I can't believe that we did this. Or that I could be this happy while my whole world is falling apart.

"Thank you." I bump him with my elbow while Harlan lines us up in his sight. "It means a lot to me."

He tilts his head, haphazard brown waves falling over his face, but not able to hide his grin. "You're welcome, Indy."

"Here, let me." I reach up and push those wild strands back. His gaze stays glued to mine. "Your eyes?"

"Heterochromia." His Adam's apple bobs. "Genetics. I was born like this."

"He was born with God's gift to women tattooed on his forehead," Harlan grumbles as he hands Theo back his device. "Should be something there for the scrapbook."

"Did you hear that, Indy?" Theo winks at me. "Some bitch is whining about my good looks like he doesn't look like a fallen angel himself."

"He has a point." I smile at Harlan. "You've got nothing to complain about."

Harlan presses a hand to his chest. "Sweet, sweet Indy."

"We should get going." Theo pushes to his feet. "But it was great to see you, Harlan."

"And you, my friend." Harlan grabs his shoulder and squeezes as they walk out to the front ahead of me. "Perhaps don't make it so long before you grace my doorstep next time. I still need to finish off that piece on your back for you."

So he does have more tattoos than the one I glimpsed.

"I'm not ready." Theo hunches into his jacket and shakes his head.

"I hope you will be one day." Harlan says to him before he turns to me. "As for you...that one is on the house. To get you hooked. So you'll come back and visit some time."

"You don't need to do that." I start digging in my purse. "I have cash. I was prepared to pay."

"Your money is no good here." He exchanges glances with Theo. Their friendship is obvious.

"Well, thank you. It means a lot."

"Come back when you want me to give you the real deal, Indy." He smiles at me. "It would be my honor to ink your skin. And bring him with you, if you can."

I hope I get the chance to do so once chemo treatment is behind me, but I suspect that I won't cross Harlan's path again. I reach up on tiptoe to kiss the man on the cheek. "Thank you."

Chapter Eight

Theo

Indy sits across the bar from me with her notepad open and the tip of her pen between her teeth while I serve one of the regular barflies. Writing a bucket list isn't for the faint of heart. You have to have some idea of what you want from life.

Indy used to know what she wanted from life, but that was before some doctor used the words "inoperable tumor" to describe her condition. It's almost fucking impossible to change the way you view your future when everything you want is ripped away.

You might as well lie down and die instead because there is nothing that will ever fill the hole that is left when some doctor obliterates your hopes and dreams. But we don't lie down and die, because it's not human nature. We choose another direction to attack from. We fight.

My phone beeps with a notification and I pull it out to check the message. A location and time for tonight's fight appears on the screen. Thank fuck.

Harlan might be the only tattooist I would trust to ink Indy's skin for real, but seeing him again—after I put so much distance between my past and my present, including hundreds of miles—it isn't surprising that I'm out of sorts and my muscles are itching to be put to use.

Some of us, like Indy, fight by redefining our future, while I prefer to obliterate memories of the past with my fists.

"You brought her to work?" Lucas's brows draw toward each other as he studies the girl at the bar. He crosses his arms over his barrel chest, staring at me, waiting... for an answer, for a confession.

"I told you she's a friend." I don't owe him an explanation, and I don't get why he's acting like such a prick these days. "I'm helping her with something."

"I bet you're helping." Heath bites his bottom lip as he sails past with a bottle of vodka. Spinning around, he walks backward toward a studious looking coed with her wallet out while sticking his tongue out at me.

"Whatever." I shake my head at the two of them as I slide my phone back into my pants. They're used to seeing me flirt with women at the bar and sometimes disappearing with them. They're used to giving me shit for my lifestyle. Or at least the parts they're aware of. But with Indy... it's different. She needs a friend who understands some of what she's going through, and I... well, I can be that person and do that one thing right.

They go back to work, and I move down the bar to where Indy is staring blankly at the shelves of liquor while the notepad in front of her appears exactly the same as it did five minutes ago. "How is it going so far?"

"Huh?" She takes the pen from between her lips as she focuses on me. Almost like she's searching for something. Her cheeks grow rosy, and she swallows. "Nothing."

I chuckle. It doesn't seem like nothing to me. It seems as though she'd like to see me stripped down to my skin. And I would be happy to oblige. Except I know it's all in my head. "What were you thinking about that has you in a tizzy?"

"I can't remember." She drops her gaze to the notepad. Picking it up, she rips off the top sheet to reveal a fresh page. "I think it might be best if I start from scratch. Perhaps break up the list into themes. Things that are brave, or passionate, or permanent."

"It must be really juicy if you don't want to share." I clean up the workbench behind the barrier in front of her. "Drink?"

"I can't drink." Her lips pull down in the corners.

"Non-alcoholic. Trust me?"

"I do, but make it ice water." She starts to scribble on the paper in front of her. "Permanent? That's hard. It was supposed to be a tattoo, but—"

"What about brave?" I fill a glass with ice and top it with cold water before sliding it in front of her. Does her fiancé still have her on a no food diet to help with the chemo? I googled the shit out of it. Even read a couple of positive studies on it. But it sounds absolutely fucking miserable. And she's already so fragile. "Ever considered dancing on a bar?"

"Dancing? On this?" She presses a finger into the glossy wood.

"Yeah, exactly that." I smirk as I lean over the barrier and steal her notepad and pen so I can write *dance at the Line 'Em Up* on the paper. "We do it every Friday night."

"All of you?" She glances at Lucas, and Heath, and Pez who has come in from the storage room carrying several cases.

"What are we talking about?" Pez dumps the drinks on the floor near the fridges and claps me on the shoulder. He makes a noise in the back of his throat. "Dancing on the bar? Yeah, it's Friday night tradition. You ever seen *Magic Mike*?"

"Sure."

"This guy puts Channing Tatum to shame with his moves."

Her eyes light up as she drags them over me.

"Something like that." I squeeze the back of my neck as heat floods me.

"What? Are you embarrassed?" Pez raises a brow at me as he wields his bluntness like a weapon to cut me down at the knees.

"No. Shut up." I can't look at Indy with Pez talking me up. As if I need a wingman to meet pretty girls.

"He is." Pez shakes me slightly. "Isn't that cute? You totally want to dance with him, don't you?"

"Maybe." She smiles at him.

"Ignore him." The tops of my ears burn. "And there's no pressure to dance with me. Or any of these jackasses."

Pez raises a brow at me.

"What other things would you want to do?" I concentrate on Indy. On the bucket list. As her friend, that's what my job is. To make sure she gets to experience the things that she wants. "There's also karaoke. Rock climbing. Uh…"

"Things in the sky." Pez nods. "Bungee jumping. Cliff diving. Paragliding."

"Whoa. Calm down, big fella." I clap him in the chest when Indy's eyes turn round. "That might be too much with the chemo."

"Fuuuuck." Pez closes his eyes and takes a deep breath before he opens them again. "I'm sorry. I didn't realize."

"It's fine. You didn't know." Indy tries to spin a positive face, but I've shoved her reality in front of her by telling him. Her eyes, ever on the verge of tears, glaze. "It's a brain tumor. Inoperable. Hence the bucket list."

Pez looks at me. While I don't talk about my past, he knows this isn't my first rodeo. That I've watched someone I care about die. It's been years and it doesn't get easier to be without her. But this is different. I went into this friendship with my eyes wide open. It's been mere weeks, but at some point that's going to mean I'll miss her. I try to convey that I chose this with a nod and a tight smile that's as brittle as it is fake.

We have limited time and one goal to accomplish, and I'd rather focus on that than the heavy truth. "What about hot air ballooning? Or feeding giraffes?"

"The idea of feeding a giraffe kind of creeps me out. Their tongue is like something from an erotic romance novel about aliens. They're all blue and weirdly flexible. It gives me the creeps."

I cough into my hand. Because my brain goes all the way to the dark side. Indy spread out and being hammered by a flexible, blue tongue. "Christ. I did not see that coming."

By the pained expression on Pez's face, he visualized something similar.

"Oh God." She covers her mouth with both hands. Her eyes are so wide they start to water. "I didn't mean to say that out loud."

And I did not mean to visualize that. But it happened anyway. I hold out my hand, palm side down to her. "Smack it."

Her gaze flicks between my face and hand several times. "What?"

"Give it a tap." I stretch my hand out another inch. "For the dirty thoughts."

"Oh." She smacks my knuckles. Then holds out her own hand. "You better do mine too."

Pez shoves both hands in his back pockets. "So what animals do you like, Indy?"

Indy wrinkles her nose. "The wolves are cool."

"Wolves, huh?" That's different. Not what I expected. But then wolves mate for life. "They're loyal. Protective of each other. Team players."

"What about you?" Indy's gaze is unwavering.

"Snow leopard." I scratch my jaw. They're sleek. Solo hunters. Great at being alone. I can handle being alone. I've even come to enjoy it.

"I personally like the turtle exhibit," Pez makes a smooth ocean motion gesture. "They glide through water and they're prehistoric."

"And they moan when they have sex," Indy says quietly, keeping her gaze on her list.

"What?" Pez frowns at me. "Did she say what I think she said?"

"I think our new friend is a little bit of a fiend." I smirk.

"Well, they do." She sticks out her hand for another slap. "It's fact."

"And on that note, I'm going to leave you two to it and get back to work." Pez covers his mouth as he walks away. His shoulders shake.

I burst into laughter. "So, no zoo for you?"

"It appears not." Her face brightens. "I have one for the list though. Oh, actually three."

"Pancakes at two in the morning." I read her list upside down as she adds shave her head and kiss in the rain. She's thinking about her fiancé when she writes down that last one, no doubt. And why does that make me uncomfortable in my own skin? "I have a place for the first one. Great pancakes. And I can totally help with the second."

But the third. It doesn't need to be said. Her pillowy lips aren't on my bucket list.

A customer comes up to the bar and saves me from damning myself. I take my time pouring pale ale into a pint glass and taking their money.

"You could add rock climbing if you wanted a challenge." I clear away her empty glass. Pour her another. "Pez is seriously gifted when it comes to the sport. I'm sure we could organize to scale a wall if that was something you wanted to do... if you're up to it."

"Maybe." She pushes her hair out of her face as her phone starts to ring. She reads the screen. "I better take this."

Probably the fiancé. I inch away to give her space.

"Hey." Her face lights up and she plays with her hair. "Tell me all about your day."

Of course she looks like a girl in love. She's dating the right guy for her. Even if I dislike the man I've never met, for absolutely no reason, other than the tight sensation in my gut.

Or perhaps it's the fact that she's here pouring over this list with me instead of him, writing words like *kiss in the rain* on a list of things she wants to do before she dies, while not eating or drinking a damn thing all day because he's decided it's a good idea.

And I can't fault him for that, even if I don't like it. Hell, I sympathize with the man. I remember being willing to do anything and everything in my power, and being aware the whole time that I was completely powerless.

No, I can't blame him for behaving how I once did. But I can totally find him lacking for not kissing her in the rain and anywhere else she might want. Not when they've been together long enough to be getting married.

Would it be absurd for me to hold a grudge over my perceived belief in his mishandling of her lips? I kind of think it might be a problem.

"Hey, there. Can I get a glass of white wine?" The woman sidles up to me from the opposite end of the bar, which is probably why I don't notice her until she's standing right in front of me. She's wearing a masculine white button down that is understated but hot.

She drops lightly onto the nearest barstool and puts her purse on the divide while I grab the white and pour it into a goblet.

She looks me up and down. "You must hear this all the time, but you have gorgeous eyes."

I smile lazily. "It never gets old."

Indy ducks her head into her hand as she laughs at whatever her fiancé said on the phone. A ruddy pink spreads in her cheeks while she draws circles on the bartop. "Well, I kind of did something out of character today. You're not going to believe it..."

The last thing I need to be doing is listening to Indy's conversation. I focus on the gorgeous blonde in front of me. Exude the full power of my unique eyes as I lean on the bar. "You're not a regular, are you?"

She runs a finger along the rim of her glass with a slight shake of her head. "How could you tell?"

"I know you were supposed to come with me," Indy's voice reaches me anyway. "And it's not permanent, so we can…"

"I don't forget beautiful women." I drag my gaze over every visible inch of the blonde. I'm not about to take her to the back room, but I could see myself asking her to come watch me fight. "What's your name?"

"Skye." She rubs her lips together and smiles. "Flattery will get you everywhere."

I lean in to impart my next line.

"Why?" Indy's voice grows louder, panicked. "Well, because… oh crap, is that the time? I'm sorry. I've gotta go."

She hangs up before her fiancé can possibly get in another word. Tosses her phone on the counter. And drops her head in her hands.

Shit. That didn't go well.

I drop the blonde, climbing up over the bar like it's any given Friday. The blonde sucks in a sharp breath as I land on my feet a foot from her. Then I'm crushing the distance to Indy whose shoulders are shaking.

"Hey," the blonde calls out after me, but she'll get the hint.

Indy is fucking distraught, and my heart is pounding in my chest. What did that asshole say to her? Okay, he's probably not an asshole and I definitely shouldn't call him one to her face, but I'm still going to think it when she looks this fucking fragile. I reach out to hug her then veer off at the last possible second, smoothing my hand over the top of my hair instead. "What happened? Is he angry?"

"Angry? He?" Indy lifts her head from her hands. Fresh tears have made her eyes watery. Her lids are already starting to puff. "That was my bestie. America. You met her. Kind of."

"The girl who rescued you from me that night in the bathroom?" The chick who looked a little like Zendaya.

"I didn't need rescuing." She wipes the wetness that brims over her lashes. "But yes, that's America. Absolutely gorgeous and super brainy. She's studying linguistics at Cambridge."

"I'm more interested in what she said to you." I use my thumb to gather up an errant tear from her jaw.

"It's more that I haven't told her." She closes her eyes against the pain as she shakes her head. "I'm keeping secrets from my best friend. We've never kept secrets. But I couldn't be the reason she didn't go to Cambridge and have this big life experience. Now I don't know how to tell her. Every time she asks how I am...it gets harder to work out the right words...everything is different...and I don't want to say goodbye. I don't want to be the reason she comes home either."

Her shoulders heave and the tears run unimpeded down her face. She carries the responsibility of her friend's overwhelming grief like she should be able to change the situation. She carries her fiancé's fears too. And probably her whole family's.

Wrapping my arms around her is a no brainer. Letting her stain my shirt with her tears is no big deal. And if that sniffle means there's snot, well, I'll go to the office and break out a fresh T-shirt when she's done using me as a tissue. Probably will have to anyway or spend the evening smelling like a flower. "It's a big step, and it's okay to not be ready to have that conversation yet."

"I'm jealous too," she whispers as she pulls away. "I can't believe I'm admitting that, but I am. She has her entire life ahead of her. She's going to get to travel and see the world. She's going to get to settle down and have the family that I always wanted. And I'm going to be a memory. And I know that's awful to be jealous of her when she's my best friend…and that I should be grateful for the life I've had—"

"Fuck that noise," I growl. I can't help it. She's trying to remain within the parameters of normalcy when there is no normal here. Death is one of the only sure events that we have in this life, but our reaction to it is never standard. If it were, I wouldn't have gotten up and walked out on everyone and everything I knew. I wouldn't have moved to a different state in an attempt to put my guilt behind me. I wouldn't be facing another month without hearing from my little sister who has decided that I find her calls a burden. "Don't be careful, Indy. Not with me. Your life is shit right now. No one is jealous of you."

"Wow." She glares at me as she wipes the wetness from her cheeks. Her spine grows straighter "Shall I… take that as a compliment?"

"My point is you don't have to be cautious. And you don't need to apologize for voicing human thoughts about your own mortality. You should be speaking your mind. To everyone. Especially the people you love. Give them the very best of you, and rage, rage against the dying of the light."

"Poetry?"

"Dylan Thomas," I say. "I minored in English Lit."

"Really?"

"In another life I might have planned to be something other than a bartender." I shrug like all those hours I spent studying law weren't a complete waste when I dropped out so close to graduating.

"That must be a real gift with the ladies." She glances over my shoulder, possibly at the blonde I forgot all about. "Let me get out of your hair so you can work your magic."

"Actually…" Part of me is aware that I should let her leave. I should go back to work. Back to the blonde who is probably still curious enough to be waiting for me to return. Keeping some distance between Indy and me would be clever for both our sakes. I snag her wrist. "Come with me."

"What are we doing?" she asks as I lead her around the bar.

Past the blonde who props her chin on her fist and guzzles her wine. Past Lucas who thrusts out his chin until the hinge swells. And Heath who laughs as I body block Indy's view of his mimed doggy style. *Dickhead.* Pez throws me a two finger salute while he gets on with his job.

"You'll see." I shove through the doors to the employee only area and grab a cardboard box from the storage room. Then, still holding onto Indy as well as the box, I head out into the alley.

She glances around the alleyway then reaches up to fiddle with the stud in her ear. "What's going on, Theo? Why are we in an alley?"

I put the box down on the ground and open it up. It's full of pint glasses. We lose a few each week so we always have backups. It's not going to matter if we lose a couple extra to a good cause. I stand, the glass weighty in my hand. I hold it out to her. "Here."

Her expression slackens. "What am I supposed to do with that?"

"You throw it at the wall."

"What? No." Her gaze follows the imagined trajectory from the glass to the wall, eyes growing wider the whole way. "I'm not going to do that. Why would I do that?"

"You're upset, right? Let it out." I wind my arm back and let the glass fly. It explodes with a loud *pop*, and Indy jumps. A small yelp bursts out of her at the same time.

I grab another one and throw that too. It's been a while, but the shatter is still satisfying. Indy watches with the inside of her cheek between her teeth.

"You want to throw one, don't you?" I pick up a third and offer it to her.

She makes a noncommittal sound in her throat but takes the glass out of my hand and faces the wall. She throws the glass with her whole body. Arm flying over her shoulder and the momentum carrying her forward a step.

The glass detonates into tiny shards.

"Oh my God. I can't believe I did that." She covers her mouth with her hands, but her eyes are bright and alive. Her pain, at least for now, is tempered by the distraction. Her anger is hopefully lessened.

"It's not wise to hold everything in." I hold out the next glass. "Do it again."

Chapter Nine

Gray

"I can't believe you got Manilow." My colleague Samson Crew fills the doorway as I turn off my laptop and grab my briefcase from its spot under the desk. It's already late. Later than I intended to finish for the day.

Samson's forehead is craggy and he's already working the tie around his neck loose. A couple of our coworkers head out behind him. He looks as tired as I feel.

Looks a little uncomfortable too, like he doesn't really want to be talking to me.

"Thanks," I reply.

"I don't know how you do it," he says as somewhere behind him a vacuum is switched on and its hum replaces the sounds of people leaving for the day. "You never stop."

Lately, that's all I want to do. I've been working my ass off at the office to get as much done as I can, so that I can be home with Indy more often over these next few months. I was planning to take a month off around the wedding anyway. To spend some time with my beautiful new wife on the beaches of Tahiti. A surprise honeymoon I organized right before she got the diagnosis.

"I'm planning to." With all the energy that chemo and radiation are sucking out of Indy I can only focus on taking care of her. Which is why landing Bryce Manilow doesn't fill me with the excitement a rising star like him usually would.

I slide the folder with the contracts I need him to sign into my briefcase. A cognac colored top loader Indy bought me for my birthday a couple years ago. I add a couple more files that I'll work on during the flight.

Leaving her for a few days so I can fly out to Baltimore and get the contracts signed sits heavily on my chest.

The vacuum cuts off and the lights in the office across from mine flicker off, and I wait for Samson to say whatever really drew him to my office. When he doesn't, it's obvious. I already know what he'll say, but I ask anyway, "Did you need something?"

"I wanted to congratulate you." He glances around until his gaze lands on the framed photo on my desk. His mouth droops even further in the corners and his brown eyes grow sympathetic.

Everyone who meets Indy loves her. My colleagues, my bosses, my friends.

"I'm sorry about Indy. I heard she was sick, and I…" He rubs at his throat. "I wanted to tell you that I can help with your clients if you need time off… or whatever. Kitty is organizing a food drive and Campbell is talking about a fundraiser."

"I have it covered." I glance at my favorite photo of Indy and me. The one from the trip we took to Fiji last summer to celebrate our five year dating anniversary. I'd surprised her with a week in an over-the-water bungalow, filled with sun and sea and alone time together.

Samson scrunches up his face and then launches into what he really thinks. "Yeah, but with Indy not working…even with insurance, the bills—"

"I can afford them." Between Indy and I we've socked away a decent sized nest egg. I've made prudent investments. We're in a much better position than most people our age.

"We all want to help. Indy is a sweetheart."

"Yeah. I get that." My shoulders drop as I give in to the good nature of the people I work with. Of course they want to help Indy. They want to feel useful. "Tell them I appreciate it."

He nods. "I'll leave you to it then."

I glance at the image of Indy and me again when he leaves. God, we were worry free then. Excited about what would come next.

I'd confessed that I wanted to marry her. She'd admitted she wanted it too. Wanted our life together, always. A family. A couple of Adirondacks around a firepit in the backyard like at her parents'.

I asked her out for the first time while we sat together in one of those wooden recliners, at Indy's parents' house. We shared our first kiss there.

We made love for the first time in one of those chairs too. We were joking around after everyone else had gone inside. Snuggled up with a blanket as the fire ebbed. She'd ended up sitting astride my lap somehow. All the oxygen had been sucked out of my chest when she realized I was hard underneath her. She'd been luminous above me and I'd threaded my hand through her hair, drawing her mouth to mine.

I let out a jagged breath as I zip my briefcase.

There's not much peace in the quiet as the last few stragglers pack up to head home. I used to enjoy when the building emptied out and the only other people here were the cleaning staff. I'd call Indy and we'd talk while I finished up whatever I was working on. About her day at school, and my day at the office. About our plans. Our dreams.

She's been my guiding light for so long. And I took it for granted that she would always be here. But now... time is finite and against us. And watching her fade away... losing her one minute at a time... is killing me. I don't know what I'll do if the treatments don't work. But I can't sit still and do nothing. Waiting for our future to be decided one way or another.

I plant my hands on the desk and struggle to breathe. I would take her place in a heartbeat. I don't have people who love me the way they love her. I have a tight ring of friends that I see a few times a year. I have no siblings. My family hasn't been close since my parents divorced over a decade ago. Indy's brother and parents are more family to me than my own. *God, don't take her from us and don't leave me here without her.* I can't do this everyday shit without her. I won't even be able to fake it.

A knock has me lifting my head, dragging myself out of the suffocating darkness.

"Hey." Indy smiles, her cheeks shining and pink like she's been getting some air.

I swallow the cold, wet lump in my throat and it sticks in my gut. Despite the ache, my heart grows in my chest and curves my mouth. She doesn't need to know how scared I truly am. "Hey yourself. What are you doing here?"

"I was close by." She's cute as ever in a flowy, black and white peasant top that she's paired with her favorite denim skirt and boots. Her hair is in wild waves under a hat she borrowed from my side of the closet and there's a black and gray scarf loose around her neck. "I thought you might still be here."

"I got Manilow." I free my tie as she walks toward my desk.

"You've worked so hard on this one. I'm so happy for you." Her hazel eyes brighten, and she breaks into a huge smile as I draw her against me.

I let her go and close the door to give us some privacy. She's getting too thin, too quickly, and I'm reminded of that every time she's in my arms.

I hate that she seems so brittle even though I'm the one who pushed the research about fasting at her doctor. I can't regret it though...I will never regret doing everything I can to fight for her life. Taking her face between my hands, I search for any tightness around her eyes or tension in her mouth that hints at her being in pain or feeling unwell. "You look happy. Today has been good?"

"So good." She wraps her fingers around mine.

"Yeah? What did you get up to?"

She takes a seat on the edge of my desk. When the treatments work... when she's healthy again, I'll take her to the best eateries in the city and buy her all her favorite comfort foods. I'll even take her to that *Pink Bits* bakery and buy her a whole box of those overly detailed dick pops. We'll do a food tour. I'll take her to other states just to try the best restaurants they boast.

"Hung out with a friend. Talked to America. Worked on a bucket list." Each item makes her smile grow.

"You've been busy." Occupied. Keeping herself from sinking into the emotions that drag her down after dinner with her family. I've caught her alone and crying on the balcony in the middle of the night too. It bothers me. The doctors warned us that she could become depressed. Go through a mental journey. Possibly even go through personality changes. They suggested end of life counselling. I should bring it up again. But not now while she's having a great day. "What's on your bucket list?"

She shrugs. "I'm still working on it."

"I hope it's nothing dangerous, like skydiving." It's a joke, but it's not. I mean it. There's no way she can go skydiving.

She laughs like it's funny, but her mouth purses and I'm not entirely sure she isn't about to tell me that's at the top of her list. She tucks a tendril of hair behind her ear while my heart holds its beat. "Nothing like that. Kissing in the rain is on my list."

My hand is shaking as I scratch under my ear. "I've never seen the appeal to standing outside and getting drenched for something that can be held off until we're warm and dry."

"Really?" She leans in and touches my chest. Curls her fingers in the cotton of my button down and brings me nearer. "You don't see the appeal in wanting someone so desperately that you don't even notice those big, fat drops hitting you?"

I reach out and touch her jaw as parts of me stir to life. "Well, I—"

Her knees fall apart to accommodate my hips. Tilting her chin, she eradicates the distance between our mouths until there's only an inch. Swallows. Her voice turns husky. "You don't care that you're wet or cold."

"You hate when it's cold." She always tells me that while she shoves her toes under my thigh or rubs the warmth back into her fingers.

"That's not the point." She pinches my ribs playfully. "You could be in the Arctic for all it matters. Because the only thing that you notice is how much you want that other person."

My nerves are on fire with the need to touch her. My breathing accelerates as she trails her hand down the buttons on my shirt until it meets my belt.

"How much you need to get closer to them." She tugs me forward and my brain stutters. I can feel her heat pressed against my aching hard-on. Her lips graze my ear and my cheek on the way to my mouth. "Feel them."

Our lips press and brush. Her lips part and she nibbles my bottom lip. I lean into the kiss, the need for intimacy overtaking thought.

We've made out more than once on top of this desk, and she tucks her legs around mine like she did those times, locking our bodies together. We're not the kind of people who can't control themselves in a public setting, but my office has always felt semi-private, especially when everyone else has left for the night.

She reaches for the buckle on my belt. "Gray..."

I pretend I don't hear her plea and kiss her like it's enough. I want it to be enough. It isn't. Not by a long shot. I'm breathing hard, and harder still between her thighs. I've never been afraid of my size. Of the strength of my hands on her skin. Of the marks that I could leave.

But she's fragile as glass. The drugs mean she bleeds and bruises more easily.

"Gray." She tries again. "It's been weeks."

"It hasn't." I went down on her that night after she took off from dinner with her family. That was...

"It's been weeks." She clasps my face between her palms. Her gaze is sad and determined and hopeful at the same time. She blinks and there's a sheen to her eyes. "I miss you."

"I'm right here." I shake my head. "I'm not going anywhere. We're going to get through this. You're going to get better."

"Don't." She covers my chest above where my heart beats. She must feel it racing and booming at the same time. Her mouth makes odd shapes like the words get stuck in her throat before they can be finalized. "Don't hang all your hopes on what could be."

I have to. Anything else is admitting defeat, and I can't do that. "But—"

"I miss you now." Her voice and the way she's looking at me tears me up inside. "I miss us. I'm scared of dying, but I'm more scared of not spending this time we do have with you. Please, Gray."

"I didn't mean for you to feel like I'm pulling away." I blink back the pain that rips through me.

"I know you didn't." She offers me a watery smile. "But it feels that way all the same."

"I never stop wanting you." I skim my hand under her skirt and over her panties. She shivers and her eyes roll back in her head on the sweetest moan. I tuck the panties to the side and press a finger into her. She grows slippery. Ready.

"Then show me." She pries my belt open and tugs down the zipper so she can wrap her hot palm around my cock. It throbs and swells in her grip.

"Fuck." I groan as I surge forward to kiss her at the same time as my hips rock forward.

Guiding me to her, she shifts position to take me.

I cup the back of her head as her heat overtakes me. Her hair smells of vanilla and roses. It's my favorite scent right after the way she smells when she's aroused. I press my lips to her temple on my way to her mouth. She opens to the slide of my tongue. Presses back while we start to move slowly.

"More, Gray." She moans into my mouth.

A ball of something in my gut keeps me holding back. I want to pound her until the desk squeaks across the floor. But what if I hurt her?

Gripping my hips, she urges me deeper.

I give in to the need to fuck her a bit harder, a little faster. Enough that she begins to tighten around me. Her breathing speeds up and her body quivers. Her cheeks flush as she shuts her eyes on a quiet cry.

The pit of my stomach draws tight and then I'm pulsing inside of her. Feeling strangely light. Lighter than I have in weeks.

"See, I didn't break." She smiles up at me, hopeful that we've turned the corner.

The alarm on my phone is jarring. It's a reminder to eat, because of the fasting. It brings all of my fears and concerns to the forefront again. Squashes the dizzy warmth that had filled my chest. I don't want it to. I smile at her as I pull out. Pretend everything is perfect.

Her stomach rumbles as she smooths down her skirt. She chuckles. "It's like I'm Pavlov's dog. Your alarm goes off and my hunger perks up."

"How about I take you to dinner?" I stuff myself back in my pants. Re-tuck my shirt. Something glistens in her hair, and I pick it out. "You have a bit of glass."

"Oh. It exploded. I was probably too close." She takes it from me and tosses it into the trash. "Where do you want to eat?"

We go to Dolce. It's our favorite restaurant. The waiter shows us to our usual table.

The lighting is diffused, and the tables are scattered with plenty of space between them. Spread with cream linens and silverware. It's intimate and quiet. A man plays tunes on the piano in the corner.

We had our first date here six years ago. I was so nervous. This was my best friend's little sister and no matter my feelings for her there was so much potential for things to go wrong. She was so certain about us. We'd laughed and talked until it was only us and the staff and they had to kick us out so they could go home.

The waiter asks if we want our usual bottle of champagne. Indy shakes her head. "I think I'd be drunk after one sip."

"I wasn't going to order alcohol anyway." I take her hand across the table like I did that first time and so many times since. "It's dehydrating and dangerous."

"You can if you want." Indy squeezes back. "I'll stick to water."

"We're in this together." I peruse the menu while I try to loosen the tension that's curled up in my jaw since we left the office. I already know what I'll have. The same thing I order every time. "I'll get the New York strip with the lobster tail and a garden salad. Indy will get the lasagna."

"Actually." She purses her lips as she mulls over her options. I don't know why. She always gets the lasagna. Sometimes she orders two. One to go so she can enjoy it the next day. She shuts her menu. "I'll get the linguine."

The server collects the menus and leaves.

"Linguine. That's different." There's this irritation between my shoulder blades that wants to convince me it means something. "I thought you didn't eat mushrooms."

She shrugs and her gaze searches for the server. "You only live once. There are a whole lot of things I need to do before I'm gone. It's why I've started a bucket list."

"Don't talk like that." I take her hand. The ring on her finger sparkles under the lights. I hate the idea that this is all we have. How am I supposed to pretend any of this is okay? "I can't stand it."

"You'll be okay." She stretches over the table to force my gaze. "Apparently, eight out of ten guys take a condom to a funeral, so it's perfectly acceptable to move on right there and then. You might—"

"That's not funny, Indy." For the first time in our relationship I want to grab her by the shoulders and shake some sense into that head of hers when she laughs anyway. She's too cavalier. "You need to take this seriously."

"I'm dying, Gray. I am taking that seriously." She sits back in her chair.

We fall into painful silence. This isn't us.

The server brings us our meals. Digging a fork into the linguine, she twirls the pasta onto the tines and lifts it to her mouth.

I have to say something when the silence continues. "I don't think you're taking it seriously enough, Indy. A bucket list? And mushrooms? And making jokes about dying?"

"I'm coping in my own way."

"You're struggling. You need counseling." Hell, I need counseling. Though I can't understand how talking will make this better.

She points her fork at me. "At some point you're going to have to accept that you can't fix me. Hoping that any of these therapies we're trying is going to work is like praying for a miracle. They only happen in Hallmark movies."

"That's not true. People do the impossible all the time. They survive when it's improbable. But not if they don't at least try." I squeeze her hand. I need her to try. I need her to fight.

"Rarely." Her voice softens and she squeezes my hand back. She watches the man playing the piano for a long time. Her eyes grow glassy. My girl has the math memorized. It's hard for her to believe anything else. "I hate that I'll leave you too. But eventually you'll be okay. You'll move on."

"I won't." There's no way I could ever.

"You will." Picking up the napkin, she dabs at her eyes. "You'll meet someone. And you will fall in love. And you will have everything that you've wished for."

"*We* wished for." I can barely breathe through the grit in my throat. My voice cracks. "And you're talking like it's a done deal. It isn't."

"I'm not saying it is."

"Then don't say it at all."

"I have to." Tears streak her cheeks, and she swallows wetly. "Because I need you to know that I want that for you. If not with me... I want you to find someone who loves you as much as I do. I want you to be happy. You deserve to be happy."

"With you." I push away my plate. I'm no longer hungry. Couldn't eat a morsel if I tried.

"Or with someone else."

"No." I surge to my feet. I'm not going to continue this conversation. I'm not interested in what happens after. Or replacing Indy with some other woman who could never make me as happy as Indy does. The impulse to put my fist through the wall is almost too much.

"We should go." Indy drops her napkin on the table.

"Yeah." The other diners are staring at me. My scalp grows sweaty. They probably think I'm an asshole. The least I can do is make myself scarce so they can enjoy the rest of their dinner. "I have to pack for Baltimore anyway."

"Baltimore?"

"I tried to get out of it." I rest my hand on the small of her back as I usher her out of the restaurant. "But Manilow will only work with me. Are you still hungry? Should we grab something to go on the way home?"

"I'm actually full." She pats her belly.

Is that because she's eating so little her stomach is shrinking or because I screwed up dinner?

"So when do you leave?" she asks in the car. "And how long are you going to be gone?"

"I'm on the red eye tonight, and I'll be gone for three days." I rest my hand on her knee. When she doesn't cover it like she normally would, I get the sense she's pulling away from me. "But after that I'll be home a lot more."

Chapter Ten

Indy

Gray is calm by the time we get back to the condo. He unknots his tie, and I kick off my boots before padding barefoot into the living area. My stomach is a hollow pit and, while part of it is the lack of food, it has more to do with the way I ruined dinner.

I have so many things that I need to tell him. That I need to tell the people that I love before it's too late.

We only have a finite amount of time in this world. Mine is shorter than most people's, but that doesn't make it any more or less precious. The fact that I can see the end…brings savagely clear perspective.

I have no clue how to make Gray understand that I need to know that he'll move on. Be happy again.

He comes up behind me and wraps his palms around my upper arms. My back relaxes to fit his chest as he kisses the top of my head. His breath warms my scalp. "I'm sorry I ruined dinner. I overreacted."

"You didn't." There is no correct reaction to losing someone. There is no tried and proven method for getting through grief. We can only do our best to come to terms. Sometimes it will ache more than is bearable. Other times it is tolerable in its own bittersweet way. It's a never-ending path that I wish I could help prepare him for. But I can't even reconcile it within myself.

"Are you sure you're not hungry? I could order something." He stills, waiting for my response. "You can eat pizza in bed while I pack."

I'm not really in the mood. For food. Or anything really. It's been a long day and my head is throbbing. "I think I'm going to take a shower and put on my pajamas."

I stifle a yawn as I march into the bedroom to grab my fluffy fleece pajama shorts and top. I take them into the bathroom with me, turning on the water while Gray grabs his suitcase from under the bed.

The hot water soothes my soul once I'm under it. And so does the gorgeous artwork on my arm. Meeting Harlan was lovely, and hanging out with Theo is so much fun. It takes my mind off the bad parts of what is happening to me. Gives me something to look forward to.

With Gray it's harder. All I can think about is that our time is running out. My heart aches with missing him. I'm scared he won't be okay after…when he isn't okay now.

"I know you're disappointed…" He comes into the bathroom and gathers his toiletries. His eyes widen. "What the hell, Indy?"

"What?" My fingers snag in my locks. Thick strands wrap around my knuckles before they're rinsed down the drain. Oh God, I'm losing my hair. Is it obvious? Do I have bald patches?

"That. On your arm." His gaze is narrowed in on the kitten in the teacup on my forearm as he strides up to the glass shower door. His jaw works like he's chewing nails while he opens the door and grabs my wrist, pulling it out from under the water. I wince as his fingertips press into my flesh.

"How could you be so irresponsible? You know that the chemo drugs make you susceptible to bleeds and infections, but you got a tattoo? The doctor said you had to be careful. It was in the pamphlets."

"But it's not—"

"You're not taking this seriously." A nerve jumps in his cheek. "You've given up."

I yank my arm free of his grip. Gray has never talked to me like this. Never acted so…angry and judgmental. Jumping to conclusions. He's always been sweet and caring and careful. And he knows me better than this. "I haven't. It's not re—"

"I can't believe you would do something so stupid." His voice rises, his expression hard.

"It's not stupid."

"Well, it isn't fucking smart, Indy."

I'm shaking as I shut off the water and grab a towel to wrap around me. My head hurts but that's not what has me barely seeing straight. He's never been condescending. Even with him being several years older than me, he's never talked down to me. "I'm not talking to you about this until you calm down."

"Fine." He storms out.

I scrub at my skin with the terry cloth until I'm dry. I'm still seething as I get into my pajamas. The ache in my head has deepened along my jaw and behind my eyes. The pain of everything about my life is almost unbearable. Now Gray thinks I'm giving up?

I march into the bedroom, but he's already vacated it. Along with his suitcase, which I find by the front door. He paces while watching the news.

"I'm not giving up." I'm not. It's just the doctors were clear about their expectations. They're not confident about any of the treatments we're trying. At this point it's all a bid to prolong my time.

Gray's phone makes a sound. His ride is here. He glances at it.

I wait for him to engulf me like he normally would. Instead we end up staring at each other from across the gap our fight has created.

Eventually his shoulders droop and he pulls me in for a one-armed hug. He kisses my temple then breathes heavily into my hair. "I love you, you know that."

My hands smooth up his back. I cling to him. "I do. And I—"

He releases me. "We'll talk when I get back."

"Okay." My voice is barely there as he collects his suitcase. "Call me when your flight arrives."

"You'll be asleep. I'll text." He closes the door behind him.

I take some pain meds and turn off the lights before curling up in bed. I squeeze my eyes shut against the ache in my head. Touching the sheets physically hurts while I wait for the pain meds to kick in. It would be easier if we hadn't found the tumor when we did. If we didn't have a clue what was coming. I wish everything could be normal again.

Eventually the meds allow me to fall asleep.

My phone beeps with a notification and I grope for it blindly, finding it on the nightstand. The torture in my head is at a level I can deal with. The screen is still hard to read, the text doubles and is fuzzy around the edges. I squint to make out that it's from Theo and not Gray, who I'm still waiting on to text me that he's landed.

Theo: Hope you're having a better night than I am. I just got puked on by a coed.

Me: Oh no.

Theo: It was like a scene out of the exorcist. Anyway, I was thinking about your list, and I think we should try to do an item on it every day.

Me: Every minute is a gift, right?

Even if it doesn't feel like it. Even if the world I love is imploding around me. I want more than hospital visits and fights about not being careful enough. I want to find joy in the misery. Peace in the painful conversations. My soul in the things that I put off for a life that I won't get to live.

Theo: Exactly. We should make them count. Talk more tomorrow?

Me: Plan on it.

He doesn't respond for so long that I'm putting my phone back on the nightstand by the time the next message comes through.

Theo: Hey, wish me luck.

Me: What do you need luck for?

Is it because he's fighting like Harlan suggested? I recall the bruising I'd seen on his torso. Is he worried he'll get hurt? Is that why he wants luck?

He's silent for a few minutes so I text him again.

Me: Good luck

Nothing more pops onto the screen so I put my phone down and make myself as comfortable as I can without Gray beside me. He's normally a space heater, but the sheet is crisp and cold under my palm as I try to fall back asleep.

"Try" is of course the word for it. I'm not used to Gray not being here. I miss his hand on my hip as we're falling asleep. His heavy, relaxed breaths. I miss the way we used to be so easy.

I can't believe he would think that I wouldn't take my own safety into consideration. Some things are different but not everything. I still put on sunscreen before I leave the house. I still carry mace in my purse in case I need to ward off an attacker. I'm careful. I haven't changed so much that he should have reason to doubt me.

My phone beeps with a notification.

It has to be Theo saying thank you for the luck. Possibly even telling me why. I light up the screen to find it's from Gray, finally safely at his hotel. It should put my mind at ease. I should be able to sleep. But that's all I get from him.

Me: The tattoo was temporary. It's not real. It's like the ones they use on kids. I wasn't being reckless.

An hour later, I throw the blankets off with a huff. The couple of mouthfuls that I managed for dinner weren't enough and my stomach is gnawing at me. Gray still hasn't apologized for overreacting. Or even responded. The message is technically still unread so there's a chance he's sleeping. And I have no idea what Theo needed luck for.

I switch on the TV for background noise and consider the contents of the pantry and fridge. We haven't been grocery shopping because we're not eating much. And the milk is out of date. This is ridiculous. I want everything to go back to the way it was.

I end up sitting in the bottom of the pantry, cuddling a box of crackers too stale to eat, with tears streaming down my face, while I scroll through social media videos of some comedian who is suddenly everywhere.

If anyone were to see me, they would think I've lost the plot.

A message notification pops up on the top of my screen.

Theo: Pretty sure you saved my ass.

What on earth? I have no clue how to respond to that.

Me: You're welcome?

Theo: You're still up?

Me: Can't sleep. Gray caught the red eye to Baltimore, and dinner was a disaster. The only thing we seem to have in our pantry are stale crackers. They're chewy and powdery and so totally wrong.

Theo: Hmmm. Been there. Brings back memories.

Me: What?

Theo: When I moved to the city, I didn't have a job or a place to live for a while. I was making all the wrong friends. Sleeping on strangers' couches. Stale crackers hit different when you're homeless.

Wow. That's the most he's opened up about himself. And it's far more serious than I expected from him, even though I got the feeling that he carries a lot more on his shoulders than he lets on when we met up with Harlan.

Me: I'm sorry you went through that.

He messages me back almost immediately. Long enough that he couldn't have typed the message prior to my last one, but quick enough that it's obvious he doesn't plan on saying any more about that subject.

Theo: How about I buy you pancakes? To thank you for the luck.

Me: You still didn't tell me why you needed it.

Theo: Meet me here.

He drops me a pin to a diner close to the bar.

Me: It's almost two.

Theo: It's on your bucket list.

I lift myself up off the pantry floor and toss the stale crackers in the trash. It's not like I'm going to curl up and go to sleep anyway. I'm wide awake and can practically taste a stack of buckwheat and buttermilk pancakes smothered in syrup and butter. The aroma of bacon is so real that I wonder if someone close by is frying the streaky meat into crispy strips as I grab a coat to put on over my pajamas and drag on my boots.

Me: I'm on my way.

Theo: You better bring your appetite.

Chapter Eleven

Theo

Indy's slender fingers are wrapped around her coffee mug while we wait for our pancakes to be delivered to the table. Her legs are bare from the hem of her coat down to the top of her tan boots, and her hair is tossed up in a messy ponytail. Strands of it have fallen out and frame her face.

It's wrong that she's so cute all bundled up in a jacket that hides whatever she's wearing under it, but whatever, it's not like I'm going to hit on her. She's the only woman in a long time I've considered a friend. One I don't want to fuck up by fucking her.

Who knew I still had it in me to be a good guy?

I take a flask out of my pocket and unscrew the cap. My cup is half-empty, and I top it up with the Jameson.

Can I call myself a good guy when I messaged her from the bathroom of the Underground after my fight while some chick sucked my dick like it was a chocolate-banana flavored lollipop?

The blow job wasn't that great. It didn't feel right. It didn't even feel wrong in an oh so right way. It was bland and boring, and I could get better stimulation from my own hand. Probably will later, after I leave here. Probably imagining Indy being impaled on a flexible blue-tongue--cock-shaped-dildo.

I almost put out my hand for her to smack it, but then I'd have to explain what I was thinking to get that slap. Yeah, I haven't been able to get that out of my head. But I'm a guy and we love weird shit so it makes sense that I would still be thinking about it.

Really, it has nothing to do with Indy and everything to do with my own dirty mind. "You wrote down sex shop."

"What?" She blinks at me.

"On your original list. You wrote it down. In case you wanted to add it to your new one."

"I... uh..." Her brows squish together. The metal around her ring finger clinks on the ceramic as she lifts it to her lips. Her gaze stays glued to my jaw as the color heightens in her cheeks. "Maybe. I'm not sure." She takes a sip without lowering her gaze from my puffy jawline. "Does that hurt?"

"Not much." I grimace at the taste of Jameson and black coffee. It's not the worst, but I'm not drinking enough for it to be great either. About half what I normally would. My opponent packed some serious strength in his hits tonight. My head throbs and my ear is ringing and if I was wise, I'd be home, choking down Tylenol and passing out in my bed. Only then I wouldn't be across the table from Indy. And her company...I don't know...I look forward to it. "I should have weaved."

"Is this what Harlan was talking about? Did you fight?" She swallows. "Were you drunk?"

"Yes. Yes. And no." I shut my eyes and lean my head against the top of the vinyl bench. "I'm sober when I fight. Otherwise I would get my ass handed to me. I drink after. And I'm not drunk. Just taking the edge off the adrenaline."

"Why?"

"Because it helps me sleep."

The server puts two heavily laden plates down on the table in front of us. Drinking helps me keep my anger and guilt from leeching into my bones and sending me down a path I barely made it back from the first time.

"Thank you," Indy tells the server as she picks up her knife and fork. She's practically drooling, and her eyes are wide as she takes in the syrup soaked sweet. "I meant why do you fight?"

"To sleep." I'm not joking.

"I thought that was the drinking." Her mouth purses into a cute little heart as she chews on a bite.

There's that thought again. Cute. Except that word isn't in my vocabulary anymore. And it's not something I'm after. What I like about Indy...what I like the most about her...is that we can hang out without it getting complicated. And without having to go into all the details that make me the kind of guy she would want to stay away from. Indy has an expiration date and therefore this friendship has a natural expiry date too.

"There's a method to my madness." I wink at her as I pour the rest of the Jameson into the syrup moat around my pancakes.

She shakes her head. "I don't get you."

"I'm living my best life," I say dryly.

"That I understand." She wraps her lips around another mouthful and tugs it free of the fork. Her jacket sleeve falls back from her hand, and I sit up straighter as I take in the dark smudges there. Considering how I spend my time in the cage...I know bruises when I see them.

She pushes her sleeve up when it falls back down, to keep it away from her food while she's cutting. I count the ovals on the inside of her wrist. Four on one side and one on the other. Neat fingerprints all in a row. Kinky bondage fun? Or something else?

I'm about ready to punch her fiancé in the face as I lean over and gently secure her wrist in my hand. The uptight prick doesn't seem like he'd be into anything fun. He has to be the reason she's wearing more bruises than I am tonight. "Tell me about these."

She pales when I turn her wrist over and brush my thumb along the row. She must realize it's too late to hide them in the sleeve of her jacket.

"Did he do this to you? Did he hurt you?" I really hope he didn't. I don't want another reason for why he isn't good enough for her. It would be such a shame if she wasted her love on a guy who didn't deserve it.

"No. It was nothing like that." She takes her hand back and puts it in her lap.

"You have bruises." *So don't tell me it's nothing.*

"I'm on medication," she reminds me. "That can cause me to bleed more. To bruise easier. Gray didn't hurt me. He was upset."

"You know what that sounds like." My voice has grown deeper. Far more than I wanted it to. I try to smooth the growl from it. "Don't you?"

"I promise that's not it at all." She flinches though. She tries to hide it. Almost succeeds, but her eyes flare. They don't lie.

So maybe she believes it, but I don't. If he's so concerned with her welfare, he should be more careful. My dislike for the man is becoming more concrete every time we hang out. I'm starting to feel inclined to do something about it. "What was he upset about?"

"My tattoo." She goes back to paying more attention to her food than to me.

I don't think that she wants to tell me about it. I think she would argue if I suggested her fiancé was a bit of douche. "He didn't like your cute little kitten in a teacup?"

"He thought it was real." She chews on a mouthful. "He thought it was risky. I explained that it's temporary. Everything will be fine when he wakes up and sees my message."

"He left?" Who the fuck is this guy? He's overprotective, but he hurts her. He berates her for her behavior without having all the answers. Then he leaves?

"For work. He didn't have a choice." She blows out a heavy breath through her nose. "Can we talk about something else?"

"Yeah, sure." I drop the conversation for her. And because it should be none of my business. We eat in silence for a bit before I ask, "How about a round of twenty questions?"

"Okay."

By the time we push our plates away and finish our coffee I know that Indy has one sibling, an older brother. Her star sign is Libra. She spent three summers working in her aunt's bookstore which is coincidentally where she learned about blue alien cock. And she has never so much as gotten a sunburn.

She knows that I'm a Taurus. And that I haven't seen my sister in three years, but I talk to Shae at least once a week so that she never feels like I don't care even though I still refuse to visit. I learned MMA from the age of six and I used to study law. And that I jumped out of a plane on my eighteenth birthday. And every birthday since. Except for that one year when the weather was bad.

She shows me this comedian that she found on social media earlier in the night. She thinks he's hilarious and cute. I tell her that I could be just as big an asshole if that would make her laugh. I promise her she doesn't need to find me cute, though I suspect she won't be able to help herself.

She laughs and then tries to hide it by pressing her teeth into her bottom lip while her gaze heats with something that makes my skin prickle with awareness. There's an attraction between us. Otherwise that first conversation in the bathroom never would have occurred. But it's not important. It doesn't mean anything. It's how easy she is to be around that makes this friendship the real deal.

It's almost four by the time we vacate the booth.

Indy is yawning so big, it makes her eyes watery. The idea of sending her home alone when she's wrecked doesn't sit well with me. And when she wobbles as we walk between tables to the exit, bumping her hip into one hard enough to leave another bruise on her delicate skin, I wrap an arm around her waist to be helpful. "You okay?"

"I'm feeling a bit off." She touches her head. "Staying up all night is probably not looking after myself, is it? Perhaps Gray has a point after all. I'm taking too many risks."

It's more likely he's blinded to how stilted she is because of his own fear. Indy wants more. I can tell that by looking at her. Add in the bucket list and her not having a reason to pretend otherwise and only a blind man couldn't see that.

"We can share an Uber." I've already ordered one and they'll be out front in a minute.

"That's okay. I can get myself home." Her eyes flutter shut as she rests her temple against my shoulder. Whether she realizes it or not, she's asking for my help.

"We'll share." It's not up for debate. I'll see her to her door, and then I'll head home to my own bed.

The Uber pulls up a few seconds later and we pile in. It's a twenty-minute drive to her apartment. Her building has a doorman. He looks at me suspiciously as I help her into the elevator because she can barely open her eyes against the dim lobby lighting.

Great. Fucking great. There's no way her fiancé isn't going to hear about this. But maybe he should. Maybe he needs to be aware that there are bigger threats to his keeping Indy than he suspects. Or at least let him think that she might be smartening up to how overbearing he is. There's still time for him to turn this around and be everything Indy needs from him before it's too late.

I wish someone had given me a reason to fly straight when there was still something I could have done. But Cooper is gone and this never-ending shit show that is my life is my constant reminder that I once was much like Indy's guy. I had the love of my life. A future so bright we needed shades to contemplate it. None of it lasted. None of it even mattered when I lost Cooper.

"Thanks for bringing me home. I can barely see straight." Indy's hand curls up in my shirt, like she's using it to hold herself up.

I'm convinced of that when her knees give. Scooping her up, I carry her out of the elevator only to realize I have no clue which door in this swanky building is her place. "What's the number, Indy?"

She directs me to the right door while she digs for her key. Holds it up triumphantly, but also without much energy. I slide her to her feet, continuing to hold onto her while I unlock the door.

She whimpers as she clutches at her head. "Shit."

"Should I be taking you to the hospital?" This is the first time I've really seen her deal with the pain from the tumor. My heart is booming. What if this is worse than I think it is? What if I'm encouraging her to make bad decisions? Being the bad influence and not taking this seriously enough?

"No." She holds her head, her eyes squinty and barely open. "I need the painkillers in the kitchen and to go to bed. There is nothing they can do at the hospital that I can't do for myself."

"I'm going to help you." I keep an arm around her as we walk through to her kitchen.

Her place is nicer than mine. Clean and filled with modern fixtures. I have a lot of retro orange and green in my apartment. They're an untouched throwback to another era.

The kitchen is full of gourmet appliances, cherry wood, and white cabinetry. Her pills are set out on the granite countertop. She directs me to pick the right ones and where to find a glass.

I fill it with chilled water from the spout on the fridge and wait for her to swallow down the meds. Then I scoop her off her feet. "Which way?"

The bedroom is cozy, but less pristine. The covers are crumpled. There's a charcoal suit jacket and matching tie hanging over the back of a high-winged armchair in the corner. Cufflinks on top of a biography of one of hockey's greatest athletes on the nightstand. A picture of Indy and a man with blond hair and ice blue eyes smiling lovingly at each other.

So that's him. Gray. The douche who left her bruised while trying to prove that she could be hurt more easily and needs to be more careful. The guy Indy loves with her whole heart and won't hear a bad word against.

"I think I'm going to hurl," she says as I put her back on her feet. She covers her mouth and sprints to the bathroom.

It sounds like Chewbacca is coughing up a hairball. Should I go in there and hold her hair back? Or bow out and let her deal with it herself?

I screw up my nose as I beat feet to the bathroom door. It's acrid and nauseatingly sweet smelling. Enough to make softer stomachs than mine sympathetic. I've been thrown up on too many times at this point, including once tonight, to yak at the smell.

She's still bent over the porcelain, her huge jacket hanging around her waist and in a puddle on the floor. The thing she is wearing underneath is a fuzzy cream colored sleep set that is too skimpy to be considered pajamas at all.

Fuck, I'm glad I had no idea or our time in the diner might have been more awkward than the whole blue-cock-tongue-dildo image I haven't been able to unsee since it popped into my head.

She wipes her mouth with the back of her hand and moans. "Those pancakes were so yummy too."

Her hair is clinging to her damp forehead and there's no color in her face. Shit, am I doing the right thing by not taking her to the hospital? "Where do you keep your washcloths?"

She points at the vanity, and I open the cupboard to grab a cloth. Wetting it under the tap, I hand it over so she can clean up. "Those meds aren't going to take. I'll order a ride to the hospital."

"Seriously, there's no need. There's another one I take. When it gets this bad." She points at the top drawer and mumbles the name of the medication.

It's a nasal spray so it bypasses the vomit problem. There was the same one in the kitchen too. I hand it to her. Once she's done, I help her to her feet and the rest of the way out of that jacket so she can be comfortable, then support her while we make the trek to the bed. "Do you need anything else?"

"I'll be fine. You should go," she murmurs between shallow breaths. She's tense like the act of lying down is hurting her as she settles into the mattress. "I've already taken up enough of your night."

"I'm going to stay until the pain meds start to work at least." In case she does need to go to the hospital. I tug the blankets up over her. "I'll hang out on the couch. If you need anything, call out."

"Thanks." Her hand covers mine. She doesn't have the energy to really squeeze it, but the motion tells me she wants me to stick around. Does fear grab her when it gets like this?

I turn off the light on my way out. Shutting the door most of the way, but not so much I won't hear if she calls out, I stall in the hallway in front of a grouping of framed photos. I'm alert to every sound she makes. Ready to react to the slightest hint that I'm needed.

The photos are mostly of Indy and the douche. There are a few with the best friend who I met that first night Indy and I crossed paths. There are pictures of her family. Her brother. They share the same eyes and jawline. They smile the same way.

When she stops whimpering and her breathing evens out, the tight coil of tension releases and I move to the couch. The buttery leather groans as I settle into it. It's nice. Reminds me of my old life. I can practically see Cooper with her blonde waves and her blue eyes beside me.

She's wearing my Yale sweatshirt over her bikini because we've come inside from the pool and the AC is too cold. She's tickling me and we're laughing and kissing. It takes me a few minutes to recall the details because it's a real moment that we shared a long time ago, and I have tried to kill a lot of brain cells since then.

She's sitting on my lap and I interrupt our make out session to talk about the trip we're planning to take when we graduate. We were going to go to Cabo for the four S's. Sex. Sand. Sun. And surf. But my dad announced over breakfast this morning that he expects me to go straight from graduation to an office at his legal firm.

I squeeze her thigh. I tell her it will be better this way. That it means we can start saving for the wedding. A honeymoon. We can get married sooner.

And she smiles and agrees that Cabo can wait. Even though we've talked about going for a few years by this point. She opens to my kiss as I stand up and carry her to the bedroom.

We have all the time in the world.

Chapter Twelve

Indy

I don't know what disturbs me, but it wakes me out of a dead-to-the-world slumber. My head still hurts, but nowhere near as violently as it did last night when Theo practically had to carry me to bed.

I press my fingers to my clammy forehead. I feel like I drank an entire bottle of tequila by myself last night. I hate the hangover that comes with these headaches. My stomach is still a tilt-o-whirl.

"I said, who the hell are you?" That's my brother's raised voice.

"EJ?" Shit. What is he doing here? What time is it? Was I aware he was coming? *Damn it, Gray. You sent my brother to check up on me?*

My face aches because I'm clenching my teeth. First the argument last night where he flat out told me he doesn't think I'm being responsible with my own health. Now he's micromanaging me via EJ? This isn't who we are.

I toss back the covers as a loud thump comes from the living room. It sounds a lot like someone hitting the ground. Oh no, what is happening? Is Theo still here? Why? Are they fighting?

Theo must have fallen asleep on the couch while he waited to make sure I was okay. It was super late, after all.

I grab my phone off the nightstand and brighten the screen. It's almost lunchtime. I've missed half a dozen calls from EJ. More from Gray. Several messages that I don't try to read yet because there are still spots in my vision, and I need to get out there and explain Theo to EJ.

Theo's voice is groggy and thick with sleep. "I'm a friend. Theo. You're Indy's brother, right?"

"EJ," my brother says. "And you're sleeping on my sister's couch because?"

"It didn't seem right to sleep on the bed." Theo's response is combatant.

"What the fuck?" EJ growls.

Oh my God, what are you doing, Theo? My muscles ache like I spent twenty-four hours straight at the gym. It takes far more effort to shuffle out of bed than it should. Everything hurts and my balance is still off, so walking across my bedroom floor is akin to being on a boat in rough seas. Or at least, I imagine it is. I keep one hand on the wall as I walk into the living room. "EJ, what are you doing here?"

"Wondering why there's a strange man sleeping on your couch." He continues glaring down at Theo, who is on the floor.

Shirtless. Bruised. Trouble of the attractive kind. To most girls. But not to me.

"And why you're not answering your phone." He marches over to me as he taps out a quick communication. A second later my phone notifies me of a message in the family chat. "No one could get hold of you. Mom is freaking out. Gray has been on my back all morning. I was supposed to be preparing for court, but since I didn't have to go into the office, I told them all I'd swing by."

"I was sleeping."

"Indy, you're sick." Feet planted wide, he crosses his arms over his chest. Then uncrosses one to rub at his eyebrow. "Sorry if we worry about you more now."

"You thought I was dead?" The truth is at some point in the near future it's going to be lights out for me. And I pray that it happens in my sleep. So I shouldn't be annoyed that they would worry when I don't respond. They're all on edge. All hypervigilant. It's not just Gray. It's my entire family.

His chin lowers toward his chest. "That thought did cross my mind."

It's too much. It's suffocating. I wrap my hand around my throat and try to pull oxygen into my lungs. I don't want them to worry about me. But I can't stop it. There's nothing I can do to help the people I love deal with what's happening to me.

"I'm going to make coffee." Theo stands and stretches as he walks out of the room. "Don't worry, I'll work out where everything is."

A muscle in EJ's jaw jumps as Theo starts opening and closing cupboards, giving us space to talk. "I felt so sick coming up here. Not knowing what I was going to find."

"I'm okay. I'm fine."

"And that guy…"

"Is a friend." I'm cold and breaking out in goosebumps so I go back to the bedroom to snag a sweater.

EJ follows me. Expression pinched, voice accusatory, he asks, "Then why don't I know him? Why haven't I heard his name before?"

Shrugging into the comfortable fleece, I tug the zipper up. "Because he's a new friend. We met recently. After the diagnosis."

"And now he's sleeping on your couch while Gray is in another city?" His eyes cut toward the noise Theo is making in the kitchen.

"Oh my God." I drag a hand through my hair. Wince when the strands tangle and come out on my fingers. "What are you trying to say, EJ?"

"I…I don't know." His brow wrinkles. "That it's weird is all."

Is he seriously being this much of an asshole? "Unbelievable."

"Indy." He follows me out of the bedroom.

Theo has worked out the coffee machine and has three mugs of piping hot brew ready to go when I enter the kitchen. He's stolen my favorite stool and is scrolling on his phone while digging into the opened corner of my mother's foil-topped casserole dish.

His jaw isn't as puffy this morning, but the bruising is vicious, and he has equally dark bags under his eyes. I should have offered him an ice pack last night. "You didn't have to stay."

He shrugs but doesn't say anything as my brother comes into the kitchen. Scooping another mouthful of loaded macaroni and cheese onto his fork he pops it between his teeth.

I collect a glass and fill it with cold water so I can take the handful of meds I call breakfast these days.

"Talk to me, Indy." EJ stands almost too close to me as I fight with the cap on one of the pill bottles. "Here, let me help."

He reaches over and snags it out of my hand. It's easy for him to unsnap the lid, but all that does is make me want to scream and punch things. I want to tell him to get out and leave me alone. Tell him that I don't need him worrying about me. But I miss him already…I don't really want to push him away. Even if it might be easier than dealing with his hurt. "I can do it."

He hands me back the container and turns on Theo. "Are you homeless?"

Theo sits back and rattles off an address like he doesn't have a care in the world. Only I don't miss the coolness in his voice or the tightness around his eyes.

"Drug dealer?" EJ snaps.

"Holy shit. Can you not be so judgmental?" I flatten my cool palms to my overheated cheeks.

"Bartender." Theo grows stiffer.

"If you must know, I was sick." I plead with EJ to drop his interrogation. That's the problem with having a lawyer in the family. They don't sugarcoat their opinions and they have a lot of them. Throw in their ability to lead and win arguments and this is all going to go downhill fast. "I couldn't sleep, and I was ravenous because dinner with Gray was a clusterfuck. So we got pancakes after Theo finished work."

I leave out the part about Theo fighting and the Jameson. And that the first time we met he was definitely on something stronger than alcohol.

"And?" EJ's gaze swings between the two of us like there's some big conspiracy here.

"And I helped her get home," Theo says. "I stuck around in case she ended up needing to go to the hospital. Fell asleep on the couch."

EJ's shoulders drop back to their normal position. "I guess I should thank you for being here then."

"You're welcome." Theo snags another mouthful of macaroni and cheese. "This is really tasty, by the way. Compliments to the chef. I haven't had a homecooked meal this delicious in years."

"It's Mom's macaroni." My mouth waters as I inhale the aroma of homemade macaroni and cheese with bits of bacon scattered through it and a crunchy breadcrumb topping. Last night's dinner was barely more than a mouthful and the pancakes Theo and I ate later didn't stay in my stomach long. I grab two forks and hand one over to EJ. "I won't tell if you don't."

"Gray said you didn't eat last night so Mom had to whip up a batch of your favorite." EJ digs his fork into the cheesy pasta as I pop the first bite in my mouth. "I won't tell him about the pancakes."

"She didn't keep them down anyway," Theo says.

EJ frowns at Theo. "How did you two meet?"

"He was at the club where I had my bachelorette party." I shrug. It was a good night...well, it was before the accident and everything that came after.

"Wasn't that prior to your diagnosis?" EJ rubs his chin.

"Yeah. We bumped into each other a few times." The pasta melts on my tongue. It's better than sex. Well, better than any sex I've had recently. No, that's not fair. Gray's being careful with me. That's all. And I'm being a bitch because I'm frustrated after our fight and because he has my brother checking up on me. Still, this macaroni is the best thing I've tasted in weeks. "Mmm. It's like I've gone to Heaven."

EJ turns ashen as he glances about the room. Anywhere, but at me. "Christ, Indy."

"It never used to matter when I said things like that..." Now, it's all a reminder that hurts my family. It wasn't that long ago he was joking around with me. I asked him to behave as if nothing had changed, but still... "What happened to acting normal?"

"You have a tumor, Indy. Nothing is normal." He sips the cup of coffee Theo made him. His jacket is slung over the back of the other stool.

I tuck into a few more comforting bites.

His lips set into a grim line. "Your behavior certainly isn't normal for you."

"So Gray told you about the tattoo?" My appetite goes as quickly as it came. He must have, right? For EJ to be putting on the big bro act. I put my fork in the sink while Theo keeps shoveling morsels into his mouth like he hasn't eaten in months.

"Yeah." EJ huffs out a breath. "What were you thinking?"

I can't believe this. Well, actually I can, because they're best friends and it isn't the first time they've ganged up on me. But if Gray had listened to one word I said last night, my brother wouldn't be here to reinforce that I did something neither of them agree with.

I tug down the zipper on my sweatshirt and strip out of one side to show him the tattoo. My voice crackles as it grows louder. "It's temporary. Temp-o-rary. Do you understand what that word means? No needles were used. There's no ink under the skin. No breakage. No chance of infection. It's a kid's tattoo, only done by a real artist. Right, Theo?"

"You're correct." Theo smiles at me while he plays on his phone.

He is different from my brother and Gray. I knew he was more laid back, but it's only as he sits here nonchalantly chewing through a pound of macaroni that it's really obvious. They're trying to hold onto me, but it feels like they're smothering me. With Theo around I can breathe.

"I still don't know who you are." EJ narrows hard eyes on Theo. "Or what business it is of yours."

"Well, we're going to rectify that." Standing, Theo slips his phone in his pocket. "I have all three of us booked into a smash room in forty-five minutes. We're going to have to hurry though because I need to pick up my truck."

"What?" EJ rears back.

"That isn't on the bucket list." But the idea of breaking things, like we did with the pint glasses, is appealing. There is something healthy about watching your emotions turn into a whirlwind of physical destruction and then walking away calm and relaxed.

"You both need an outlet." Theo dumps his cup and fork in the sink.

"Bucket list?" EJ turns to me. "What are you talking about?"

"He's helping me do the things that I want to do before I die. He's helping me have the experiences I want to have while I'm still here. I have a list." When his face crumples I keep going. He needs to understand how important this is to me. "You and Gray both think that I'm not taking any of this seriously enough, but I am. That's why Theo is here. The treatments aren't going to fix me the way everyone hopes. They're to help prolong the time I have. Theo is helping me to get as much out of that time as possible and come to terms with the life that I have."

"Like a therapist?" EJ looks at Theo through new eyes. "A death coach, or whatever they're called?"

"Sort of." I press my hands together as I glance at Theo. It's a fairly accurate summation of our friendship, isn't it?

He nods. "Basically."

"Good." EJ loses the stand-offish tension that he's been wearing since he woke us up. "Do I need anything for this smash room?"

Chapter Thirteen

Indy

We're in a small basement below street level with harsh florescent strip lighting. There's a two-seat sofa and a table loaded with magazines. Along one wall is a bay of blue metal lockers. I pick up a *People* magazine while Theo leans over the kiosk to talk to the woman running the smash rooms.

He's all charm and interest as they go over the details of our booking. I flick through the glossy pages. The woman is giggling and blushing and falling all over herself to help Theo with the PPE that is stored in cubbies along the wall behind her.

"So is this something you do now?" EJ stands with his feet apart and his arms crossed over his chest. He went home and swapped out his suit for a polo and chinos. Theo went with him to pick up his truck and then swung back to get me.

"Huh?" Okay, I'll admit that Theo's attractive, but he's also looking worse for wear with the bruising along his jaw. It could be she doesn't notice because she's too busy staring into his eyes. Those pretty boy eyes are magnetic.

"You come to smash rooms?" EJ hums in his throat. "To break things."

"It's my first time." It's a bit much, isn't it? Does he ever get sick of flirting with every girl he talks to? And they lap it up like no one else has ever paid them attention. "Last time we broke glasses at the bar."

"You're spending time in a bar?" My brother is staring at Theo too. Expression tight, he juts out his chin as he inclines his head in my direction. "I have to ask…does Gray know about him?"

"It's where Theo works. I've been once. And of course I've told Gray about him. I can't believe you would ask that." It's like they don't trust me at all. I can feel my blood pressure rising. "Since when did I become a completely different person?"

"You're not…" He bunches his jaw and shakes his head. "But Gray never mentioned him. He never said anything about you having someone you were talking about this stuff too. Or a bucket list."

"I've told Gray about Theo." I'm sure I have. "And the bucket list. Perhaps he didn't think you needed to know."

My brother and Gray share almost everything. The only thing they don't talk about is what Gray and I get up to in the bedroom.

EJ raises a single brow at me.

"You're right." That was a dumb thing to say. "I don't know why he hasn't told you. He's been busy getting Manilow to contract though, so maybe it slipped his mind."

"If it were me. If that guy was hanging out with my girl…" EJ stares at his palms as if they might hold the answers.

"What's that supposed to mean?" I concentrate on his palms too. But there is nothing there to explain what the heck he is on about.

"Ready?" Theo comes over with an armful of protective wear and the attendant in his wake.

The woman briefs us on safety and hands out coveralls and helmets.

"Are you sure you should be doing this, Indy?" EJ holds up the helmet that looks somewhat like a motocross helmet. It has a full visor and will cover our entire heads. "What if you get hurt? This is too dangerous."

"She can get hurt if someone grabs her the wrong way these days." Theo clenches his jaw as he strips out of his jacket and places it with my bag in one of the lockers. "Do you have anything you want stowed?"

EJ empties his pockets, placing his stuff with ours. "What is that supposed to mean?"

"It's nothing." I reach inside the coverall and tug at my sleeve. Gray wasn't hurting me. It's the chemo drugs that are the issue. "And I get to choose whether this is too dangerous."

"But—"

Theo drags the coverall up over his wide shoulders as he comes toward us. "Fine, man, you're afraid of what could go wrong if we hand your sister a mallet and let her go to town on some crockery. Those shards can be sharp. Plus there's three of us... so if one of us accidentally swings the wrong way it could cause a lot of damage."

"Exactly. This is what I'm saying, Indy."

"Yeah, but your sister is dying anyway. So what does it matter?"

"Excuse me?" EJ's nostrils flare.

"Your sister is dying." Theo enunciates each word with care. "She's going to die, and you can't stop it. Or slow it down. Or control it in any way."

"But that doesn't mean she needs to take risks," EJ snaps back. "That's not you, Indy. You've always been careful."

"Well, maybe I regret that," I say softly before I pull on the helmet and pick up a baseball bat from the milk crate outside the entrance to the rage room.

The walls and floor are painted concrete, which has been chipped and beaten in places. It's filled with cheap bookshelves holding all kinds of vases and ceramics. Several small tables are stacked with glassware and plates. An old TV sits on the floor at one end.

Theo puts his helmet on with one hand while he hauls a long-handled metal mallet inside. He steps up close to me. His voice is muffled behind the protective gear. "Are you going to be all right?"

"Never better."

My brother is freaking out about everything. My fiancé is trying to fix me and keep me bubble wrapped. My mother is terrified. My father is barely talking. The only person who seems to understand what I need at all is Theo. And I am so sick of crying. It isn't fucking fair that I only have six months to live, and I still don't have a clue what will make all this worth it.

He touches my elbow. "So what are we going to do?"

I lift the bat up around my shoulder and swing it as hard as I can into the glassware on the table. Some of it explodes on impact. Some shatters when it tumbles to the floor. The noise eases the sickness in my soul. "We're going to rage."

"That a girl." He hoots before he lifts that hammer over his shoulder and sends it crashing into a pile of plates.

EJ joins us in the room, gripping the handle of a golf club. He watches at first while Theo and I smash everything our weapons touch. But then Theo goes over to him, and he must say something to my brother because EJ starts swinging that golf club into everything in range.

We're surrounded by dust and debris at the end of our session, each of us dripping in sweat as we take off our helmets. Our breathing is loud and fast.

"How are you feeling?" Theo asks me with a knowing smile curving his mouth.

I bounce on the balls of my feet. "Fantastic."

He lifts my feet off the floor and swings me around. "You're a total fucking badass."

I get caught up in the gleam in his eye. In the heady sweetness of letting everything but the here and now fall to the side. His lips part on a giddy shout.

I'm way too aware of how much thicker the bottom lip is to the top one. Of the scar on his chin. There's another across the bridge of his nose. Another on the thin skin between brow and eyelid. Are they all from fighting?

When my toes touch the ground again reality seeps in. I'm hyperaware that I'm too close to Theo. It takes me far too long to remove my hands from his shoulders. He mustn't like it because his smile fades.

My brother is staring straight at us with a wrinkle between his heavy eyebrows.

Theo's soft eyes harden. Tension thickens the muscles across his shoulders. Turning his back on me, he strides out of the room.

EJ is still staring at me.

"He's a good guy." I'm not looking for an argument. I don't want EJ's opinion on what I'm trying to accomplish with Theo's help. I press a hand to the wall and hang my head as I catch my breath. It takes longer now. Everything is more tiring than it used to be, but coming here and smashing things… totally worth it. "And he's helping."

"I can see that." EJ leans against the wall beside me, his club propped against his leg.

"Good." I hate arguing with him. It eases the tightness between my shoulder blades to have him see things from my side.

He rests his head against the concrete. "I'm scared, Indy. You're my little sister. I've been told my whole life to take care of you. I've dealt with you being a pain in the ass. And forgiven you for stealing my best friend. It isn't supposed to be this way. You're not supposed to be sick. And I don't know what to do or how to feel…"

"I'm scared too." My knees turn to water every time I think of the end. Will I close my eyes and go to sleep? Or will it be ugly? Will it hurt? What comes after? I struggle to breathe through the lump in my throat. "I'm scared of dying and leaving everyone I love behind. I'm scared that I won't get to do the things that I want to do. All this time I've had to live, and I've only recently realized that I don't know what would make me happy. I want to experience life. I want to have lived. But I don't want to hurt anyone either. I'm scared and sad and angry as hell."

"Yeah, I got that." He snorts under his breath as he runs his gaze around everything we smashed in the room. He starts to chuckle.

I laugh too. It feels good to have this conversation with him. Nothing has changed. I still have an inoperable brain tumor. But it's nice to be on the same page as EJ again.

"We should go." EJ pushes away from the wall as he sobers up. "Save that woman at the front from the charms of your death coach."

"I don't think she minds his charm at all." Even if he's over the top with it.

"I have to admit I find him a little bit charming myself." His laugh fades too quickly. "It makes me wonder if I should warn you to be careful."

"Would anything stop you?" I flick my gaze to the ceiling in a bratty display of eyerolling.

Theo is half out of his blue coverall. His sweat-soaked T-shirt sticks to every well-formed muscle of his back. He's not pumped up like one of those bodybuilders. He's all sleek lines and understated, agile strength from fighting and the type of workouts that must entail. Still, the material is stretched thin around his shoulders and biceps, ink is barely visible through the white cotton as he talks to the woman at the counter.

I'm disappointed I can't make out what picture the ink makes as she hands him three bottles of water. I've been curious about his tattoos since Theo said that every tattoo should have a meaning.

I strip out of the top half of my coverall. "What did he say to you to get you swinging that golf club?"

"He told me…" EJ has already shed his protective garment when he grips my arm and lifts it up. His gaze narrow on the fingerprints on my wrist. They've gotten darker overnight and look worse than they are. He tsks under his breath. "What the hell?"

"Theo didn't do that." My throat closes up as I tug my wrist free from his loose grip so I can finish stripping off the coverall. I don't want to go back to him thinking poorly of Theo, but I also don't want him to be upset with Gray.

"This is what Theo meant by you can get hurt by someone grabbing you the wrong way, isn't it?" His brown eyes search mine like he's looking for it to be worse than it is but hoping that it's all a big mistake. Which it is. He captures my wrist again. "Was it Gray?"

"It's nothing." I can't look him in the eyes. "I wouldn't have bruised if it weren't for the meds."

"I can't imagine what he was thinking." He examines the marks carefully. "I'll talk to him."

"No, you won't." I clear my throat. If I wasn't sick I wouldn't have bruised, and if I hadn't bruised EJ wouldn't feel obligated to pull the big brother card with his best friend. He'd let us sort out our own issues. And that's what I need from him now.

"Water?" Theo thrusts two bottles in our direction.

"Thanks." EJ lets go of my wrist to take a bottle. He twists the lid off and takes a long slug.

"EJ?" *Let me have control of my own life and don't get involved.* "When I'm gone Gray is going to need you, and you're going to need him. Don't complicate it out of some misguided sense of responsibility. It's the meds that are the problem. Not Gray. And you know it."

"Yeah, okay." He huffs out a breath. "I won't say anything."

"Thank you." I take a swig from my own water as he collects his keys and wallet and phone.

He switches on the device and the notifications start pouring in. He gives them a cursory glance. "Apparently my day for working from home is over. I need to get to the office. Do you want me to drop you off first?"

"It's in the opposite direction." I put the cap on my bottle. "It makes no sense for you to take me when I can order a ride."

"I'm going in that direction." Theo hands me my bag. "I'll take her home."

Chapter Fourteen

Theo

Indy's personal life has literally nothing to do with me. She has months to live, and I have a ton of guilt on my shoulders that I need to work through. That's it. All we have in common. The extent of our friendship. The problem is I'm having trouble remembering that's what I signed up for.

I figured it would be easy to help Indy with her bucket list because I didn't have to care about her. I just had to care about her need to complete her bucket list. And if I didn't get attached then it wouldn't hurt much when she was gone. Yeah, I'd think about her from time to time. But in that rose-colored way where it was a great adventure at the time.

Now, I have an opinion on the guy she's with. And I suspect I'm really going to miss her. But what's worse is that when I swung her around in that room full of debris, I was so invested in her that I forgot everything that matters.

All I was aware of is the way her hands felt on my shoulders and the way my palms fit the curve of her waist. How each time I stare into them, I see more little flecks of gold and cinnamon in her whisky colored eyes. She smells like vanilla and endless blue skies. And there is the faintest hint of flowers in her hair.

God, I wanted to kiss her. I wanted to bring her lips down on mine so I could taste their sweetness. I forgot that she's with him. I forgot that she's dying. And I forgot every reason I have for never getting involved with anyone beyond meaningless club hookups in dark, seedy corners. Until it all came flooding back in.

I can feel her warmth in my hands still, as I hunt my keys from my pocket. It was only a hug. There was no grazing of bare skin. No intention to take it further. It didn't mean anything. It doesn't change anything. But I feel it.

Like I feel the bruise along my jaw. In that sensitive way where you want to press on that raw spot and feel the sweet ache over and over again. It's a new sensation.

I'm used to the numb exhaustion of a hard fight. This is different… when Indy is happy she lights up something inside me that shouldn't exist. And that feeling…that sweetness…it doubles my guilt.

I should have supported and encouraged Cooper the way I am Indy. I should have taken her to Cabo, and I should have poured over a list of all the things we wanted to do. Checking them off one by one.

Instead, I took everything from her. Failing her eats me alive. Hurting her has me clenching my fists. Wanting to kiss Indy turns me inside out. I let Cooper fade into the background… I let her disappear in the moment, because I'm selfish.

Being around Indy is turning out to be a balm to my soul. And that's not what I signed up for. That's not what I want. I can't let it happen again.

"So are we going to make this a weekly thing?" EJ asks as we stand around on the pavement. "Should we invite Mom and Dad and Gray next time? I bet Dad could use the chance to pound on something."

My jaw tightens. Hell no, I don't want to spend time in a room full of weapons with Indy's boyfriend. That sounds like a fucking recipe for disaster.

"We'll organize an outing at family dinner," Indy tells him as he climbs into his sleek silver BMW. It purrs as it leaves the parking lot then roars as it picks up speed.

"That is a nice car." I used to love flashy cars. Fast motorcycles. Expensive boats. I appreciate them still. But I don't have the same level of interest in them I once did. The appeal of owning something like that is long gone.

"It's his baby." Indy wrinkles her nose as she starts toward my old truck.

The truck was new thirty years ago and had a dozen owners before I bought it so I could claim that I had a roof over my head while I was finding my feet. It's nostalgia that makes me hold onto what is essentially a junker.

"Do you think we could find a karaoke bar at this time of day?" Indy peers up at me as I peel open the truck door for her. "Cross another thing off my list?"

I can think of at least three places we could go at this time of day to sing some terrible rendition of Journey's "Don't Stop Believin'," or Linkin Park's "In the End." Or perhaps Indy is hiding a beautiful voice and it wouldn't be so awful, but I've got a craving for Jameson that won't be quelled until I black out on the ugly orange carpet in my apartment. Although I would pass on the Jameson for a decent fight.

I have my phone in my hand, and a message in Sigh's inbox before I can help myself. If there's anyone who won't mind me scaring up a fight in the middle of the day, it's the guy who got me hooked on them in the first place. "I'm dropping you home."

"Oh. Okay." She climbs up into the cab. A frown mars her perfect features as I pull out of the parking lot. "Is something wrong?"

"No." I twist my hands on the steering wheel. I'm aware I'm stilted. That she's picking up on my not-so-subtle mood change. But I can't come out and tell her the truth. There are things that I will never let myself forget. That I need to be punished for. And she somehow made those memories hurt less. She granted me a reprieve and for that I can't be around her. For that I need to bleed. Like I made Cooper bleed. That's the kind of fucked up conversation no one wants to have.

She gets a notification that draws all her attention to her phone. Her wide-eyed gaze spins across the screen.

"It's him. Isn't it?" How long did her brother wait before he hit speed dial?

"Yeah." She taps away at the screen.

Did he chew his best friend out for the bruises he left on her too? I really fucking hope so. "There better be an apology."

"He's asking about you. Asking why I didn't tell him." She purses her lips. "But I did. I know I did."

They text back and forward while I stew in my own frustration. I'll grind my teeth down to stumps, trying to make sense of how he can't see that she needs him to believe in what she's attempting to do. He's going to regret it. He might even become a shadow of a man, going through his days on autopilot. Fighting to breathe. Holding onto the memories because that's the only way to hold onto her.

Eventually, she slides the device back into her bag.

"Everything okay?"

"It will be. We'll talk it out when he gets back from Baltimore." She twirls the ring that is far too loose on her finger. Only her knuckle has any hope of keeping that thing in place.

I squeeze the life out of the steering wheel like I'm wringing his neck. Perhaps I'm not being fair. Everything with Indy is complicated. He's losing her, and that's got to hurt. He's having to deal with her hanging out with me and I wouldn't be cool about that either. It could be that my own feelings about Indy are making me biased. "If you need me to bring him to a smash room..."

She jerks her chin. "Okay. I'll keep that in mind."

"Great." Fuck my life.

"I thought smashing things was supposed to make us all feel better," she says a few minutes later.

"It was." I deflate. Have I ruined this for her? "You don't?"

"Neither do you." Her eyebrows squish together as she takes in my rigid posture and scowl. "You and EJ talked. Did he say something?"

"No." I grit my teeth. If anything I thought he was going to take that golf club to me when I told him he'd regret not talking to her about how her diagnosis was affecting him. And that he better get on board with her choices unless he wanted to be the asshole that holds her back from getting the most out of her time. I may have lumped him in with the fiancé who is definitely doing that.

"Or, um...did you strike out with the attendant? You were super into her."

I chuckle mirthlessly. "She's not my type. It's called being friendly."

"Uh... people can be friendly without making fuck me eyes at each other." She strengthens her jaw and stares me down.

"Can they?" I try to make it into a joke. By the expression on her face, my attempt to lighten up falls flat. I rest my elbow on the window as we drive through traffic. Press the top of my tongue to the roof of my downturned mouth. "I wasn't giving her fuck me eyes."

"You could have fooled me." She turns her attention to the diamond on her engagement band.

My heart skips so much it makes my stomach hurt. Does she know that I wanted to kiss her? That I was so close to doing so? Did she catch me making fuck me eyes at her? But logic settles in. If she did, she wouldn't be in my truck. She would have gotten her brother to drive her home. Or arranged a ride.

I would be looking at a text from her outlining all the reasons we should not hang out anymore. The bucket list would be kaput.

I'm so not ready for that. "Look, I didn't—"

"I don't care. It's none of my business." Her tone is clipped. She takes a breath, and her next words are softer. "I mean, you shouldn't feel like you need to not make fuck me eyes at the attendant at the smash room because I'm around. I don't want to cramp your style. We're friends."

"You don't." She's not the problem. It's me.

"Oh, I one thousand percent do." She straightens the seam in her pants. "I'm more than you bargained for. You didn't sign up to put me to bed because I'm blinded by pain or hold my hair back because the nausea makes it impossible for me to keep anything down for long. You didn't think you'd be woken and tried by my lawyer brother after a long night of babysitting me. And then there's my drama with Gray, and it's a lot. I wouldn't blame you if you wanted to change your mind about helping me with my list."

Sigh's answer finally comes through and it's not what I want to hear. He's been dealing with the police this morning. Some jackass provided information on the fights to help himself out and it's causing some heat.

It's nothing unusual considering the activity and the gambling that take place, but it means I'm going to have to wait until the next matches are announced like everyone else. Whenever that might be. I slam my hand on the steering wheel. "Damn it."

Indy recoils.

"It's not you." That bottle of Jameson is looking mighty fine. I might make fuck me eyes at it before I tongue the inside of the glass clean. "That wasn't at you. You're fun. And I like... hanging out with you."

"Sounds like it." She rolls bratty eyes at me. Exhales a short, sharp breath through her nose.

"Fucking hell." That does something to me too. It's a jolt of adrenaline, making my spine straight and my body hum. If she were anyone else... but she's not. There's no treating her rough. There's no stripping her bare and forgetting her name by the time I've had my fill. There's no being such an asshole she wants to hurt me for it. "Attitude much?"

She sticks out her tongue.

I snort. Perhaps its best she isn't like those girls. I think I'd find her hard to move on from.

Her eyes light up and she reaches across the cab to grab my arm. "I have an idea. Turn left."

Chapter Fifteen

Indy

"Come on, hurry up." I jump out of the truck and stride toward the building with the big vinyl sign hanging on the side. It has a colorful picture of two people wrestling in a toddler pool full of squishy blocks of red gelatin and claims it's famous for its Jell-O tournaments.

Jell-O was my favorite dessert when I was a kid. I loved the sweetness, and its wibbly wobbly texture. Even better with vanilla ice cream on the side, of course. But that's so not the point.

"This is what has you all excited?" Theo stops beside me. He folds his arms over his chest, but I can tell by the way he thrusts his chest out that he's feeling this too. One corner of his mouth lifts. "Are we adding it to the bucket list?"

"No point. We're going to mark it straight off." I grab his wrist and drag him into the building. A crowd is gathered around a high-sided kiddy pool where two women are slipping and sliding in the bright red Jell-O.

"Are you sure about this?" Theo raises a brow at me.

"Yes." I step up to the bar and crane my neck until I spot the sign-up form. When I catch the eye of the bartender, I smile. "Can you pass me that?"

"Sure, doll." He collects the clipboard and places it in front of me.

I pick up the pen and take a deep breath. I wasn't oblivious to the message Theo checked in the truck. I caught a glimpse of the SOS that he sent out to his friend about a fight before he angled the screen to hide it. He's been wound up tighter than one of those big metal springs since EJ left. I'm not dense. I can tell that something happened at the smash room. I have no clue what because he doesn't open up.

I wish he would. He's the one who told me it's not wise to bottle everything up. I want to be his friend the way he's been mine. I want to help him. If only to pay him back. But I don't know how to break through his walls. They're built so high and thick. At least this might help release some of that tension he's carrying around with him. "You have to sign up with me."

"What?" He stands behind me, his palm on the bar next to my elbow as he leans in.

"I know it's not the kind of fighting you take part in normally, and I know that you don't think I can help with whatever is on your mind, but I want to try. And since you don't want to talk about it…" I shrug. "We're wrestling."

"Indy, no."

"I'm doing this, Theo. I can't wrestle myself, can I?" My mind immediately goes to a dirty place.

Theo drags his hand over his mouth, his gaze dancing with humor.

"Put out your hand." I hold mine up ready to dole out punishment. "I could see what you were thinking. It was written all over your face."

"Only because you were thinking it too." He chuckles as he taps the back of my fingers when I'm finished with his.

"So you're going to do this with me, right? You're going to get all sticky and gross with me?"

"Indy, I'm bigger than you. Stronger. And this is a contact sport. I could hurt you. And I don't wanna do that."

"Anything could hurt me." I print my name on the signup sheet. "You told EJ that earlier. It takes nothing to bruise me. But risking a few bruises is my decision. I trust that you won't hurt me. Not really."

"You probably shouldn't." He studies the wrestling pool like he's mapping out how a fight would take place inside it. Worry lines form on his forehead.

He's concerned, but he doesn't want to decide for me. So I make it easy. I pick out one of the fiercest looking competitors. A guy with more biceps than hair. He's currently prepping by arm wrestling another burly looking man. "I'm going to do it anyway. I will find someone to jump in with me. Maybe that guy."

"Fine." He grabs my hand, tugging it down when I point at the man. "We'll wrestle."

We order drinks—coffee for him and iced water for me—and watch the other wrestlers while we wait for our turn. The matches only go for a few minutes and then the winner moves up the list to take part in round two. Everyone comes out of the ring wet and sticky.

Finally our names are called.

Theo takes off his jacket and drapes it over the back of a chair. He kicks off his boots and tugs off his socks before grabbing the hem of his T-shirt and drawing it up over his head.

"Show off," I tease while I drop my bag on the seat.

He ducks his head but grins unabashedly. His torso is lean but ridiculously well-defined, the bruising there subtler than that on his jaw for some reason. He stretches and his muscles undulate from his hips all the way up his torso and arms. The striations between his ribs become more prominent. The top of the tattoo I noticed the first time we met peeks out from the waist band of his jeans. I still can't work out what it is. But he said it has meaning, and that makes me want to see a little more than I otherwise would.

I bend down to take off my socks and shoes. Then get rid of my sweatshirt too. Stripped down to a tank top and pants, I won't be removing any more clothes.

He waits for me by the side of the pool. Offers me his hand and a smirk. "You first."

"We're enemies from this point forward." I stare him in the eye like I have any chance of intimidating him when he fights guys like himself every few days. And I need to balance myself with a grip on his bicep as I climb over the inflated side. Yeah, I'm real intimidating.

The Jell-O is squishy and cold between my toes. It's not the most pleasant sensation, but then I'm finding life is full of unpleasant moments that lead to great things.

"I'm going to ask one last time…" He peers into my eyes like he's trying to see so much deeper. "Are you sure you want to do this?"

The bell sounds.

I launch myself at him as I sound my battle cry. The surprise is enough for me to get the upper hand. The Jell-O makes everything slippery, and he might be light on his feet, but that doesn't matter when there's nothing grippy about what you're standing in.

He grabs me around the waist as he falls, dragging me with him. Protecting me, with the way he makes sure I land on top of him and not on the hard floor. "Oof. Holy shit, Indy."

He's trying to drag raspberry scented oxygen into his lungs, and I'm not going to waste the opportunity. I scramble up to straddle him. My knees are slipping and sliding and I'm essentially squirming on top of him with my hands pawing his bare muscles in an attempt to keep him in place long enough to be declared the winner.

It's awkward as hell, and I'm already panting and puffing. I'm not a wrestler. I've never done this before. I literally have no idea how to win here. So it's not surprising when he rolls over and takes me with him like I'm barely an inconvenience.

He manages to hold my hands to the floor, while the gelatin seeps into the back of my pants and tank top. The slimy texture makes everything that much more difficult. Somehow I twist free and get to my knees, but my back is to him, and I need to turn around in the slippery goo so I can tackle him again.

The other competitors are encouraging us on. They've picked sides and most of them are on mine. Probably because it's clear that I need all the help I can get. I'm tiring quickly and Theo's barely breaking a sticky sweat.

"Come here." He growls as he bands one arm around me.

"That's my boob," I squeak when he accidentally grabs a handful.

"Fuck. Shit. Sorry." He yanks his hand back like I've burned him, and I start to fall face first into the slime. Until he grabs a fistful of my tank top, and it tears as if it's made of tissue paper. But his hold on the material is enough for him to yank me back.

"Oh my God." I tumble into him, and we both fall on our asses. The material of my tank falls around my waist. Now the crowd is cheering because they're getting an eyeful of blue lace and more cleavage than I would ever willingly show.

Theo grabs me around the waist. He moves with animalistic fluidity. It's as though he's gotten a handle on the slipping and sliding while I've exhausted myself. He beams down at me with such smug confidence as he holds my wrists above my head. "You might as well give up. You're never going to win this one."

His gaze drops. He swipes his bottom lip with his tongue. Swallows. My chest prickles with heat. My cheeks too. But there's another sensation unfurling inside me. An awkward, uncomfortable awareness that this is too intimate.

He doesn't even notice that I slip my hand free. Not until I form a fist and drive it into his junk.

He coughs and splutters as he bows over me. There are tears in his squinted eyes and his face is taking on a pallor. He rolls into the fetal position beside me, his hands cradling his balls. "What the hell, Indy?"

I might have overreacted a tad. I didn't mean to cause him as much pain as I have. That doesn't mean I won't use it to my benefit. I straddle his hip and make a V with my arms. "I'm the winner."

He groans, still acting like a baby. "Friends don't punch friends in the junk."

I lean down and whisper in his ear, "Friends don't stare at their friend's boobs either, but here we are."

"I didn't do it on purpose." He manages to shove up onto his elbows as I climb out of the kiddy pool. Someone tells me I'm disqualified so Theo is the winner by default.

"Oops." I pretend that I didn't fully understand the rules we were told before we entered the pool while I wait for Theo to crawl out of the Jell-O. He's covered head to toe. Traces of it stick to his chest and his back and his jeans. There's a glop of it in his eyelashes. "You look a sight."

"Oh, I look a sight?" He still looks pained as he drags a hand through his hair releasing pearls of the red sludge onto the oilcloth under our feet. He starts to chuckle as he reaches over and brushes a big chunk out of my hair.

"At least I didn't hurt you too bad." I hold my tattered top to my chest, still conscious of all the people around us. And the way he looked at me while he held me down on the bottom of the pool. The way I fizzed up inside.

"You cheated." He glares at me.

"You were staring."

"I wasn't staring on purpose, but I'm a guy. I'm gonna notice when a woman, any woman, flashes her boobs at me." He limps over and picks up his T-shirt, holding out to me. "Here. Take it."

I grow hot again. This time it's all embarrassment. Of course Theo wasn't staring at my boobs because he wanted to. It was purely the surprise of my bra being suddenly on display that caught his attention. And my awkwardness is unnecessary. It isn't like I...want Theo. And if I'm attracted to him, it's because he's attractive. So is Zac Efron but I don't make a big deal out of that. "Thanks, but I'll be okay with my sweatshirt."

"Sure." He tugs the stretchy-soft cotton over his shoulder and down his torso.

I pick up the warm pink fleece and tug it over my head. Only once I'm covered up do I strip off my ruined tank. "You got hurt, didn't you? Your ankle..."

"I twisted it when you attacked me the first time." He drops to the floor to put on his socks and boots. "It's not a big deal."

"Oh, that's good."

"What about you? Any sore spots?" He gets up in one fluid movement and watches me carefully while I put on my shoes. "I tried to be careful, but you were a little heathen. When you jumped me, I thought for sure it was going to end up in disaster."

"You protected me. The whole time. That's the only reason the match wasn't immediately over, isn't it?" He could have had me pinned as soon as we stepped inside the ring. I rub my bruised wrist. Of course he could.

"Oops. Busted." He squints with one eye. Lays that pretty boy smile on me. He offers his hand and lifts me to my feet. Steadies me with a hand cupping my elbow. "So. Injuries?"

"Uh..." I take stock of my body and its aches. I'm still dealing with the headache hangover and my muscles are almost shaky after swinging a baseball bat and then with the effort to topple Theo. "Nothing new."

Sticky and gross, we hang around to watch more wrestlers fight it out. Theo gets back in the pool twice more as he moves through the rounds. He loses in the third round to a Finnish man who is as solid as a tree trunk and is possibly a real lumberjack. But he's grinning from ear-to-ear as he limps back to me with his boots and jacket in hand.

I can't help but beam up at him. I like seeing him relaxed like this. It makes him appear boyish, like he doesn't have any big cares, or he hasn't experienced whatever has jaded him.

"I think I have Jell-O in my ass crack." He laughs as he shoves his socked feet into his boots.

I wrinkle my nose as I stand up and brush a wet blob from his cheek. "And everywhere else. You're coated in it."

"Yeah?" He stares at me funny, and it makes my pulse weird out.

Wrapping an arm around me, he drags me up against him and covers me in a fresh smattering of the sticky goop. "You're all covered in it too."

"Oh my God, stop it," I squeal. I'm still tacky, but at least I'd managed to flick away the bits of Jell-O as they'd dried. Now, I'll have to start again.

He laughs as he lets me go. "Consider that payback for junk punching me earlier."

My heart is racing, but it could be the tumor. It could be another sign of my impending doom. My nerves fluttering could definitely be the tumor. This light-headedness, well, I probably overextended myself. I haven't eaten since the macaroni. I turned down Theo's offer to buy me lunch.

"Theodore Valentine?" a gruff, masculine voice calls out.

"Fuck." Theo's eyes widen and his face turns as white as a sheet. Taking my hand, he tugs me toward the exit.

The guy follows us as people try to stop Theo to talk about his wrestling prowess or commiserate on his losing the match to the Finn. Our tail is an older man with dark hair and salt and pepper in his wild beard. His blue eyes flick to me for a second before they go back to burning into Theo's back.

"Do you know him?" I ask.

"Used to." Theo doesn't slow down, but he draws me ahead of him. Presses his palm to the middle of my hips as he shoves open the door and ushers me into the cool evening.

We were here longer than I realized. The door opens and closes again. "Why is he following us?"

Or more importantly, why is Theo practically running from him?

Theo ignores the question. His whole body language has changed since the guy approached. He hurries me across the parking lot.

"Hey, I want to talk to you, Valentine," the man yells, an edge to every word.

"He's still coming." My pulse is racing, and this is definitely not the tumor. The hair on the back of my neck is standing on end.

Theo unlocks the truck and yanks open the door. "Get in, Indy. Get in now."

I scramble up into the seat and when I'm free of the door he closes it. The locks click as he hits the button on the fob, sealing me inside.

The man shoves Theo against the door. Pushes a thick finger in his face. "I knew it was you, you piece of shit."

"Don't do this, Nelson." Theo lifts his hands as though he's surrendering to this guy.

I don't understand. He fights. He's skilled at it. He told me over pancakes that he's trained in martial arts his entire life. Shouldn't he be protecting himself? I fumble my phone as I light up the screen, tapping in 9-1-1.

"Please." He bows his head. "Not in front of her. You don't want to scare her."

Scare me? I'm on edge, pumped full of adrenaline. I'm terrified.

The man locks stares with me through the glass. He doesn't blink. "Did you tell her? Does she know what you are?"

Chapter Sixteen

Theo

Fuck my life.

I knew Cooper's dad would catch up with me eventually. I might have run from my life like a dog with my tail between my legs after Cooper passed, but it's not as if I hid from the man who had treated me as a son for years before I took away his baby girl's life.

I think I always wanted him to find me. I deserve his hate and his retribution. The few months I spent behind bars—my sentence whittled down to almost nothing because of my bigshot lawyer father and his team—was never going to be enough.

He pulls a gun from somewhere and shoves the barrel against my ribs. I don't flinch, because I was never worthy of this second chance I was given when it's my fault Cooper is gone. But Indy doesn't deserve to be caught up in this. If she gets hurt because of me…

"Does she know you're a murderer?" His breath is heavy and hot against my cheek while he stares at her over my shoulder. He's mostly calm, his voice wavering a little with the emotion he's trying to keep reserved.

He's probably dreamed about this day. Obsessed over it. Considered every scenario. Nelson Mitchell is a kind man, a loving father. If those things have been buried, it's in an avalanche of my making. "Nelson, please. You're scaring her."

"Are you his girlfriend?" he glances at her and then back to me. "Is this Cooper's replacement?"

"No." Indy will never be mine. She will be Gray's until the day she dies. She loves him. She'll marry him in a few short weeks. When she takes her last breath, he'll be the man by her side. All we can be is friends, even if being around her brings me a peace that I hate. "She's just some girl. She doesn't need to be a part of this."

"He killed my daughter." His composure is cracking. There are tears in his blue eyes. "He hurt my baby girl. She died…"

I can't hear or see how Indy responds to him. I can't tell how scared she is or whether the warmth that was in her eyes earlier has been replaced with fear. There's no way she'll ever look at me again without seeing the truth. I'm not a good man. I'm not even a decent one.

"Every day I wake up and I remember the choices I made that led up to the accident." The back of my throat goes wet. If I had slept longer before we took that trip…if I hadn't had too much to drink. If I'd insisted we wait until a little later in the day or told my dad to go to hell. There are so many things I could have done differently. The guilt eats me up inside. The pain of it has become an addiction to my soul. "The way I felt about your daughter…how I destroyed the best thing in my life. I live with what I did. It never goes away."

"Don't call it an accident." He jams the gun into my ribs hard enough to bruise. "What you did wasn't an accident. It was a decision. You chose to kill my baby. My wife has since left me. I have nothing because of you. I welcomed you into my home and you took everything."

"I'm so sorry." My shoulders shake. My vision is blurry. Seeing him after so long… it makes everything fresh again. The guilt. The pain. "I would do anything to take it back."

"I'm going to kill you." He sobs, gulping air as he wipes at his eyes, the gun in his shaking hand. "I promised myself that when I saw you again, I would put a bullet between your worthless fucking eyes."

"You don't want to do that."

"Shut up." He snarls and spittle hits me in the face.

My lungs seize. I'm chilled to the bone. And the whole while my heart is booming like a big drum. I'm staring at the gun waiting for a bullet I won't see coming. Shot by a man who I used to consider a father figure. "It won't bring her back. It won't make it hurt less. And you're a good man, Nelson. If you shoot me... you won't get what you want."

"Yes, I will." He straightens his arm.

"No, I will." I point at my chest. "You'll take the guilt away. I won't feel it anymore. And I don't think that's what you really want."

"You're in pain? But I saw you with your friend inside..." He glances at her. "She makes you happy."

"She's no one." I swallow. Please don't let him focus on her. Don't let me be the reason Indy gets hurt. I'll never forgive myself for dragging her into my mess.

"No." The muzzle of the gun inches away from the center of my chest. "You were laughing. Smiling."

"I like her." As fucking crazy as it is for me to feel an emotional connection to anyone. "I like her a lot, but it doesn't matter. She's in love with someone else. She's engaged to him. And even if that wasn't the case...she's dying."

"You're dying?" He looks to her for confirmation.

Sirens sound in the distance.

"I have a few months." She clears her throat as she cracks the window. "Inoperable brain tumor."

"And I'm still in love with your daughter." I'm no good for anyone else. She was it for me. She was my everything. No one else can ever compare. Certainly not a girl who only has a few months left before she's wearing a toe tag. And even if Indy was free, what would be the point? I could never love someone I know is dying. It hurts too much to be the last one standing. "I live with her loss every day."

"The cops are on their way, Nelson." Indy is trying to be as calm as possible, but the strength of her voice wavers. "I'm so sorry about what happened but please don't shoot him."

He glances over his shoulder, but the police aren't close enough yet. He still has time. He roars in frustration, but he tucks the piece back into the waistband of his pants. "You remember my girl every day for the rest of your damn life, you hear me?"

"I will. I promise." It's not like I could forget what I had... and what I did. Or the love that I lost. The entire life that it cost me.

He grabs my collar with both fists. He's a tall man and he lifts me part way off my feet while he bares his teeth. "You don't get to move on."

"I won't."

"I can see the cruiser," Indy says. "They'll be here any second, Nelson."

He shoves me away. "If I ever hear that you've forgotten Cooper...or that you're happy..."

"I've got it." He'll find me again. He won't hesitate.

He takes off running as the cruiser tears along the block, and I collapse against the side of the truck.

"Theo." Indy is calling my name as she struggles to get out of the truck.

I mash the unlock button on the key fob and yank the heavy door open. She's crying, tears streaking her cheeks.

I wrap her up in my arms.

"Oh my God, I was so scared." Indy sniffles. Her cheek is pressed to my chest and her hands are on my back, inside my jacket.

I was so scared too. I was terrified that she'd have to watch him shoot me. That he'd turn that gun on her after he was done with me. "He needs psychological help."

I might need psychological help too, considering that if Indy hadn't been here, I would have probably grabbed the barrel and held it against my forehead. Egged him on.

The cruiser pulls up beside us and the officers jump out. "Are you two all right?"

"Yes." I release Indy. My chest cools noticeably without her warmth against it.

"Can you tell us which way the man went?" One of the officers—he looks like Sam Elliot with his white hair and bushy as fuck mustache—has his hand on his weapon though he keeps it holstered. "Did he only have the one weapon?"

"Um." I glance around and point out the direction I last saw Nelson. "As far as I know. He didn't hurt us. He's not a criminal. He lost his daughter...he just...he needs help."

"Stay here," the second officer orders.

I stay by Indy's door while they check out the area surrounding the parking lot. I'm cold and stickier than Bubble Yum bubble gum by the time they split up to take our statements. Eventually they're done and I climb into the truck, cranking the heat as they drive away.

Indy doesn't say anything. Doesn't utter a single question about Cooper. Or ask if I lied when I told Nelson that I have feelings for her. She sits next to me with her eyes facing forward.

It kills me that I dragged her into my mess. And that Nelson is a ghost of the man I once knew. My breath is choppy, and my head is spinning. I can't breathe properly. The oxygen is all stuck in my throat.

I rub the heel of my palm against my chest. God, I miss Cooper. It aches so fucking much. I bury my face in my hands as the pain takes me under. It's like a wave with its troughs and its peaks. Sometimes I coast along the surface, able to keep from diving too deep, but tonight Nelson has pushed my head under the water and held me there.

I walked away from the wreck, but I can never walk away from what I caused.

Eventually I get my emotions under control. Opening the console, I pull out a handful of napkins so I can dry my eyes and wipe my hands. Then I pass the rest to Indy in case she wants to clean up. "I'll take you home."

"Thank you." Her voice is barely there as I drive out of the parking lot. She clutches the napkins in her lap.

She doesn't utter another word until I'm parked outside her building. Then she turns to face me. "You lost someone you loved. That's why you're helping me?"

"Yes."

"Hmmm." She tugs at the sleeves of her sweatshirt, dragging them down over her hands.

I can't tell what she's thinking. She's always talking to me, telling me things, but she's put a wall up between us. She knows that I'm to blame for Cooper's death. She knows I can't be trusted. Maybe that should be enough, but I find myself wanting to clarify.

"I'm not a murderer. Not the way it sounds, anyway. I loved Cooper. I didn't set out to hurt her. It was an accident."

Indy stays quiet for a long while before she asks, "Then why did he say you did it on purpose?"

"Because it was my fault she died. My stupidity." I hold onto the steering wheel with one hand like it's a buoy, keeping me from being dragged away by the undertow of what happened back then and what occurred tonight. "We had a motorcycle accident. Lost traction in a corner and hit gravel. The bike pinned me, travelling a few yards. I came to in the back of the ambulance. Cooper was being airlifted."

Indy covers my hand with her own, and it helps.

"She made it to the hospital, and they thought that if they could get the swelling around her brain to go down that she would be okay. But there was internal damage no one knew about. Her organs started shutting down."

"I'm so sorry." Indy shakes her head. "I'm so sorry you went through that."

I don't deserve her empathy. "It was my fault. I was exhausted from the interning hours I was doing at my dad's law firm. And under the influence…Cooper and I had fought the night before and I'd handled it badly. Then handled it with a bottle of Jameson. Cooper wanted to do so many things and I should have made them happen. I should have put my career on hold. I should have put her first."

"Like you're doing with me." Indy withdraws her hand from on top of mine. She finally gets that everything I've done isn't selfless.

I've done it for me. Except for being drawn to her the way I am. The way I don't want to be. "I didn't mean it—"

"You said that you liked me?"

I clear my throat. I can still salvage this. I can take it back. "I told Nelson what he needed to hear."

She stares out the windshield at the lobby of her building. "That makes sense."

"If he thought we were lovers he might have shot you." I chew on my lip. Hopefully she's buying this as easily as she bought that me looking at her tits was a guy thing. "I couldn't risk that."

"I guess." She presses her lips together.

A man comes out of her building. I recognize his blonde hair and blue eyes from the pictures in her house. His eyes flare as he takes in the sight of his fiancée in my truck.

"Gray?" Indy straightens. "What is he doing home already? Oh crap, he looks mad."

"You didn't do anything wrong," I remind her. It's me that made our friendship weird.

He starts to march toward us, and she shoves open her door. "I've gotta go."

"Should I stay?" Because I will. I'm more than happy to help this idiot get real clear on how his behavior is affecting Indy.

Chapter Seventeen

Indy

"You should go." I slam the door closed and hurry toward Gray, meeting him a few feet from the hood of Theo's truck.

"This is the guy you're hanging out with behind my back?" He glares over the top of my head, the cords in his neck prominent.

"It's not like that." I press both hands into his chest when he tries to storm around me. His jaw pulses with the way he's grinding it. I've been so freaking stupid. "Gray, it's really not. Let's just go inside and talk—"

"The guy literally spent the night in our apartment the minute I left town." He finally looks at me. His eyes widen as he notices my tangled, clumping hair and the messy state of my clothes. "What the hell?"

"Are you okay, Indy?" Theo's voice is hard as a door shuts behind me.

Damn it. Theo isn't leaving. I told him to go.

Gray's whole body becomes rigid and his gaze cools as he lifts it.

"I'm fine." I reach down and cover one of Gray's hands. It's bunched into a tight fist at his side. My heart hurts at the raw emotion on his face. My Gray is patient and compassionate. He's not angry all the time. He doesn't have a violent bone in his body.

But then I've never been the girl who goes out with another man in the middle of the night for pancakes. Or spends the day Jell-O wrestling with him. Or looks forward to the next time I see him with an almost giddy excitement. I've never been the girl that Gray is losing day-by-day to an illness that will eventually take me completely.

I can't believe how ridiculously I've been acting. How unthinking…It's not bad enough that he has to accept that our future is short? I threw him this curveball with Theo. I'm such an idiot.

I didn't see what was happening between me and Theo until tonight while I watched him beg that man to leave me out of it. While my heart was in my mouth because I was so certain that he wasn't going to make it out of the situation alive. Even if Theo lied to Nelson about having feelings for me, the truth is…I've started feeling things for Theo. Feelings I shouldn't have.

I grasp Gray's face and drag his attention to me. I pointedly ignore the man watching on from behind me. "Let's go inside and talk, okay?"

Theo interjects again. "Indy, are you—"

"Go home, Theo." I only have enough attention for one man. That's the way it has to be. The way I want it to be. When Gray wraps his hand around my fingers my heart loosens. I'm done with the bucket list and Theo. I can't be his penance or redemption or whatever he thinks helping me is doing for him. I can't be around him when it's stirring up these unwanted feelings inside me. Now that I know that's what's happening… it isn't fair to Gray. "Please, Gray."

"Yes, we should talk." Gray lets me lead him toward the building.

The truck door closes and the engine roars to life. By the time we make it into the lobby Theo is gone.

Gray drops my hand, walking ahead of me into the elevator. He stares at his tacky palm like he wants to throw up. "Is this what I think it is?"

"Yes." I'll never see Theo again. I make the decision without batting an eyelid while we take the elevator up. Gray is my world. I'm going to make sure he knows it. I'm going to concentrate on the wedding. Concentrate on trying to stay alive for as long as I can.

"That's...God..." Gray turns his head and belches into his clean hand as he turns green. "Foul."

I forgot how Gray reacts to Jell-O. It's been so long since I've had any because of the way it makes him gag.

The elevator stops on our floor and I follow him into our apartment. Gray's suitcase is still by the door, as though he's prepared himself that he might not be staying. There's a six-pack of beer on the coffee table, three of which have been opened. His jacket lies in a crumpled heap where he tossed it on the arm of the couch.

"I'll go wash up. Shower." Then we can talk. When I have these thoughts and emotions under control.

"Not until we've talked this through." He's audibly hurking at this point. "But I need to wash this...*hurk*...off."

He races into the kitchen. The water turns on.

I stand in the middle of the living room. Arms hugging myself. Everything is falling apart, and I can't stand that I hurt Gray. That's the last thing I want to do.

Eventually he comes back, though he keeps distance between us. He scrubs his hands with a kitchen towel. "What is going on with you, Indy? You're lying to me. Hanging out with some guy."

"I didn't mean to hurt you." I rub my biceps. I'm still sore and sticky. It's been such a long night. "But I didn't lie to you either. I didn't hide what I was doing. I told you about Theo."

"No. No, you didn't, Indy." He paces a small square on the living room rug. "If you'd told me you were hanging out with another man...I wouldn't forget that."

"I told you about catching up with him and going to the bakery." I put my hands palm up in front of me. I didn't hide anything. At least I didn't until tonight. I'm not going to tell him about Nelson. Or what Theo told me in the truck. Or that there are emotions… It doesn't matter now. "I told you that we were hanging out. He's been helping me with my bucket list."

Recognition flares in his pale blues. "I thought your friend was one of the girls from college. You never told me your friend was a guy. Never gave me a name."

"I…" I replay those conversations in my head. Of course I told him about Theo in the same way I talk about all my friends. I've never hidden anything from him on purpose, but I can see how he feels like I did. "I'm so sorry."

For hurting him. For making him feel like I could betray him. For leaving him behind when our time is so short.

"When EJ called and told me about him…" He shakes his head. "I lost my goddamn mind, babe."

"Didn't he tell you that Theo is helping me with my bucket list?"

"Yeah." He scrubs his hand through his hair. "EJ said he took you both to a smash room. That he's some kind of death coach. But honestly, I have a bad feeling about the guy, Indy. We can find you a proper therapist. We can—"

"Okay." It's for the best. Staying away from Theo is my plan anyway.

"I'll help you with your bucket list." He takes a step toward me before he seems to think better of it. The bridge of his nose wrinkles. "I'll do anything for you, Indy. I love you so much."

"I love you too, Gray." I blink back tears. Less than two hours ago, I was oblivious to my growing feelings for Theo. Not anymore. I hate that I've caused Gray so much anguish. "Please forgive me?"

He takes in the tears that have wobbled free from my eyelashes and slid down my cheek, before taking in the rest of me. His lips part and then press. "There's nothing to forgive. It was miscommunication. Why don't you take a shower? Get cleaned up."

"Yes. That's a good idea." Numb, I drag myself to the bathroom and strip down while I wait for the water to heat up. Tonight has been too much.

I climb under the spray and let it slick away the remnants of the slime from my hair and skin. Another tear finally escapes and then they keep coming. It's probably shock. It's most definitely stress at almost losing everything I care about.

Gray, who loves me like he can't survive without me. Who would do anything in his power to look after me.

Theo, who has shown me what my life could have been if only I hadn't been so focused on the future. I was too busy sticking to the plan to experience it. He's made me feel more joyous and carefree than I ever have in my life. But it's over. It has to be. I'm too aware of the line that I've straddled.

It happened so quickly. Theo and I have been friends for such a short amount of time. But I've already come too close to crossing that line. Spending any more time with Theo would be wrong. And I'm not that person. I'm not the girl who falls for another guy weeks out from her wedding to the man she has loved all her adult life.

When every trace of Jell-O is cleansed from my body, I climb into my pajamas and take my meds. Gray unpacks his suitcase and leaves to pick up salads and grilled chicken from his favorite eatery.

I run a load of laundry then curl up on the corner of the couch and turn the TV on for company. Dragging the fuzzy blanket from the middle of the couch, I arrange it over me and pull it up to my neck. It smells a little like Theo. He must have pulled it over him last night.

I hate myself as I dig my nose in and inhale. I hate that my heart leaps when a message pops up on my phone and it has his name on it.

I swipe it away without looking at it. It hurts like I'm ignoring a part of myself, but ghosting Theo is for the best. I'm making the right decision to stay away from him. I just wish it didn't feel like my heart is shrinking. Gray doesn't deserve this.

When he returns, we eat together on the couch. He notices the bruises on my wrist and cries when he realizes where they came from. He holds it so gently as he presses his lips to each one carefully and repeatedly apologizes.

I tell him that it's okay. That the stress is getting to both of us. That the meds are the problem. I know it isn't him.

He touches me like I never tried to build a wall between us. And I fall into it because I love him so much and I want him to know it.

We make love on the couch, him hovering over me, one hand on my hip while his weight is balanced on his other arm. It's sweet and careful and emotional. But it's not like it used to be, and I'm not sure if that's because my body is changing with the tumor and the meds, or because my heart is no longer completely his.

When we're spent, he carries me to bed.

"I love you," he tells me with his hand on my hip. "We'll find a real therapist. We'll work on your bucket list."

I'm not ready to talk to someone new about my illness and my fears. I'm not ready to admit to what is going on inside my head and my heart. "It can wait until after the wedding."

"Indy—"

I take his face between both my hands and pour every ounce of love into my gaze. "I want to focus on the wedding. We're getting married in a few weeks. That's what I want to put my energy into. You and me and our marriage."

"Okay," he finally says, after a long pause, his body relaxing against mine. "We'll concentrate on the wedding."

Chapter Eighteen

Theo

Me: How did it go with Gray? Is everything okay?

Me: I was thinking we could cross karaoke off your bucket list. There's a place. Want to meet me later?

Me: I don't know if you're freaked out because of what happened with Nelson...or if you're avoiding me because of Gray...but if you could text me back, I'd appreciate it.

Me: Hey, Indy. It's been a few days. I wanted to clarify... when I said I had feelings for you...it wasn't true. Sorry if I made things weird, but they don't need to be. We can go back to how it was before.

Me: Serious question. Gray isn't holding you hostage or anything, is he?

"Hey, this is Indy. I'm a tad busy right now. You know what to do."

My phone glued to my ear, I pace the small storage room in the back of the bar. It's been a week since everything went to shit.

Beep.

"Indy, it's me. Er, it's Theo." I shove my hand into my hair. What can I say to her that will change this place that we've ended up? She won't talk to me. She hasn't read my messages. And there are so many things that I should apologize for. "It's been almost a week and I haven't heard from you. I don't know why you're freezing me out…"

I collapse against the concrete wall. "Not that I don't deserve it after what happened with Nelson. What I said…"

What I am. That's probably why I'm missing having her around. As much as I tried to fight it…Indy made me feel like I was redeemable. Made me want to eke a little more out of life than being numb. I would do anything to have her back in my corner. To feel that way again.

"You probably don't trust me anymore…"

And she shouldn't. I didn't help her out of the kindness of my heart. I helped her for my own gain. I used her to save my own life while Nelson had that gun pointed at me too. I lift my hand up in front of my face. I start to shake every time I remember the event.

"But I—"

Pez strides into the room and picks up a carton of glasses. "Going to be much longer? It's a madhouse out there. We need all hands on deck."

"Oh, right."

"Is that…Indy?"

I jerk my chin down. I haven't told him about Nelson or any of it. He still thinks Indy and I are hanging out.

"Hey, Indy," he calls out as he passes me on his way back, then he mouths at me, "Hurry."

"Right. I've got to go." I take a deep breath that doesn't alleviate the heavy feeling. "Uh, call me when you get this I guess."

"Hey, this is Indy…"

I can barely hear her voicemail message, but it doesn't matter; I have it memorized at this point. I take another swig from the half-empty bottle of Jameson in my other hand.

Tonight's fight was rough. I got clocked a couple of times and there's a ringing sound in my ear and the strobe lights are making me want to kill a fucker, they're so bright. But this girl is nibbling on my neck and it's not the worst feeling in the world. If I close my eyes, I can imagine it's Indy.

I can give in to that dark voice in the back of my head that tells me what I told Nelson about Indy is true. I'm into her.

"Want me to…" The girl grabs my belt and gives it a tug. I go with it…let her lead me into a dimly lit alcove. Watch her drop to her knees.

Beep.

Shit. I forgot I was on the phone. "It's me. I know I said I liked you, but I don't. I want to set the record straight. It was all bullshit."

"Who are you talking to?" The girl looks up at me, her hand on my zipper. "Me? You told me you wanted this."

"Not you." I sway on my feet. I miss Indy. Miss her voice and her smile. Miss her perfume. Her inappropriate facts. The way her eyes light up when she's excited.

"So, you want me to? Or no?"

I collapse against the wall and drag down the zipper myself. "Yeah."

Her hand wraps around me and then her lips. Her head bobbles back and forward.

I shut my eyes. Imagine Indy on her knees with her mouth around me. But then she's in the truck behind me and Nelson is holding that barrel to my face. The back of my throat starts to burn. My phone is still pressed to my ear. "Unless it's because I killed Cooper."

"Oh my God, you killed someone?" The girl on the floor pulls back, her eyes wider than her mouth was when it was wrapped around me.

I scowl down at her.

"That's so hot." She dives back in greedily. What the fuck is wrong with this girl? Shouldn't she be running away?

Indy did. That girl is smart. "I keep thinking about all the things that we haven't done yet. I think we should get back to it. Call me back, Indy. God, just call me back."

"Hey, this is Indy…"

I kick the baseboard of the bar while I listen to her voice. It's been weeks since I heard a single word from her. I've left so many messages at this point. Too many. Like a desperate idiot who likes his friend more than he should.

Not that it matters because she's made it clear that she's sticking with her fiancé.

Beep.

"Uh…It's me again. I'm going to go out on a limb here and assume Gray doesn't have you locked up somewhere so you can't get to your phone." I exhale and my shoulders fall. It's pretty obvious that our friendship is over. "You're avoiding me for one or all of the many reasons I've given you."

"Hey, can I get a drink?" A woman calls out impatiently. When I glance at her, her eyes widen, and she licks her lips.

I turn my back on her. "I'm just…I'm worried about you. Worried whether you're still…here. I'm going crazy not knowing. So if you could, text me. Anything. Even an emoji."

My chest tightens all the way down to my gut. I need to let Indy go, but I can't stop thinking about her. Wondering if she's working on her bucket list without me. Or with him. Or if she's thinking about me too.

She's started to crowd Cooper out, and it terrifies me that I would consider letting her do it if she would answer my damn messages. I can't be obsessed with another girl who will be cold in the ground long before her time. There's only enough room for one. And for my guilt. But I'm not going to be okay until I hear from her. "Message me, and I'll back off. I'll leave you alone."

I hang up and turn back to the woman in need of a drink. "What will it be?"

"White wine."

I pour her goblet while she runs her gaze up and down my torso. She pays, and I hand her back her card. The minute she walks away, I light up my screen.

Nothing. Indy isn't listening to my messages. She's banished me from her life completely. Of course she has. As if there were any other way this would play out.

"You look like my sister after one of those assholes she dates ghosts her." Wade walks past me with several cases tucked under one arm. He puts them down in front of the fridges.

He's a decent bartender. Younger than the rest of us. Quiet. He doesn't annoy me the way Lucas does. Isn't in love with himself as much as Heath is. But that he would equate me looking at my phone to his sister getting dumped… I shove my phone back in my pocket. "Go fuck right off."

"I didn't mean…sorry about your relationship, man."

"It wasn't a relationship. We were friends." Now we're not. It's fucking life. That's how it was always going to go, right? It's just, I have this feeling that I'm not done with Indy yet. And it's probably not even about her. It's about the bucket list. About Cooper and how she didn't get to do everything she wanted.

No, it's not about Indy at all.

Chapter Nineteen

Gray

"Here." I drop the thick blanket around Indy's shoulders. She doesn't seem to notice when I tuck it around her and take a seat behind her on the Adirondack in her parents' backyard. I press a kiss to her temple. "Are you feeling okay?"

"Mmhmm." She stares into the small flames flickering in the fire pit. She's lost in thought. Or lost in something worse.

The woman I adore isn't really here with me. When I wrap my arms around her and she rests her head against my chest, she's a million miles away. It's been weeks, and I don't know how to bring her back. Every day I can feel her slipping away a little more. It's ripping me to shreds, watching her give up.

"Hey, do you want to grab a beer?" EJ's mouth is pinched, and his stare is pointed. I'm not the only one who has noticed that Indy isn't okay.

"I'll be right back, babe." I climb to my feet and follow her brother into the house.

He liberates a couple of IPLs from the fridge while Indy's mom bustles around putting the finishing touches on a salad to go with the lemony roast chicken still in the oven. Stalking through to the living room where her father is immersed in ESPN, EJ leads the way out to the front porch.

We take a seat on the steps, like we did so many times as kids. Only with beer instead of lemonade popsicles. Quiet, serious thoughts plaguing us now, when it used to be girls and sport and cars.

"She's not well." EJ twists the lid from his bottle, but he doesn't drink. "She's going downhill too fast, Gray."

"The headaches have been getting worse. The nausea too." Her hair is falling out. She's lost so much weight. Far more than I ever thought she could. "We had to schedule another fitting for her dress to make sure it would fit because she's not eating at all anymore."

He opens his mouth to say something.

My throat thickens and I grab at the tightness in my chest that doesn't ever seem to ease these days. "That's not what I wanted. You know that. You read the same studies I did."

He peels the corner edge of the label on the bottle. "But it's gone too far. We have to do something."

"I don't know what to do." My eyes grow wet, and I pinch the bridge of my nose to stop it. She cries all the time. She thinks I don't notice, but how can I not when her eyes are always red-rimmed and puffy? She barely gets out of bed unless we have somewhere to go. It's killing me that I can't work out how to help her. "She says she's not depressed. She won't try a new therapist."

"I'm scared." He takes a swig from his beer. "Mom and Dad won't say anything, but they're freaking out. Things have changed these past two weeks. She's given up."

"America called me." I put my unopened bottle on the step.

"She called me too," he says.

Indy hasn't talked to her best friend in weeks. America can tell something is up. That we've been keeping things from her. "I don't think she's worked out what's going on. But I think we have to tell her."

"America would come straight home if she knew." He stares into the opening of his beer like he expects it to provide something other than liquid.

"But we promised." As much as I hate the idea of letting Indy down, it's fast becoming obvious that we're going to have to.

"Maybe seeing America would help." He leans in. "Maybe if she got America involved in the bucket list—"

"Indy isn't doing the bucket list anymore."

He pauses with his beer halfway to his lips. The gleam of hope fades from his eyes. "She's not?"

"She wanted to focus on the wedding."

"What about the death coach?" He frowns. "Going to that smash room with them really helped me deal with my anger. Not that it's gone. It's still not fucking fair that my baby sister is going through this shit. Or that we're going to lose her. But it helped me articulate what was going on in my head."

I didn't like the way this asshole moved in on my girl the moment I stepped away. I didn't trust that his motives were to help Indy and not to benefit himself in some way. I didn't like the way he tried to insert himself in our relationship that night on the curb either.

That could have been borne from Indy not realizing she didn't give me all the details. It could be because our relationship has been rocky of late. "You told me you didn't like the look of the guy."

"I didn't." His mouth puckers like he's sucking on a lemon. "But that was before we spent an hour smashing things. And he told me that my biggest regret would be not saying everything I needed to say to Indy while she's still here. We don't know when this tumor will take her from us, but it will without a doubt be far too soon and before we're ready."

I'll never be ready to lose her.

"I think she needs the bucket list, Gray," he says quietly. Seriously. "I think focusing on the bucket list was giving her something to look forward to."

"But the wedding—"

"Reminds her of the future she wanted but won't have." He blows out a long breath. "Don't you think? Doesn't it make you think about how soon it might all change?"

I don't want to think about it. I force those thoughts out of my head when they try to creep in. Indy is going to get better. The tumor is going to shrink, and the doctors will cut it out, and this will all be a blip that will make us appreciate everything we have.

I imagine her, belly round, carrying my child. I imagine her growing old with me. I refuse to give up because everyone else has accepted that there's nothing more to be done.

Standing, I leave EJ on the steps and make my way through the house and back to Indy. Her dad is sitting on the wooden lounger beside her. He looks gutted all the time since the diagnosis.

He gets up when I join them, his gaze glittering as he nods at me. Then he strides inside, leaving Indy and me alone.

I straddle the Adirondack behind her. Wrapping an arm around her waist, I bury my face in the crook of her shoulder and neck. We made out so many times on this very spot. The crackling flames keeping the chill away, not that we noticed anything. We were so into each other.

"Do you need anything? Can I get you anything?"

"No. I'm okay." She meets my gaze with her own soft one, before relaxing into me.

My chest aches. If I can't find a way to pull Indy out of her funk and cling to positivity, how can we possibly stand a chance?

"So, the bucket list?" I ask EJ while Indy rests on the couch after dinner. She barely managed a couple of mouthfuls, and I almost broke down. I wasn't the only one. Her mom had to walk away from the table to rein in her emotions. "Do you know where it is?"

He nods. "She keeps it in a notepad in her bag."

Her bag is on the hook in the hallway, the same place she hung her school bag way back in middle and high school. The notepad is palm sized, one of mine. It's open to a page of her handwriting. Some of it is already crossed off, like her temporary tattoo.

Karaoke. Kissing in the rain. Shaving her head. Dancing on a bar. Going to an adult store.

"It's all simple things that most of us have done." EJ reads over my shoulder.

Indy has never been like most of us though. She's always been careful. Always shied away from anything the littlest bit crazy. If this is what she needs to feel alive…which one of these is going to jolt her the hardest? "Do you think we can find somewhere for her to dance on a bar?"

"Uh, there's this place. One of my colleagues told me about it. She said it's not a strip joint, but the bartenders dance on the bar every Friday. And usually invite girls up out of the crowd. It's called Line 'Em Up."

"I'll start there then." I pull up notes on my phone and make a memo. It's two days until Friday. That gives me time to make sure it'll be safe enough. "Will you come with us?"

"Can't," EJ says. "I have a, uh…date."

The big surfer type guy behind the dimly lit bar is singing along to that Spice Girls song everyone knows. The one about getting with the friends. He seems to have every single word memorized.

It's an upscale venue. Fairly modern, and if I had to guess, renovated in the last six months or so. Everything is in great condition considering the wall-to-wall drink-and-dance crowd it serves. EJ said his colleague told him it's one of the most popular clubs in the city, especially on a Friday night. "Excuse me."

"Oh, hey." He turns from his focus on arranging bottles on the top shelf. "What can I get you?"

"I want to speak to your manager." I'm not going to beat around the bush when it comes to Indy's safety. I'm going straight to the top to get the assurances I need.

The guy grins widely, showing pearly teeth. "The name is Hudson. I'm management."

"I'm Grayson Ford. I need my girl to dance on your bar."

"Bud, it doesn't work like that." Hudson crosses his arms over his barrel chest as another guy comes into the bar with several cases under his arm. He crouches down to put them on the floor so that he can unpack them. "Although if she comes on a Friday night she has as much chance—"

"Hear me out." I put my hand up to cut Hudson off. "My fiancée has a brain tumor. It's inoperable."

"Oh." He drags his golden mane back with a hand, his gaze filling with sympathy.

The other guy pauses in what he's doing. Everyone who hears about Indy has a reaction. Mostly this *oh shit, deer in the headlights, what do I say* expression that makes me want to scream.

Hudson rests his palm on the bar. "Shit. I'm so sorry."

Of course he is. There is nothing on God's green earth that anyone can say that will make this better. The only exception would be the doctor telling us that she's gone into remission.

"Thanks. It hasn't been easy." It's excruciating on a day-to-day basis actually, but that kind of conversation is for the therapist I'll need in the future. Once Indy is no longer my future. I have a feeling I'll be swept out to sea at that point, with no idea how to get back to who I was before the diagnosis turned our world upside down. "The thing is that she has this bucket list that she wants to complete before she…dies. And dancing on a bar is on it."

"Well, we have to make that happen." Hudson leans on the counter. "You bring her on Friday night. I'll make sure the guys know. All she'll need to do is tell them that it's for her bucket list."

"I need a guarantee she'll be safe. She's on medication that makes her more susceptible to bleeds and bruises. She's fragile." Struggling. If I bring her here and this doesn't work, I don't know what I'll do. "I need your guarantee that your guys will be extra careful with her."

"We won't let anything happen to her." He stands up straighter, somehow grows impossibly taller as he thrusts out his chest. "I'll word all the guys up."

The other guy stands too. "Yeah, man, we've got her. We'll make sure to treat her as if she is family."

Hud glances over his shoulder at the guy, and the man shrugs and walks away. Turning to me, Hudson smiles. "They'll treat her like she's one of their own. You have my word she'll be totally safe."

"Alright." I'm still not entirely convinced. But Indy needs this. And I need her.

Chapter Twenty

Indy

Gray comes into the bedroom. "Babe, you need to get up."

He turns on the light and I blink at the sudden brightness. Drag the blanket up higher. I've cocooned myself in these layers. In this bed. I'm mired in this awful fog that has nothing to do with my head, and I can't seem to shake it off. I miss Theo more than I should. Or even expected I could. "I'm so tired, Gray."

"You've slept for hours." The mattress sinks as he sits on the edge. Leaning over, he kisses my forehead. "You can get out of bed for a little while. There's somewhere I want to take you."

"Please, I think I just need to sleep some more." Block out the terrible person that I am. Because I'm too weak to delete Theo's voice messages without listening to them first. Because the craving to respond to even one text still hits me each time he sends a new one. I'm doing the right thing by deleting them and not responding, so why does it feel like the worst choice?

Gray sighs heavily. Pats my hip through the blankets. "Indy, you're not sleeping because you need it. You're sleeping because you're sad."

"I'm dying." Isn't that enough reason for me to stay in bed? I need to go out and find more reasons to feel miserable? "Let me sleep."

"I can't do that." He stands and pulls the blankets off me before scooping me up. "I need you positive and strong. I need you to fight for your life, Indy. This...what you're doing...it's not helping you."

He places me on my feet in the bathroom before turning on the shower.

"I'm sorry, Gray." My cheek and his shirt grow wet as my emotions leak from my eyes. I'm so sorry that I'm leaving him. That we won't get our happy ever after. That in the time we had left I went and met someone else who makes me feel alive in a way I didn't know I could, and now I don't have a clue how to put the pieces of us back together. Gray deserves so much better than that. "You're right. Where do you want to take me?"

"It's a surprise." He holds me so close, his chest rising and falling against my cheek. His lips press to the top of my head. "Shower. I'll pick you out an outfit."

An hour later Gray drives us through Friday night traffic. I tug at the hem of my favorite dress. It has layers of white lace and pairs well with my favorite mid-calf, tan boots. "Are you going to tell me yet?"

"We're almost there." His mouth curves in that cute *I know something you don't know* way.

My heart skips a beat when we turn onto a familiar street. The bar where Theo works is up ahead, and the closer we get to it the faster my pulse races. My whole body turns hot and then cold when Gray pulls into a space out front and turns off the engine. Ice settles in the pit of my stomach when he climbs out to open my door and offer me his hand.

"This is where we're going?" Please, no. Let this be a coincidence. Why would he bring me here? Does he realize this is where Theo works?

"Line 'Em Up." His chest puffs up. "You can dance on the bar here on a Friday night. It's on your bucket list."

"The bucket list is stupid." I turn my back on the bar, while my heart urges me to race inside and lay eyes on the man that has consumed my thoughts since I ghosted him.

Gray grasps my bicep and ushers me toward the entrance to the club. "It's not. It was helping you. So we're going to keep doing it."

I drag my feet. "But—"

"Stage fright, babe. That's all this hesitation is." He leads me past the bouncers and inside where it's noisy and crowded.

"That's not it at all." The bitterness of beer and a cacophony of women's perfume sticks in the back of my nose. My heart stills at my first glimpse of the man across the room juggling bottles of tequila and Bacardi. Even with Gray beside me, I want to go to Theo.

His gaze finds mine through the crowd, and I forget how to breathe. His brow wrinkles as he looks me up and down. There are questions in his eyes. Hurt too.

We were friends and then we were nothing. But it feels like we're alone in this overly crowded room. If I put one foot in front of the other the chasm between us will disappear. The words I haven't said will come tumbling out. *I like you too, Theo. I like you a lot. Way more than I should. That's why I had to stay away. It's why I shouldn't be here tonight.*

"Come on." Gray leads me forward. Somehow he doesn't notice Theo or the way I reacted to seeing him. He finds me a spot in front of Pez. "You were the guy who was here yesterday."

"Right." Pez points a finger at him as though he's recalling the details. Then he smiles at me. "Hey, Indy, how are you? How's the bucket list?"

"What?" Gray's expression slackens as he glances between Pez and me. "You know each other?"

"Pez." I grab the edge of the bar and lean in. I need him to keep Theo away.

But then he's in front of me, pressing a hand to Pez's shoulder as though using him as leverage to close the distance. He climbs the divide and vaults over the glossy wood to stand in front of me. "Indy, what are you doing here?"

"I came to cross dance on the bar off the bucket list." He looks so good up close, but he has new bruises. On his neck. On his jaw. He stares into me, and I feel so bared to him. It's as if he should be able to read in my eyes the reason I vanished on him.

Gray tugs me into him, my back against his chest. Away from Theo. Gray's breaths are shallow and his grip while gentle is full of tension. "This guy works here? Your death coach is a stripper?"

"I'm not a stripper," Theo growls. The music switches and the crowd around us swells as everyone rushes to get the best vantage point for the guys' performance.

"Oh, right." Gray sneers at Theo. "You're just some bartender that takes his shirt off and dances on a bar every Friday night."

"Gray." I gasp.

Theo shakes his head, his jaw bulging. Planting his hands on the bar he pulls himself up before holding out his hand. "Come on, Indy. You've only got one life. What is it going to be?"

I can't. Doesn't Theo see? I put my fingers to the fire and almost burned them. Dancing with him now...it's too much. "I really shouldn't."

"It's one dance, Indy." Gray's arm around my waist loosens as his chest caves at my back. "It's what we came here for. Your bucket list."

"It doesn't matter. I told you I'm not doing that anymore." I turn in his arms and put my hands on his shoulders. "Take me home, Gray."

Gray shakes his head as he strokes my hair back from my face. He flicks glances at the rest of the bartenders who are already partnered up. "I wish it didn't have to be with that guy."

"It doesn't." Because it can't. Because the temptation is too great, and that's the last thing that I want. "Let's just go."

One side of his mouth lifts into a sad smile. "At least I'll know you'll be in safe hands while you're up there. Your brother thinks he's a good guy."

"Gray." I hold onto him.

He takes my hands from his shoulders. Turns me around and inches me forward. "Go. You get your dance, but after that we go home."

I take a deep breath as Theo bends to offer me his hand again.

Okay, I can do this. I can say goodbye to Theo. Close this chapter. Move on—no, move back to my old life for as long as I have to live it. And I can focus on loving Gray.

I slip my hand into his. It's a mistake of course. His big one encloses mine and the heat, the spark, the knowing there's more between us makes me hyperaware of his touch.

He wraps a hand around my hip and steps in so close the hair on the back of my neck stands as though reaching for him. His palm smooths over the middle of my torso and my belly fills with butterflies. The move is intimate, and my body responds by wanting more.

"You didn't say a word to me for weeks, Indy." His fingertips leave a trail of sparks as he runs them along my ribcage and up my arm, lifting my hand to cup the back of his neck.

"You left me a voicemail while you were getting head." It's almost impossible to breathe as I tilt my face to look at him. I'd heard him come for another woman. Heard the way his breathing grew harsher. The groans. I'd wanted so very much to be disgusted. "Who does that?"

"It wasn't my finest hour, but even after that I called. I texted. You couldn't even manage a simple emoji?"

"I'm sorry." If he feels even a fraction of what I do, then he has to understand that I had to do what was best for everyone. But God, I missed him.

I can feel every inch of where our bodies connect. His chest moves against my back. His hands explore my body in a PG way that feels entirely R-rated. His lips caress my ear. He's a little more unkempt than usual. His facial hair tickles. "Why did you cut me out?"

"Does it matter?" I whimper as he drags his hand up my thigh, lifting the hem of my dress as he goes. Sparks fly under his fingertips. Coil in my belly.

He spins me around and I have to put both hands on his chest to find my balance. He covers one of them with one of his, holding me there as he brings his face to within an inch of mine. His breath feathers my skin. "I thought we were friends."

"We are." Friends shouldn't want to kiss, though. They shouldn't lick their lips while they imagine lunging forward and pressing their mouths together.

He huffs out another breath. "I thought you understood that I only told Nelson I liked you because of the situation. But then you ghost me...and I can't work out if it's your fiancé..."

Gray. Oh God, I forgot about Gray. I twist clumsily in Theo's arms.

The cords in Gray's neck stand out. His jaw is solid as marble. But it's the hard, flinty look in those pale blues that are usually so warm that makes my heart shrink.

"Or if it's because I killed someone." Theo's voice has a painful edge to it.

"No, it's not that. What happened...you said it yourself. It was an accident." I don't ever want him to think that I'm scared of him because of the mistakes he made. Yes, it's tragic that someone died, but it was never deliberate. He made poor choices that led to a tragedy.

My choices right now are poor too. Staying instead of making Gray take me home. Continuing this conversation instead of climbing down from the bar. No one will die because of my decisions, but they are destroying Gray and that's not fair.

"So then why avoid me?" Theo asks as the music cuts out.

I shake my head. If I answer that question, then everyone will know. I'll destroy Gray. I'll hurt Theo. I'll create chaos in my family. And for what? I'm dying anyway. There's no future here. There's nothing here that can possibly last. "I had a wedding to plan."

The girls are helped to the ground. The guys follow.

Theo stares at me for the longest time. Then he climbs down from the bar and storms off.

"Hey, Indy. Let me?" Pez holds out a hand for me.

I can't drag my gaze away from Theo as he starts chatting to the first woman who approaches him. She touches his chest and I want to scream. He smiles at her, and I will never be the same. When our eyes meet, I can't breathe. And when he lets his hand linger on her waist, I can't look any longer. Wetness slicks the back of my throat as they walk away together.

I nod as I take Pez's hand. His gaze is sympathetic as he puts me on my feet right before he goes back to serving drinks.

"What the fuck, Indy?" Gray crowds me before I can catch my bearings. He grabs my arm and drags me away from the bar. His nostrils flare. "Do you want to tell me why I watched that prick make love to my fiancée in front of my eyes?"

"That's not...we were dancing. We were fully dressed." But I'd felt it too. How intimately we'd acted. Two lost souls finding peace in each other. Feeling the same ache. The same thrill in living.

"You had your clothes on. I'll give you that." He rushes me through the crowd toward the exit. I'm barely able to keep my feet. "And he immediately found some other woman to be involved with, but I saw the way he looked at you, Indy."

"What are you talking about?" The cold air hits my sweaty body, cooling me down considerably as soon as we're on the pavement. "Stop, Gray. We should talk about this."

"Talk?" He lets out a pained chuckle as he pulls me away from the other club goers. Towering over me as my back finds the brick wall, he scrubs one hand down his face. "I've been trying to talk to you for weeks. Ever since you stopped talking to that…" His expression crumples. "I see my mistake."

"Hey," Theo shouts.

Suddenly Gray isn't touching me anymore. Theo has him by the collar of his shirt and is glaring at him like he wants to murder him. "Don't fucking treat her like that, asshole."

"Who the fuck do you think you are?" Gray roars as he turns on Theo. He shoves him in the chest with both hands. "Indy is my fiancée. She's my girl. What is going on between us is none of your business."

"It is when you leave bruises on her, fuckstick."

"Stop it." My hands shake as I wrap my arms around my waist. I don't want Gray to get hurt. I don't want Theo to act like he cares when he walked into the arms of another girl as soon as he walked away from me.

"I would never hurt her. I would never toy with her." Gray shoves Theo again. "You though…I can't work out your agenda. Other than ruining people's lives."

"I saw the bruises, man. For someone who claims to care as much as you do…you're doing a shitty job of everything when it comes to Indy."

Gray's eyes bulge and he roars as he throws a fist. It might be his first ever punch. My Gray has always been so sweet, but his knuckles hit Theo's jaw with an audible thump that makes me wince.

I lurch forward before Theo can swing back. He has more than twenty years of martial arts training and fights regularly. The only reason Gray got a shot in at all is probably because Theo didn't expect it. Gray will lose this one. He will get hurt. Because of me. And I can't bear to let that happen. Getting between them, I press my hands to their chests. "Stop it. Stop it. Please. You have to stop."

Pez and Lucas come running out of the club. They race toward us, but Theo has already dropped his fist.

"Are you okay?" Pez asks me while he watches Theo and Gray with the intent of someone who is used to reading body language and is ready to jump in if necessary.

"He had her fucking cornered," Theo growls. "He's angry and he's not being careful enough with her."

"Theo," I cry. "Just stop. Gray has never hurt me. He would never hurt me."

"Move out of the way, Indy." Gray chews his words. "He doesn't get to come into our lives and turn them upside down. Accusing me of hurting you. What are your motives, huh? Do you get a thrill out of getting a dying girl to fall for you?"

"No, that's not what happened. And you know it, Gray. The diagnosis changed everything." It isn't Theo's fault that we're a mess. Or that I feel this connection to him. He never pretended to be the kind of guy I'd want to get mixed up with.

"Indy, let me take you inside." Theo wraps his hand around my upper arm.

"No." I shake him off. "But you should go back inside. You aren't a part of this conversation. You should never have gotten involved."

Theo draws away like I'm a flame and standing too close will burn him. His gaze swings from Gray to me. There's a rawness to the emotions in those eyes that make my stomach flip-flop. "Indy—"

"He's my fiancé, Theo." I tilt my chin up. He has to understand that I will always love Gray. Nothing could ever change that. Not my feelings for him. Nor my dying. If I have to be harsh with Theo for Gray's sake then I will. "You're only the bartender who helped me with my bucket list."

The color leeches from his face. "Do you really mean that?"

I glance at Gray; he has his hands in his hair and a look of absolute pain on his face. It isn't as simple as walking away. We have so much history. I need the time to deal with this correctly. Give Gray the conversation he needs. End things properly.

Holy shit, did I really just think those words? Do I really want to call it quits with Gray? The man who, until this very moment, I believed I would spend the rest of my life with? Or at least the next few months?

But even with our time limited, I want out. I don't want to hurt Gray, but doesn't the fact that I don't want to spend the rest of my life with him tell me all I need to know?

I don't have time to waste on a relationship that isn't making me happy anymore. If that bucket list—if Theo—has taught me anything, it's that I should choose to do things that make me happy. No matter how messy. Not to settle. Not to accept what I have because that's what I'm supposed to do... because we can't keep going like this. It isn't working for either of us. "I mean it."

"Okay, yeah. Fuck it." Theo grits his teeth as he stomps away.

Pez shrugs an apology and he and Lucas follow their friend.

Gray puts his arm around my waist and tugs me into his side. I glance up at him as he guides me into the car. I always imagined Gray was my future. But that future no longer exists.

He climbs into the driver's seat. He doesn't start the car. Doesn't say anything. He stares out the window for the longest time. "This isn't you, Indy. And this isn't me either."

"I know." I curl my fingers into the lace on my lap.

It's funny how when it comes time to say goodbye to someone you notice all the little things that have gone unseen. Like the golden prickly growth along his jaw that has become a part of his style these past few months. Like how dark the bags under his eyes really are. The lines have deepened around his eyes too, aging him. They soften my heart. Make me want to cling to the past. But I can't cling to the past any more than I can grasp for the future. All I have is the present. It's time we face that reality. "I'm dying and there's nothing we can do to change that. There's nothing I can do to stop it from hurting you."

God, how I want to. But the doctor was clear about my prognosis and my last scans didn't show any promising changes. There is no miracle this time. No cure. Gray can't save me by wrapping me up in cotton wool and locking me in his tower. He can't love me better.

I wish he could. I love that he tried.

"I don't want you to stop it from hurting, Indy. I'm losing the love of my life. We're getting married. We were going to have a family. We were supposed to have our entire lives in front of us. And now we're not. Damn it." His hand turns into a fist and thumps against the center of the steering wheel. "It's supposed to hurt. Losing you is supposed to ache so much I can barely stand to breathe. But it isn't supposed to happen now. I'm supposed to have months to love and cherish you enough for an entire lifetime. That's what the doctors said. So why are you already out the door? And with that guy?"

My own eyes burn and then spill. I love him so much. I hate that I'm breaking his heart. "There's nothing between Theo and me. Not like that."

"Bullshit." He grinds his teeth. "I'm not blind. Are you in love with him? Is that why you've been so sad?"

I scrunch the lace in my hand. I know love. I have Gray's love. It is rock solid. It is comfort. It is always having him in my corner. And I love that about Gray even now when everything is falling apart. I love who he is and who he has always been to me.

Theo is the very opposite of that. When I'm with him I'm scared, but in a good way. He makes me want to see what could happen if I spread my wings, and follow my dreams, and all those other cliché things that people embroider on throw cushions and are absolutely what make life liveable.

For so long I avoided taking any kind of risk because I didn't want to hurt my family or Gray. But I didn't live. And they're hurting anyway.

"Don't tell me." He exhales audibly. "Let's just go home."

"I'm not going home with you." I can barely get the words out. "And I don't think I can marry you."

"Baby." He takes my face between his hands. We're both crying. Our hearts are breaking in sync. "Please don't do this."

"I have to." I cover his hand with mine and remove it from my cheek. Then I remove the other as I back as far away from him as I can in the confined space. Part of me will always yearn to bridge that distance. "We are not the same people we were when we were happy, Gray. And I want to live. Not protect every last moment like that might somehow change my diagnosis, because it won't."

"I can do better," he says. "Be less cautious. Work on your bucket list."

"I slept with him." I blurt it out. I don't want Gray to hate me, but I think he needs to. That's the only way he's going to let me go. He'll hold on as long as he loves me. So I'll tell him what he needs to hear to be able to let me go. If I hurt him enough maybe that will ease the pain long-term.

"I slept with Theo. When I'm with him I feel alive in a way that I can't remember ever feeling before."

His lips part on a harsh intake of breath as he sits there as rigidly as stone. Closing his eyes, he covers his mouth with his hand. Eventually he opens his eyes and peels his hand from his face. "When?"

"While you were in Baltimore." It's easy enough to say that it happened the night Theo stayed at the condo. I work my engagement ring up over my knuckle.

"In our home? In our bed?" I can see his heart breaking in his eyes. The confusion in his voice turns to disbelief. "No, baby, you wouldn't—"

"It happened." I take his hand and put my ring in the center of it before I open the car door. There is no point in prolonging this torture for either of us. "Being with him is exhilarating and addictive. He encourages me to find happiness in the time I have left. He doesn't try to stop me from living."

"And I do?" Gray's features turn hawklike. His knuckles are white on the steering wheel as he starts to shake. "I used to know you so well. I have no clue who you are anymore."

"Maybe you don't." Who I am is a mystery to me too. I thought I had it figured out. I was his fiancée and EJ's little sister. I was Sharon and Oswald Jones's daughter. I was a woman with goals and a promising career. And now I have no goals and no career. I have no future with Gray. I am the daughter and sister and fiancée who is dying. I will be the daughter and sister that died before long. But none of those things is who I am.

I hold myself together as I stand on the pavement, and he drives away. Did I really blow up my entire life?

"Are you okay, Indy?" Pez joins me on the footpath. He must have been watching from inside the entrance.

As good as I can get. "I didn't mean it when I said he was just a bartender. I don't believe that. I don't believe that about any of you."

"I didn't think anything," he says. "Emotions were high. It must have been a hard situation for you."

"It's over." And it hurts. It's still the right decision. I turn toward the club. "Where is Theo?"

He makes a face like I won't like his answer. "He got his stuff and he left. Took a bottle of Irish whiskey with him. I'd say he's gone to work some things out."

So he's spoiling for a fight. "Do you have any idea where he would go?"

Chapter Twenty-One

Theo

*C*rack.

The brute in front of me rocks his fist into my chin. My head flies back with the momentum and my body follows. I stumble backwards into the metal cage surrounding the fight.

People scream for him. Others yell encouragement at me with the desperation of more money than they can afford on the line.

He shouldn't have landed that blow. I should have blocked it easily. I grip onto the honeycombed wire. I'm so fucking distracted tonight. I need to get my head straight. Need to do it or I might as well lay down and hand him the win.

What the fuck does she see in that guy? What does he hold over her that makes her stick to him when he's not right for her? As if I'd be any better...As if I want to be. But with him in the picture I'm not. And God, I miss her so fucking much.

I can practically see two of her through my blurred vision and the sweat dripping down my face as I turn to face my opponent again. She's so clear it's almost like she's here.

And she brought Pez. That makes sense. He's the only person she knows who would be able to locate me. They stand side-by-side outside the cage.

Another head-spinning punch has my lights flickering.

Indy's eyes grow so big. She covers her mouth as though choking back a scream.

Shit. She's real. Indy is really here. I scramble to get my balance. To refocus on the guy who will knock me out cold if I give him the chance. But having her outside the cage makes my heart bottom out.

She shouldn't be here amongst the bloodthirsty men and woman crowding the cage. She should be with him…that's what she wants. So why did Pez bring her here? I catch another fist to the chest, and when she screams, I'm done.

The other guy isn't prepared for me to turn the tables. I've been lethargic in my blocking all night, taking more hits than I needed to. Unable to concentrate with a head full of Indy. I come at him hard. Punch after punch. Until he's stumbling like a drunk. I don't stop until there's no chance that he's getting up again.

After the fight is declared I leave the cage.

"Theo?" Indy calls out as they try to push through the crowd.

Turning my back on her, I make my way to my bag. I take a minute to remove the perspiration and all visible traces of blood from my face, hands, and torso before tossing the towel back in my bag and pulling out a fresh T-shirt.

"Hey, man," Pez announces that they've joined me.

I tug the cotton over my head and smooth it down my torso. He brought her here. Am I supposed to be grateful or pissed?

"Theo, can we talk?" Her voice is a trembling caress on my skin.

When did this girl with one foot in the grave become more than a way to ease my guilt? I snag the bottle of Jameson and zip up my bag. My plan is to get very drunk, but not until I find out what Indy has to say. "Thanks for looking after her. But you shouldn't have brought her here."

"I made Pez bring me." She sticks out her chin.

"She can be a stubborn one when she wants to be." He ruffles his hair as he shrugs.

"And I can take it from here," she says.

"I'll make sure she gets home." And if that means getting in her asshole fiancé's face and taunting him with how she came running to me, it'll be my pleasure.

"All right." Pez leaves, disappearing into the crowded aisle.

"Do you want to sit?" Nothing could ever replace the love I had for Cooper, but the way Indy is making me feel...I'm so fucking relieved to see her. Bated breath stupid.

"Yes." She walks past me into the row, taking a seat in the middle.

I sit down beside her on the bench. The way I feel around her makes no fucking sense, and I don't even care, because her thigh is pressed to mine. And if I don't squeeze my arms to my sides then our shoulders rub too. "What are you doing here, Indy?"

"I needed to make sure you were all right." Her eyes are red rimmed. "And to apologize for ghosting you. Things got too complicated with Gray."

Indy crying twists me up inside. "Tell me you didn't come here to make it clear that we're not going to see each other anymore."

"No." She stares straight ahead, her fingers gripping the edge of the bench.

"Gray must be furious." His name leaves a bad taste in my mouth.

"We broke up." She rubs a fingertip along the skin under her eyes.

"I'm sorry." I don't mean it. At least not when it means she's here. But a part of me does wish that it didn't mean she has to hurt. And it's clear that she is. "Perhaps give him time to cool down."

"It was my decision." She lifts and drops her shoulders. "I gave him his ring back."

"Oh." I have no clue what to say. I seek out that diamond that has been on her finger since the beginning. She's right…it's no longer there. Only the faintest tan line hints that it used to be. My grip on the bottle between my hands tightens. My heart pounds far harder than it did in the fight. "So what now?"

"Friends, I guess." She lifts those pretty whisky orbs to meet mine.

"Friends…" It makes sense.

"Maybe we can start working on the bucket list again?" She stares at me expectantly while she holds her breath.

"I'd like that." Spending time with her and helping her with her bucket list is enough. "Why don't I find a bathroom to wash up in and then we go get some food and figure out a game plan? We've got some catching up to do."

She nods so I take her hand and guide her through the crowd, leaving the unopened bottle of Jameson on my seat.

I'm quick in the bathroom and then we find the club exit.

"Where do you want to go?" she asks as I hold the door open for her.

"I know this great place to get pancakes." I smile.

"It seems fitting." She chuckles as we walk toward my truck.

A big, fat drop of rain splats on my face. Another follows it.

"It's raining." She stretches out her arms to catch the drops as she tips her face to the sky.

Kissing in the rain. It's on her list. But it was supposed to be Gray she was kissing. Gray who held onto her so tightly she could barely breathe. Now she's free… "How did you convince him to let you go?"

Her eyes widen. She shoves damp tresses away from her face. "I told him I slept with you."

"Yeah?" My whole body starts to tremble, I want to kiss her so bad. I want it to mean that she feels what's between us as much as I do. "But we both know that's a lie."

"I lied. Does it matter?" She darts the tip of her tongue over her bottom lip and swallows.

"I didn't."

"What are you—?"

"To Nelson. I didn't lie to him." Clasping her face with both of my hands, I capture her mouth softly...determinedly. When she parts to me, I slide my tongue between her teeth and taste her. I've been dreaming of this. Wanting her sweetness all for myself. Living somewhere between prayers and hope.

She kisses me back, her hands covering mine as she lifts up on tiptoe. Her tongue tangles with mine.

All this pent-up want is kindling and we've lit the spark. The flames are burning us from the inside out. Our mouths are fused, and her hands are around my neck as her back meets the side of my truck. Her body bows so that every inch of us is pressed together.

Our hands frantically search and shape the other's body.

She moans into my mouth when I squeeze her ass and grind against her. The hem of my T-shirt rides halfway up my back as her hands explore. "Oh God, Theo."

I unlock the door to the truck and lift her into the seat. It's all the distance she gets before I'm kissing her again. Climbing up into the passenger side and scooping her onto my lap while I keep kissing her.

The rain hits harder as I drag the door closed, encasing us in the dry cabin. The fat drops pound on the metal and glass, blocking out the outside world and creating a space that is ours alone.

She straddles my thighs and settles her weight right over my cock while she whimpers into my mouth. Her heat and her sounds make me hard. Make my damn eyes cross with the exquisite torture. I find the zipper on the back of her dress. Loosen it little by little. Enough that I can slide my hand inside to feel her warm, dry skin. The small side-curve of her tits. "I've been dreaming about kissing you."

"You have?" Her cheeks are radiant as her gaze slides shyly away. She toys with my shirt sleeve. "I've wanted it too."

I tip her chin up and take in the naked truth in her eyes. She feels guilty.

She cut off all contact with me for weeks in an attempt to stay true to him. If he hadn't accidentally brought us back together tonight, I have no doubt she would have ended up marrying him. Thinking about it makes me want to punch something. "Do you regret it now that it's happened?"

She doesn't scramble off my lap like I expect her to. Doesn't announce that she's made a mistake. Or run back to him. "No."

"Thank God." I surge forward and claim her lips.

We kiss for a long time. Her hands wander over my chest and under the hem of my T-shirt. Mine stroke her bare skin but keep it at second base. We're experiencing being with each other without taking it too far before she is ready.

My heart feels two times its usual size. I suck her bottom lip between my teeth and bite down ridiculously gently. I like her weight on me. I like the vanilla rose scent when I nestle my nose against her hair. I like the way her hands push up the hem of my shirt and skate across my abs.

The rain has eased up by the time we break apart. I'm breathing like a freight train, needing more from her and fighting for self-control. Wanting to touch her and taste her and cover her in me so that she forgets all about him.

"What's wrong?" she asks. "You're tense."

I'm used to being drunk or high, and I am not used to caring too much about the person I'm with. Indy heightens every one of my senses. She makes me see stars. How can she not know what she's doing to me? How can she not feel how worked up I am? "Nothing."

"Theo, don't start treating me as though I'm incapable of handling whatever it is." She pushes off my chest. "Please don't change on me. Tell me what's wrong."

"That's not it." I cup her cheek.

"Then tell me what you're thinking."

"Tell you?"

"Yes." Her eyes flare.

I take a deep breath. "I want you to touch me so much. I want your hand wrapped around my cock until I come. I want to see whether your mouth can handle my piercings. And I want inside you so fucking much I can barely think straight. Christ, I want to put your ass on the bucket list."

"Okay, well, that's..." she giggles, "a lot to unpack. You have piercings?"

"Yes." Across the road is a neon sign on a building that screams adult store.

"And you want to..."

"Very much so." I grasp her ass cheeks in my hands and squeeze.

Her eyes darken. "Maybe you do need to start a bucket list."

"Well, everything I admitted to you is pretty much what would be on that list." I grin at her. "But you have adult store on your list and..." I nod at the venue, "it's no longer raining. So how about we go and check it out?"

Chapter Twenty-Two

Indy

I always thought the only man who would touch me would be Gray. He was my first and he was gentle, sweet, and patient. He made me orgasm that first time when most of the girls I went to school with didn't get to experience that even after multiple partners. I promised him he would be my last when I said yes to marrying him.

Until tonight, I believed that would be the extent of my experience. The way Theo told me what he wanted to do to me still has my mind reeling. The fact that he has piercings…I'm curious enough that I consider untying the drawstring in his shorts and tugging the waistband away from his abs so I can see.

Now he's holding my hand as we walk into the well-lit shop with its front window of mannequins dressed as nurses, and cops, or in nothing but a leather halter and gimp mask. So weird.

It's going to take a breath to get used to Gray not being my home. But Theo is helping it hurt a lot less than I thought it would. Parts of my heart will always belong to Gray, but Theo holds some too. He's crowding out the pain and the doubt.

He wraps an arm around my waist as we walk around looking at the dildos and vibrators. At the wall of handcuffs and hot wax candles and feather whips. At the rainbow of dildos in all different sizes. At the sex swings and harnesses and collars.

The heat in my cheeks must be a beacon. This girl has never set foot in an adult store before. I do own a vibrator, but that was an online purchase; and yet still became embarrassing when it was accidentally delivered to my neighbors—the discreet box damaged enough to be obvious what was inside. I really loved the way they looked at me when they brought it over to our house.

"Hey." Theo presses his lips to my temple. "Remember how you thought giraffes were creepy with their weirdly erotic blue tongues?"

"Of course." I follow the direction he points; to a display of blue alien looking vibrators that also somehow kind of look like tongues.

"Oh God." I cover my mouth as an awkward laugh escapes.

"We have to take a closer look, don't we?" His breath is hot on my skin. The growl in his voice makes my breath catch.

Curiosity has me walking over to the display. I want to say I'm not intrigued, but the idea of what it would feel like...it stirs something inside me. Makes my belly quiver.

"Do you know what I imagined when you were telling me about that?"

"Whatever it was, it was dirty." I clear my throat. Swallow the excess saliva. He'd told me as much, made me slap his hand.

"You." He smooths his hands from my elbows to my shoulders. Lifts my wet hair from my nape and puts it all over one shoulder so he can kiss the side of my neck. "Naked. Splayed on my bed. That vibrator stretching your pussy and making you orgasm."

"That's what you imagined?" My voice is barely there. My whole body is on fire as I envision it too.

"Many, many times." He bites my earlobe. "I'd watch you take it. I'd control the vibration. It would be the hottest fucking thing I've ever seen. And when you were done with the toy, I'd fill you with the real thing and you'd take it all, wouldn't you? All of me?"

"Theo." My breath quickens, and I close my eyes. God, I want that. I want to experience it all. I want to feel the kind of alive that I only feel with him. "You've been thinking about that this entire time?"

"I have." He drops a hand to my belly, fingers pointed down, then inches them that little bit further to the apex of my thighs. "I want to put it on my bucket list. If you'll let me?"

Maybe the guy at the counter can see or maybe he can't. Theo isn't actually touching me inappropriately, but my whole body is on fire with anticipation. I nod as I turn and pull him against me. Press up on my toes and kiss him.

Like before, we combust. He crowds me back against the wall as he tortures my mouth with the sweet promise of more.

Blue vibrators fall off the shelves around us as he lifts me up and uses the display wall to balance us. One bonks him on the head.

"Hey, stop that." The man leaves the counter to come and yell at us.

Theo laughs as he slides me down his body. He lets me go to grab the closest blue alien vibrator in a box. He holds it out to the man with a look of contrition. "We'll take this one. And whatever lube you recommend."

He pays for the vibrator, and we step back into the night. It's super late and I'm not sure what happens next. Do we go back to his place and immediately put that blue alien vibrator to use or…?

"What now?" He opens the truck for me to climb in. Then goes around to the other side. "Should I take you home?"

"I…don't have a home." I moved into Gray's condo because we were getting married, but now…I'll have to pack up my things. I'll have to move everything back to my parents' house. EJ is going to take it the hardest. I've broken his best friend's heart. How do I smooth things over for my brother and parents? They don't deserve to lose another person they care about. We're going to have to find a way to coexist. Perhaps I should have thought about that before I lied about sleeping with Theo.

"Indy?" Theo covers my knee. "My place is a dump, but it's yours for as long as you need it."

"I don't want to crowd you."

He clasps my face and brushes his thumb along my cheek. "I want you to. I want you in my bed. I was going to be so disappointed if you'd told me to take you home."

I latch my seatbelt. "Show me your place."

His apartment is hideous. A mixture of oranges and browns and greens that probably should have been forgotten decades ago. It's barely furnished and has no pictures on the walls or keepsakes lying about. Two recliners, a sofa, and a coffee table don't adequately fill the living room. A TV and the same gaming system my brother owns is on the opposite wall.

A bottle of Jameson is on the top of the fridge and several mason jars are in the drainer by the sink. There are a couple of pictures on the fridge. Cooper, maybe? She's very pretty and she looks at the person behind the camera with love in her blue eyes.

The other must be his younger sister. They have such similar features. Same cheeks and nose and dark hair. But where Theo's eyes are breathtaking in their uniqueness, her eyes are singularly blue.

"That's Shae." He nods at the photo I was staring at.

"I can see the resemblance." Almost a decade younger than him, she sounds nice, if a little complex. He told me that she has ADHD and that sometimes it really messes with her head. Sometimes she takes rejection hard and that she'll stop talking to him when she thinks she's being a bother. I think he feels guilty that he hasn't been there for her more. When he talks about her it's with affection, but also with regret.

"I didn't think to ask..." He pours water from a bottle in the fridge into two mason jars and hands one to me. "Are you okay for meds?"

"I have enough of everything in my purse to last through the next twenty-four hours. I'll have to text Gray about collecting my things." I sip the cold water. It's been awkward between us the entire ride here. We went from hot and heavy to reeling at the repercussions of my breakup with Gray. Well, no, that's me. Theo would probably happily go back to the part where I wanted him to fill me with blue alien cock. "I'll arrange to get the rest of my medication tomorrow."

"I can help..." He shrugs. "If you need me."

I tuck my chin to my shoulder. I appreciate his offer, but he can't help me with this. I have to deal with Gray myself. I owe him that. And the wedding...there will be vendors to call. I'll need to tell everyone that the whole thing is cancelled. "I need to tell America."

"Huh?" He puts his glass down at the same time I do.

"I need to call my best friend." My eyes water as I search for my phone. "I'm going to have to tell her the truth. I'm going to have to tell her that I'm dying. I have to do it before she hears it from anyone else. Shit, my battery is dead."

"I have a charging station." He strides into the living room and comes back with a flat rectangular battery and cord, which he plugs in before placing my device on it.

My breath is caught until the battery on my screen lights up. I'm going to have to wait to call America. I'm scared of how she'll react and that she'll be angry that I kept it all from her. I'd be upset if the shoe was on the other foot. I'd be angry if I wasn't there for her. But I'd understand that she'd want me to live my life too. I hope she sees it the same way.

Theo wraps his arms around my waist. I lean against him, soaking up his warmth and his strength.

"You look tired." His lips caress the shell of my ear. "It's been a long day. Maybe you should get some sleep."

I turn in his arms. Lift up on tiptoe and wrap my hands around his neck. Press my lips to his throat. My world is a scary place. I'm a mess. And he is the only thing that feels right to me. "I'm not ready. I don't want to close my eyes. I'm scared I'll wake up tomorrow and this whole night will have been a dream."

He wraps his hand around my throat. His fingertips rest against my pulse point. Lowering his mouth, he kisses me. "It's not a dream, Indy. And if you wake up anywhere but in my bed, I'll come find you. I promise."

His lips enclose on mine again and I fall into the kiss we share. Until I'm on fire with the need to touch and press and discover.

I shove up the cotton of his shirt and he yanks it over his head and tosses it aside before lifting me onto the counter. His hands explore my body, and I explore him right back. Every touch makes me want more.

When he steps between my legs and presses against me, I can't think of anything else but having him inside me. "Take me to bed, Theo."

Hands stilling on my waist, he bows his head to my ear. His breath stirs against my skin. "You sure? You won't regret it?"

My belly knots. But it's not regret about being with Theo. "I won't."

"Good." Grasping my ass, he lifts me up as he fuses our lips together. He carries me through his apartment and the whole time his tongue is exploring my mouth.

I've blown up my relationship with Gray. Our wedding. My family is going to be pissed. And I'm still dying. But at least I can be real with Theo. I can be free. I don't have to make the safe choice around him; he doesn't expect me to. He's strong enough to let me live the life that I want. To keep me safe. To handle the short time we get to spend together. Time I won't waste.

He places me on my feet in the bedroom. My toes sink into the shag. He has a perfectly made double bed and a two drawer nightstand. A discarded cool gel pack sits next to a bare-bulbed lamp and an empty mason jar with only the dried up hint of amber liquid in it.

He turns on the lamp while I tug at the zipper on the back of my dress.

"Let me." He gathers up my hair before working the zipper down. When my dress is loose, he pulls it over my head. Discarding it, he inches my bra straps down my arms and then unlatches the hooks.

I let it fall away and then wriggle out of my panties before I turn to face him.

"Fuck, I knew you'd be a wet dream." His eyes darken—all pupil—as he drinks me in. His voice is a husky feral growl that makes my pussy clench and my insides hot.

"Your turn." I bite my lip. I want to know what I'm working with. My mouth waters as he tugs the drawstring in his shorts free and then pushes them off his hips to reveal a decent cock and one…two…three…

"You really weren't joking about being pierced. You have…" My fingers scale the ridge with its ladder of piercings. "Four?"

"Five." He groans like me touching him is the best feeling in the whole world.

"Five." I run my fingers over the row of five shiny barbells. Nerves flutter in my belly. Oh wow!

He closes his eyes and rocks back on his feet as he hisses between his teeth. "Fuck, Indy."

My fingertips wander over his flushed shaft. It jumps under my touch. "What does it feel like for you?"

"Extra sensitive."

America told me, after her first experience with a pierced cock, that it feels like using an extra ribbed condom. I'm nervous. My body doesn't work properly anymore. "Will it hurt? If I can't get wet enough?"

"Is that a problem for you?" he watches me keenly through heavily lidded eyes.

I duck my head. "It never used to be. But these past few weeks...I don't seem to be able to anymore."

"Because of the meds?" He lifts my chin.

"Yeah."

"I'll make sure you're wet enough." He threads his hand through my hair and brings our mouths together. "I'll make sure you're really ready. I won't hurt you, Indy. I'll never hurt you."

"I know you won't." Only Theo could manage to wrestle me in a vat of Jell-O and keep me completely safe. He would do the same here.

He gathers me into his arms and lays me down on the bed. His lips move over my skin in a series of light brushing movements. My body sparks everywhere that he touches. Trembles under each butterfly kiss.

All the way down he goes with those little fire starters. My breath quickens.

His hand finds my knee and bends it, arranging my leg over his shoulder. "I want to taste you."

"Mmhmm." I nod as I cover my eyes with my hand.

"Indy?" He stretches out a hand to grasp mine.

I squeeze back. I'm here. I'm all the way in this.

He drops his mouth to my pussy and runs the flat of his tongue up my slit. He has a mouth built for sin. The way he uses the tip of his tongue...I arch off the bed with a whimper. He teases me slowly until I drop the hand from my eyes so that I can see him between my thighs.

He watches me with dark, molten eyes as he sucks my clit between his teeth before releasing it. The view is so sexy. So debauched. Replacing his mouth with his fingers, he eases the tip of one inside me. "Indy, I'm going to spit on you. Make it wetter."

"Please." I just want him. To experience being with him. My body is aching for it.

He sucks his cheeks in to gather saliva and then spits it onto my pussy. The warm fluid rolls down my slit, and my insides clench. It's dirty and hot when he starts pushing it inside me with his finger. Using it as lubricant. I've never been so turned on.

"That's it," he croons as he opens me up slowly, using his mouth on my clit and his fingers to stretch me so that it won't hurt when we finally come together. "You're taking my fingers so beautifully. Two of them now."

I close my eyes when he adds that second digit. But my body is relaxed and it's barely uncomfortable.

He squeezes my hand. "You need lube, don't you? Before we go any further?"

He's still holding my hand. He's been holding it the whole time. "I'm sorry I'm not—"

"You're everything." He smiles at me. "But you don't need to be perfect. And you don't need to make apologies because I need to put in a little extra work."

He doesn't make this about me being sick, even though it is. With him I get to be exactly who I am in this moment. Right here. Right now.

I nod. "I need lube."

"I'll go grab it." He crawls off the bed.

A minute later he's back with the bottle of water-based gel. He pours some on his fingers and rubs them together to warm it up while he lies down beside me. When his finger curls inside me more sparks fly.

"Better?" He adds the second finger and there's no discomfort. My eyes close while my body starts to move.

"So much." I whimper right before he kisses me. Opening my eyes, I thread a hand through his hair as our tongues tease and taste.

The heel of his palm grinds on my clit as he adjusts his hand. "How does that feel?"

"Amazing." I can feel an orgasm building as I become hypersensitive to every stroke of his fingers.

"You're taking three of my fingers." He stares at me like I'm something mythical. "You could take my cock so well."

"Then do it. Give it to me." I bow off the bed. I'm so close.

"Let me get a condom." He pulls away.

I grab his wrist. "It's not necessary."

He peers into my eyes, and he must find what he's looking for, because he lays on his back. "Come here then."

I straddle him, his hard cock with all its metal between my thighs.

"Take control." He wraps his hands around my hips. "Show me what you want. Take what you need."

I grip him and his cock pulses as a groan slips from between his teeth. Guiding him to my entrance, I notch him there then ease down. He's thick; even with all the preparation I can feel each bit of metal, but it's pleasure not pain. It's more than I expected, but in a good way.

When he moves inside me he hits spots that feel so fantastic as the piercings drag against my most sensitive places.

"Nice and slow." He lifts me easily, not guiding, but steadying, letting me control the depth and the tempo. "Whatever you need from me, Indy."

I need to see stars. I need to soar. He has me so close to the edge with all this sweet friction. I want to fall headlong into this orgasm he's bringing on with his pierced cock and his words. I want him to push me. I want to be swept away. "Take control."

"What do you want? Deeper? Harder? Faster?"

"All of it."

Our positions are changed in the blink of an eye. I'm on my back underneath him. He has my knee over his shoulder and the pressure as he pushes in is exquisite. He hits deeper inside me like this and he rides my clit with his thumb.

The orgasm starts like an earthquake. Low and rumbling. Building in intensity with every sure thrust. All those piercings create shockwaves of pleasure so deep and delicious. My thighs start to shake. My toes curl.

"Fuck yes, sweetheart." He growls as my climax takes me over. He thrusts more urgently. Groans as his cock pulses inside me with his own release.

It floods me in hot waves, setting off a last mini-quake. We rock together until the aftershocks wear off.

Rolling to his side, he takes me with him. His hand rests on my waist while he searches my face as though seeing something he didn't expect to see. One corner of his mouth tugs up a fraction. "Fucking hell, Indy."

Chapter Twenty-Three

Theo

We climb out of bed and I give her one of my shirts. It swamps her, the hem hitting mid-thigh. Her hair is all teased up at the back thanks to her being on her back while I moved her up the bed with my thrusts. She's more than I ever expected. Perhaps more than I know how to handle.

Cooper was my everything. She became my love and my grief and my guilt. I guess it would make sense that I would find someone who could make me feel again, only to have to lose her. It's penance, right? My life without Cooper is supposed to be agony. I don't get to forget her. And I wouldn't want to.

But Indy makes me wish for so much more.

"What?" She wrinkles her nose when she catches me staring. "Why do you keep looking at me like that?"

"No reason." I concentrate on pulling on sweatpants. "Your phone should be charged. Do you want to call your friend?"

In the kitchen, she turns on her phone. The screen lights as it boots up.

"I hope he hasn't told anyone yet." She takes a determined breath and lifts her phone to her ear. "Hey, I'm glad I caught you."

Her friend is loud despite the phone and continents in between. "Indy, what on earth is going on? You don't answer my calls. You don't talk to me anymore. Something is going on with you…this isn't…we've never kept secrets from each other. You're freaking me out."

"I don't even know where to start." Indy wanders away from me to the other side of the counter. She lowers her voice and turns her back on me. "I…left Gray."

"You did what?" her friend screams, as Indy takes her call into the living room.

She doesn't need me eavesdropping, so I scope out the fridge for something to eat. But I'm never here, which means the fridge is empty apart from a couple of beers Pez brought over one night and a half-gallon of milk. The pantry yields similar results. Except for a half block of chocolate. Score.

I put it in a pot on the ancient stove and pour in a couple of mugs of milk then light the hob. I'm going to have to do better than this if Indy is staying. We need groceries. Vegetables and fruit and whatever else she eats. Less alcohol. Less pills. Less fighting.

That's if staying is what she wants. She might not. Tomorrow could bring regrets and changes of heart. God, I hope she doesn't go back to him. I need the time we have. I need to show her the world she wants to live in.

When the milk is heated and the chocolate has melted, I pour it into two mugs and go to find her. She's curled up in my recliner, her phone cradled in her hands on her lap. She has a strand of hair between her lips while her eyes stare at the wall unseeing.

"Indy, sweetheart." I sit on the coffee table. It wobbles, but it's sturdy enough. I've stood on this thing before and haven't fallen through it. Putting down the mugs, I reach out and cover her hand. "Are you okay?"

She blinks and her gaze meets mine. "Sorry?"

"Here." I offer a mug. "It's hot."

"Thanks." She handles it carefully. Her eyes glisten with the tears she's cried over the course of the phone call. Her eyelashes are webbed.

"How'd she take it?" Stupid question. No one is ever going to take the kind of news Indy had to share well.

"Like her best friend is dying." Her eyes grow wetter and she hiccups. She takes a sip of the hot chocolate. "This is really good."

"It is." I wait for her to open up to me. It's her choice to tell me more. I won't push her to talk to me when she isn't ready.

"She wanted to get on the next flight home. She was looking at tickets while we were talking." She tugs at the hem of my shirt. Rubs the pad of her finger on the middle of her bottom lip. "I convinced her to stick to her original plan and fly back in a few weeks."

"Do you think she will?" I found it took a lot more than persuasion to keep loved ones at bay. Drugs and hard liquor helped a lot more than yelling in their faces. When you push them away hard enough, eventually people give up on you.

But that's not Indy. She cares about everyone. And she cares about living even if it is short term. I numbed to survive. She's surviving by putting her energy into living. It's a lesson I'm so fucking grateful for.

"I guess we'll see." She yawns. "I just wish I could go over there to see her. But now I'm going to have to cancel the wedding and move all my stuff. My parents are going to be beside themselves. EJ is going to be so upset with me."

"You did what you needed to do." I take her mug and put it next to mine before I stand. Holding my hand out to her, I wait until she takes it and then I lift her into my arms. If she hadn't broken his heart, I would not be the one kissing her tonight. I would not be the lucky son of a bitch carrying her to bed. And I would not be the one to strip her bare and take her soft and slow until she cries out my name while she comes.

Sunlight seeps in around the blinds, lighting up the room and making me squint as my eyes adjust. My arm is still around Indy and my morning chub is nestled against her ass. It gets harder now that I'm aware of her naked body pressed on mine. Until she shakes against me. "Indy?"

"Sorry." Her voice is thick and wet and she lifts a hand to her face.

Shit. My heart catches. That swampy feeling sticks in the back of my throat. Waking up to her tears after last night was my fear going to sleep. I brush her hair away from her cheek. "You're crying? For him?"

"Yes."

It kills me to hear her admit it. Is she done with me already? "Are you going to go back to him?"

"No." She turns in my arms. Plastering herself against me, she seeks my mouth with her own in a damp and salty kiss. "No, I'm not going back to Gray."

"Do you regret—"

"That's not…I don't regret what is happening between us. Or that I left him." She sniffles. "But he was my first love. And even before that he meant so much to me. He's my family, my brother's best friend, my parents' figuratively adopted son, and I hurt him so much last night. I don't know how we get past that in the time that I have left. Or maybe I just have to think of it like he's someone I've already said goodbye to. Either way it hurts, Theo. I loved him so much. I love him still. I will probably love him in some way until the day that I die."

"I understand." How much it can hurt to love someone and have to leave them behind. How a heart can rip itself in two in order to have strong feelings for two people at the same time, but still have those feelings for each person with their whole heart. Loving and missing someone doesn't just go away because we find happiness in another.

"I'm going to mourn the way Gray and I used to be. It breaks my heart."

I hold her tighter. "It's okay."

"I don't want to ruin this." Her gaze falls to my chest.

"You won't." I press my lips to her forehead. "It takes time to get over loss and heartache. That doesn't mean that something good can't grow at the same time."

She lifts that whisky gaze. "I'm so glad I met you."

"Glad I met you too, Indy." I roll onto my back. Prop my head on one hand as I draw her over me. "You know, I just realized I don't even know your last name. All this time we've spent together and—"

"Yours is Valentine, right?"

"It is." I smile against her hair. "Girls always kind of like my last name. It's why I don't tell them what it is most of the time."

"I've got you beat." She chuckles.

"Oh really? What is it?"

"Jones." Her fingers draw pictures on my chest and trail down to the slight trail of hair that leads to her next orgasm.

She pulls at it with her fingers and my cock twitches with a neediness that has me rolling her under me in a heartbeat. "Indy Jones? What's your middle name?"

"Anna." She grins.

"Bullshit. Your name is not Indy Anna Jones?" This girl was born to live her own adventure? All this time she's been trying to shoehorn herself into a box that makes no sense for her. And now she tells me her name is basically Indiana fucking Jones?

"Not bullshit." She wriggles under me, her hand wrapping around my erection and giving a gentle tug. "My dad loves Harrison Ford."

"Oh fuck." I groan as my hips shove my cock deeper into her hand.

She lets go before I'm ready for it. Touches the tattoo at the bottom of my abs. "Tell me about this? What does it mean?"

"It's a dragon eating its tail. Means everything is a cycle. Life and death. Love and grief. Good times and bad."

"And the one that still needs to be finished? The one on your back? It's wings, right? All those feathers." She bites her lip like she's trying not to be curious.

"Should I sit up so you can examine it?"

"Will you?" Her eyes brighten.

I would give anything to keep her sadness at bay, so I sit on the edge of the bed and give her my back.

The bed dips as she kneels behind me. Her fingers are warm brushing over the image. Angel wings in jet black. "Harlan is so talented. They look so fluffy and ethereal. I fully expected them to be soft to the touch. Are they for her?"

"They're for Coop. She loved everything fantasy. Especially angels. For her eighteenth birthday she had these giant white wings made to wear to her party. But they were so heavy that they wouldn't stay on properly." I laugh at the memory of her in those huge wings. She was so indignant. So cute. "They'd dragged on the floor all night and ended up covered in beer and dirt. There was no saving them, unfortunately."

There was no saving her either. Fuck, the happiness followed by the sad still steals my breath. I'm pulled back to that hospital room. Saying goodbye to her while I'm in handcuffs, my dad and two cops watching. It's why I haven't had the tattoo finished. Why years have passed since I sat for Harlan.

Indy wraps her arms around me and presses her cheek to the spot between my shoulders. Without a word, she eases the weight.

I don't know how long we stay like that. Eventually I suggest a shower and she agrees. I check my phone and let her use my toothbrush while I adjust the temperature of the water then lather her up until she smells of my shower gel. Having my scent all over her makes me want to put my mouth all over her. My cock inside of her.

I kiss the side of her neck down to her shoulder before she turns in my arms. I lift her up and press her into the cool tiles. She reacts eagerly, throwing her arms around my neck and pressing her tits against my chest.

I graze her ass crack with my fingers. It's definitely on my bucket list. She shivers and lets out a little moan.

"You ever?"

"Never."

I raise a brow. "Pity. One day."

She stills and so does my ability to breathe. We're both aware that our time is finite. Later and one day aren't guaranteed.

"I want to experience it all." She kisses me. "Everything with you."

Now that we're not hiding what we want from ourselves and each other we can barely keep our hands off of one another. But if we don't finish this shower, sex will be the only thing we do today.

I slide her body down my front as I put her back on her feet. Squeezing shampoo into my hand, I lather up her hair as gently as I can. It falls out in fat strings around my fingers. I noticed last night how much it's thinning. There's no hiding how much her scalp shows through under those lights above the bar. So I made the call and texted someone who could help while I was making the hot chocolate last night. "We better finish up. We have somewhere to be."

Chapter Twenty-Four

Indy

"The bar is where we needed to be?" A half-finished warm beverage in each hand, I ignore the itch to look at my phone. I'd probably drop one or both of the drinks and my phone if I tried to juggle all three. But I need Gray to text me back.

"It is." Theo nods as he unlocks the door then pockets his keys.

I hand him back his coffee so I can finally check my notifications. I texted Gray almost an hour ago, before we left Theo's to grab breakfast and coffee and come here. I'm wearing last night's dress. I'm wearing the same panties. I need to pick up the rest of my meds and some of my things.

"He's not responding?" Theo holds the door open for me as I slide my phone back into my purse.

"Would you want to respond?" I broke Gray's heart last night. Under normal circumstances he probably needs space, but I told him I cheated on him. He needs time without having to see my face. I need my meds more. "If he won't talk to me I'll have to beg EJ to collect my medication for me. I only have enough supply to get me through tonight."

"If he cares as much as he says he does, he won't want you to not have them." Theo follows me inside, closing the door behind him. "I can take you."

"Thank you, but I don't think that would help the situation." It's silent in here. A complete reversal of how loud and boisterous it was last night.

The glasses and empty bottles have been cleared away. The floor and bar cleaned and polished.

There's the spot where we danced on the bar. Where my world finally shattered into a million unfixable fragments and I could no longer deny what was between us. And that's where Gray stood, no doubt watching us the entire time while it dawned on him that I wanted another man. It all seems so much worse in the quiet without the people swarming around. I recall Gray's face when my feet were finally back on the floor…how angry he was when he drove away.

I hurt him. And that hurts me. Breaking Gray's heart was never going to be something I came away from unscathed. I put my cup of hot chocolate on the counter. My stomach is too unsettled to finish it. I wrap my hands around my elbows as though that can stop my heart from shrinking.

"You didn't do anything wrong." Theo slides an arm around my shoulder, his hand resting above my heart. His chest against my back chases away the emotional chill. He presses his lips to my temple. "Not one damn thing. You care about everyone, Indy. You care so much that you don't want anyone to hurt. But you can't stop pain. Trust me, I'm the king of trying to numb away everything that matters. It still makes itself known. It has to be felt as much as happiness or anger or love."

I turn for his comfort. For his kiss. Because being with him makes everything hurt a little bit less. Taking his jaw in my hand, I bring his mouth down on mine.

He sneaks his tongue between my lips, and I whimper at the possession. There's happiness here. Affection. Lust. Things that I want to feel no matter how fleeting they might be.

A feminine clearing of the throat breaks us apart before the kiss becomes naked and vertical dancing on the bar.

Theo lifts his gaze over my shoulder and his mouth curves widely. "You're here."

"It took longer than I anticipated," the woman says breathlessly as I turn around. Long blonde box braids flow down her back as she drops her bags on the floor and strips out of a leather jacket that would look at home beside Theo's. And she has the cutest baby bump.

Theo meets her at the entrance. "Thanks for doing this."

She smiles up at him affectionately as she presses a hand to the small of her back. "Any time. You know that. Now grab my bags, because those bastards are too heavy to be carrying in my condition. And introduce me to your girl."

"Indy, this is Sadie." He takes her bags and carries them over to one of the tables. "She's top shelf when it comes to hair and beauty, and her husband is one of my bosses."

"You've never introduced any of us to a friend before." She peruses me with a pursed mouth and her brows drawn close together.

"You know I don't play well with others." His grin is cocky and followed by a wink.

"A real solitary creature." Her eyes gleam. "Somehow I don't believe you're as much of a loner as you want everyone to believe you are."

"That sounds about right." I press my teeth into my lip and smile at him.

He chuckles. "Yeah, maybe I'm not so much anymore."

What he doesn't add is *for now*. But I see the thought in his gaze as the humor fades. When I'm gone I don't want him to go back to the way he was when we met. I don't want him to be alone and succumbing to his misery. Or trying to numb it with pills and booze and fighting.

I run my thumb over the spot where my ring used to sit. Gray will have my family, but Theo…he doesn't even talk to his. Except his sister. He barely opens up to the people who would call themselves his friends.

"I'm sorry to hear you're sick," Sadie says quietly and with a squeeze to my arm. "That's rough."

"It's not what I would have wished for." But I'm not sure I regret knowing that I'm dying. I've met people I never would have met and done things I would never have done. I've had more fun and experienced more than I did for the entirety of my life before the diagnosis.

"Well, we're going to do our best to mark an item off your bucket list today." She glances at Theo over her shoulder while he unwinds an electrical cord. "I brought my clippers if you're ready to rock a sexy short do, Indy. And if not, I have a selection of wigs. We'll find what you're after. Or I can dye a wig to the color that you want."

"You can do that?" I touch the tail of my pony gingerly.

"I can."

It's irrational but every time I touch my hair my gut clenches and I expect it all to come out in my hands. I have dreams about it. I can't hide the way my scalp shows through anymore. At least I'm in control of how I lose it. And if I cover it. "I want to shave it all off. And then try on wigs."

"Let's get you set up then." She ushers me over to where Theo has set up her equipment, and once I'm seated, tosses a cape around me. "Do you have any colors in mind?"

"I'm not sure..." It wasn't really an option, so I didn't let myself think about the details. Now my options are limitless.

"Orange." Theo smirks at me from where he leans on the chair across from us. "It would be hot. Like flames."

"Or like Cheetos." I roll my eyes at him. "Somehow I don't think I'm an orange girl."

"Red?" Sadie sections off my long locks. "Or purple? Or pink? There are some gorgeous pinks and I can dye the wig whatever shade you like. We can even do ombre. Or rainbow hair. Or pastels."

I chew my lip as I consider all the options. "What about blue?"

"We can do blue." Sadie starts to cut.

"What do you think?" I ask Theo.

"You'll look fucking gorgeous in blue." His voice is throaty and his gaze is piercing. He holds out his hand to me. "But you're going to have to slap it."

"Alien tongue?" Because my mind went there too.

He grins, and I smack the top of his hand, then he taps my fingers with his.

"Alien tongue?" Sadie stops snipping. "Do I want to know?"

"Inside joke." Theo winks at me.

Sadie shows me my ponytail. "We're ready for the clippers I think."

There's something about all that hair not being attached to me that is so freeing. I feel lighter all over. Like a bubble or a balloon. I grin at Theo. "Oh my God."

"Is that a good O.M.G. or a bad oh my God?" Sadie asks.

"It's real good." Theo beams back at me. His hands knead the back of the chair he's leaning on.

"Great. Come here." She grabs his arm and drags him behind me. "It's your turn."

"But—"

"Have you ever used clippers before?"

"Of course, but I—"

Her tone is soft and encouraging. "You're going to do just fine, I promise."

"Indy." He squeezes my shoulder. "Are you cool with this?"

It's weirdly intimate that he'll be the one to shave my head, but this bucket list has become as much his as it is mine. We're in this together until the end. I cover his hand with mine. "Yes."

"Okay, let's make you look like a badass." He withdraws his hand.

My eyes sting even as I smile. "Let's do it."

He readies the clippers while Sadie wanders behind the bar and helps herself to a bottle of water. One big hand gently tilts my head so that he can glide the shears through the strands. My scalp tingles from his touch and the vibration of the clippers. Tiny bits of my hair fall around me.

A tear slips down my nose when he switches blade size and removes even more hair from my head. He's become someone who means the world to me. Someone I trust with every part of me. Things I never thought I would do…when he's with me I feel capable of handling them all. But this whole act is bittersweet.

"Are you doing okay, Indy?" Sadie asks as she takes a seat to watch Theo work.

"I'm just missing my best friend." If anyone was going to be the one to hold the clippers, I would have thought it would be America.

"She's not local?" Sadie props one cute motorcycle boot on a chair and pats her baby bump.

"She's living in the UK at the moment." I straighten as Theo turns off the clippers. "It's weird but I always thought she would be here for something like this."

"It's kind of a big deal." She smiles softly at me. "When you have reasons like yours."

Theo puts down the clippers and turns me and my chair. He brings his face down to mine as he takes in my new 'do. His mouth curves brightly. "You look awesome. Like a badass bowling ball."

A laugh escapes me. "That awful, huh?"

"Oh my God, you asshole." Sadie grunts as she leans forward to whack him with her water bottle. "You cannot say things like that. It's not a compliment."

"Ease up." He lifts his hand to ward off another attack, though his gaze doesn't leave me. "I know it isn't a compliment. It was to make her laugh. Which it did."

"It did."

"You…" he tips my head this way and that with the crook of his finger to my chin, "have me so fucking hard right now."

"Also not a compliment," Sadie shrieks.

My chest and neck and cheeks grow hot, but not as heated as the look he's giving me. Like he could pluck me out of this chair and onto his lap in front of Sadie because he can't wait to get me alone. As if he likes what he sees so much he can barely keep his hands off me. "I'll take it as one. This time."

"You're so fucking beautiful, Indy." He takes my face between both hands and meshes our mouths together. His tongue and mine play wicked games with each other.

I'm about to leap out of my chair and straddle him when Sadie stands up and coughs. "Take her to see while I sweep up."

"Come on." He takes my hand and pulls me up from my chair. Tiny pieces of hair fall from the cape onto the floor.

"Hang on, let me." Sadie moves behind me to unhook the cape and take it away.

I'm practically floating the entire way to the bathroom. My heart skips too, though. What if I look ridiculous? Like a not so badass bowling ball. What if it makes me look as sick as I am? I might have made a huge mistake.

Theo pushes open the door to the bathroom and before I can freak out I'm in front of the mirror. The girl looking back at me… is me. But she also… isn't. My hair… "It's all gone."

In its place is a bit of peach fuzz and the palest scalp in the whole world. Not one drop of sun has graced this scalp. My whole head looks bigger without hair. My eyelashes and eyebrows and cheekbones are more pronounced. And I don't hate it. It's got an attitude and I could use one of those.

"Weird, huh?" Theo grins as he leans a hip on the counter. He turns on the tap and washes shard-like bits of hair from his hands.

"So weird." A little more than I was prepared for. But it's too late now. I can't take it back. Can't change my mind. Can barely get air into my lungs while I run my hands over my head. It prickles under my fingers. Not quite smooth, but almost.

"But you like it?"

"I do." It feels a little like control, if I'm being honest, and that goes a long way in a world where I no longer have any. It's liberating.

"You are so gorgeous…" He stands behind me and rests his hands on the counter at my hips while his lips caress my ear. "So intensely sexy."

I tap my tongue to the center of my bottom lip. Rub them together to moisten them as he watches. His gaze is so intense, my pulse quickens. His hardness at my hip makes me feel sexy. Heat floods me. I spin around and he hikes me up onto the counter and steps between my legs.

His kisses are a drug. One hit and I became an addict. He explores with just the right amount of pressure and movement. A simple kiss can reach down into my core and light off a whole box of fireworks. Have me wanting to beg.

I follow the hard lines of his abs and then follow the bumps of his spine up his back. All that muscle is begging to be explored. His flesh is hot and supple under my palms. It jumps with his jagged breathing. The closer I get to the waist of his jeans…the harsher his breath gets.

His palms squeeze and knead my thighs. His fingers brush lightly against my panties before he tugs them to the side. He tests and teases me so gently while I wrap my hand around him and play with his barbells.

The crown of his cock weeps and becomes slick. It kills me that my body doesn't respond the way it should. That as turned on as I am, I don't get wet anymore. Pulling back, I press into his shoulders to break us apart. "We can't."

"Can't what?" His voice is husky.

"Have sex." I squirm.

He takes one side of my throat in his hand while he kisses down the other side of the column. "I can still make you come."

I swallow, my throat lubricating itself the way my pussy should.

"Do you want me to get on my knees? Should I treat you like the seductive queen you are? One word, Indy, and I will worship you."

"Holy fuck." I nod.

"Yes?"

"Yes." I lick my lips.

He falls to his knees on the bathroom floor, his mouth level with my thighs. One hand on my belly, he presses me back and I brace with one hand on the counter and one in his hair. I whimper at the first lick of his tongue along my slit.

He licks me wet with his tongue and his spit. He uses his fingers to hold me open so he can thrust the tip inside me while his thumb rubs my clit into a frenzy of sensation.

It feels so good and I feel so sexy, perched above him while he eats me like I'm his last meal.

He groans when I tighten my hold on his hair, push his face closer. "Fuck, sweetheart. You don't know what that does to me when you assert yourself like that."

His praise makes my chest fuzzy. My body reacts with a rush of heat. And his tongue does the rest, torturing me into an orgasm that has me gripping his hair even tighter. His responding groan against my clit sets off more pleasurable quakes. It's such a vicious circle of sweet relief.

When it ends and he takes his mouth from between my thighs, they're shaking. My breathing is sharp and quick.

He stands and his mouth and jaw have the shine of good head. He clasps the back of my head and kisses me. "Indy, you take my breath away."

"I feel the same way." I'm satisfied in a way I don't think I've ever been. With me. Who I am. My decisions. And how I am choosing to spend the rest of my time. Who I'm choosing to spend that time with.

There's a knock on the door and then it opens a crack. Sadie's voice comes through it. "If you're done in here...I'm ready for you to try on wigs, Indy."

"That's great." I raise my eyebrows at Theo. I can't believe we almost got caught. "Thank you."

He winks at me, a smirk tilting up the corners of his mouth as he turns on the tap and starts to wash up. "We'll be right out."

Sadie retreats and we tidy up. He dries his hands with the noisy machine on the wall. I straighten my panties and dress. Then we head out to see the wigs Sadie has lined up.

She shows me the different types of wigs, some of which are dyed bright colors. Then a book full of colors and styles. All of which is possible if I decide on one that I want. I try on the ones that she's brought. Pinks and purples and even an orange one, which does indeed make me look like a Cheeto.

I eventually settle on one. The cut and wave is somewhat similar to how my hair used to be. It has roots that run into a bright but pale ombre blue.

"You look stunning." Sadie claps her hands together in front of her chest.

Theo just drinks me in.

My phone rings. My upbeat mood disintegrates when I see EJ's name on the screen. It was only a matter of time before Gray told him about us. I'm so not ready for this conversation. I accept the call anyway. I can't hide from life. I don't have the time. "Hello."

"Just checking that you remember family dinner is tonight, right?"

"What?" That's not how I expected this conversation to start. And it's the wrong night.

"We changed it last week because I have to go out of town to meet with a client tomorrow," he says. "But I figured you might have forgotten. You weren't in the best headspace."

"Yeah." I can't clearly remember our last family dinner. Between the headache and missing Theo I'd been practically comatose. I clear my throat. "Have you heard from Gray?"

"I haven't, but I figured he was preoccupied..." His voice lightens. "You sound like you're in better spirits."

"I...am." I clasp my stomach. He will not like the reason. How do I tell him I broke up with Gray? Or do I wait and let Gray do it since my brother is his best friend? I curl a blue lock around my finger. "I might have done something."

"Like what?"

"Shaved my head. And I'm buying a wig." I bring the vivid blue strands up to eye level. They're super pretty. "How do you think Mom is going to take it if I rock up with no hair or wearing a bright blue wig?"

"Probably not well." He exhales heavily. "But I'll warn them so they're prepared."

Mom hasn't taken anything well recently. "I'm not sure—"

"Seriously, Indy, you have to come to dinner. They are really struggling and your absence will make it worse." A quick intake of breath is followed by more exuberance. "Actually, you know what they need? That death coach you were using. I know you were taking a break from your bucket list, but are you still in contact with him?"

"Yes." It comes out strangled.

"You should bring him to dinner. It'll be great. It will really help Mom and Dad. Maybe we can convince them to go to a smash room."

"You think I should bring Theo to dinner?" I glance at the man in question. Clearly Gray hasn't told EJ that we've broken up yet, so I can't imagine he would show up to dinner tonight. I chew the inside of my cheek.

"All I'm saying is...he helped me. Maybe he can help with this too."

I should tell him about the break up, shouldn't I? No, I should tell my family, but it should be in person. About Gray. And my new living arrangements.

At some point I'll have to talk to my parents about moving back in with them too. Staying with Theo can only be a short-term solution. Eventually I'm going to get sicker. Able to do less. Unable to look after myself. And I will not ask Theo to take that on. I will not be his burden to shoulder. But dinner tonight with my parents... "I'll ask him."

Chapter Twenty-Five

Theo

I clasp Indy's elbow and gently bring her to my chest when we're at the top of the steps to her parents' house. She's jittery tonight. She couldn't stop fidgeting on the way over here. She keeps tugging at the hem of the floral dress I bought her at the mall after we finished up with Sadie. Touching the blue strands that fall about her shoulders. "You look amazing. The hair is fire."

"Mom is going to freak out." She looks up at me beseechingly. "I think we should leave now. I'll call them and tell them I don't feel well."

"The Indy I know doesn't back down from the hard things." I slip a tendril of hair behind her ear. "She's baller and incredibly brave."

"It doesn't feel like it."

"But it's true. You're brave enough to go in there and deal with their reaction to your break up with Gray. And the hair too." Her mom will probably need a minute to catch her breath. But that's all. "It's clear that your family loves you dearly. I hope that epic macaroni casserole is on the menu tonight."

She smiles at that. "You ate a lot of it."

"And I would do it again if I got the chance." I take her hand in mine, interlock our fingers. "Which I won't if we keep standing out here."

"My mom is really struggling." Her eyes glisten and she presses her lips together. "And all this change. When I'm supposed to gone by Christmas."

"It's hard."

She nods. "That's an understatement."

"Well, that's why I'm here. To make it easier." If they're going to have a problem with anyone, it's going to be me. I'm the interloper here. The one who broke up Gray and Indy. Or at least that's how they'll see it.

I'm surprised her brother suggested this in the first place. Unless it was all a ruse to get me here so he could take a baseball bat to my knees. Which is totally possible. I've seen him swing a golf club. A bat is not that different.

"Okay." She drops my hand and opens the front door.

We step into a small foyer full of warm woods and muted taupe walls. Vases of fresh cut flowers and the aroma of warm apple pie make me suddenly nostalgic for the late-night raids that Shae and I used to partake in when our parents would leave me to look after her. A lot of the time Cooper would join us. We'd fill our bowls full of whatever mom had baked for her network cooking show, adding all kinds of sugary treats. Actually, I don't know how any of us slept or didn't have stomach aches on those nights.

My stomach growls.

EJ chuckles as he rounds the corner and comes into view. "Good to hear you brought your appetite."

I pat my flat abs. "Indy is rubbing off on me. I skipped lunch. But honestly, if there was any chance your mom was making that macaroni bake...I wanted to be ready."

"When I mentioned Indy was working with a death coach, I told Mom how much you liked her casserole. So she cooked two. One for dinner. One for you to take home with you." EJ wraps his arms around Indy and pulls her into a hug. "You look better, Sis. I was worried about you these last couple of weeks. And I like the hair. It's vibrant. That was on the bucket list, right? You wanted to shave your head. And color your hair a bright color too."

"You've seen my bucket list?"

"I helped Gray pick out what to help you mark off it. We figured it might get you out of your funk. And it looks like it worked." He leads the way to the kitchen.

"Uh…" Indy wrings her hands.

She's so nervous about telling them about the breakup. And how they'll react. Her whole family loves the guy. We rehearsed what she'd tell them in the truck on the drive over. About him. About us.

It's going to be difficult for her, but better to rip the Band-Aid off. Especially with the wedding to call off as well.

We reach the heart of the house where Indy's mom is watching a pot on the stove while sipping from a goblet of white wine. Her eyes turn round as she greets Indy. "My baby. I love your hair."

"It's a wig, Mom. No dye."

"I know." The older version of Indy sniffles. "Your brother told me."

"I warned them," EJ says at the same time.

"It looks great. Truly." Indy's mom holds her gaze and smiles softly. A lot is conveyed without words in that look. Eventually, Indy's mom turns her attention on me. "You must be Theo. I'm Sharon. It's so nice to meet the man who is helping our baby girl."

I let her drag me into a crushing hug. It's been a long time since anyone has shown me parental affection. It fills a need in me that I didn't realize I had. Makes me want to call my mom just to hear her voice. Reminds me that I should check in on Shae as well. "It's great to meet you too."

"EJ told us you're a death coach." She keeps hold of my arm as she steps back.

Indy suggested to her brother that being with me was like therapy the one time, and her entire family seems to be running with it. "That's not exactly—"

"I'm so glad you're helping our Indy."

I catch Indy's gaze and her encouraging nod. I'm not sure what the right step is here. Tell them I'm not a death coach or skirt around it. "I'm happy to be able to support her."

"EJ also said that we should make a plan to go to a smash room. I'm not sure what that is." She laughs depreciatively. "I'm showing my age, aren't I?"

"No, ma'am." I stiffen as a big bear of a man comes into the room.

Mr. Jones moves lethargically and when his gaze lands on Indy it sticks. He joins his wife on the other side of the counter without taking his eyes off his daughter.

He reminds me so much of Nelson in those last days. Withdrawn. Going through his suffering in silence. If I needed to get any of them into a smash room it's him. "A Smash room is a room full of breakable items that you can smash. You wear protective gear and can use a baseball bat or a hammer."

"Or a golf club." EJ pretends to swing a putter. "And you don't have to clean up the mess."

"It helps, Mom," Indy says.

"Well then, we'll plan a family trip." Sharon glances behind us. "Is Gray stuck at work again? Well, we can organize it when he arrives."

"Gray said he's running late, by the way," EJ announces.

"Gray's running late?" Indy's eyes flare.

What does he mean, Gray is running late? I scratch my temple. My gut tightens. I was certain he wasn't coming. So was Indy. Otherwise she never would have asked me to come with her. And I never would have agreed to joining their family dinner. The last thing I want to do is be the cause of the trouble this is sure to stir up.

"He didn't tell you?" EJ's brow furrows.

"Erm, well..." Indy curls her fingers around the strands that touch her neck. "The thing is..."

"Where's your ring, baby?" Sharon covers her mouth. "Oh my God, did you lose it? I thought it looked loose the other day. I should have said something."

"No, Mom." Indy's eyes fill with tears as she walks over to comfort her mother. She turns to include her dad. "I'm sorry. Gray and I broke off the engagement."

"What?" Her brother's gaze turns cold and hard as it lands on me. He folds his arms over his chest, bunching his fists into his armpits. He most likely knows his friend well enough to know that this isn't his choice. "Why?"

"Because we're not our best selves when we're together anymore." Indy dashes away the wetness from her eyelashes. "And because we shouldn't be getting married when I'm dying. It isn't helping me and it isn't helping him either."

"And if I ask Gray what happened?" There's a kaleidoscope of emotions warring in EJ's expression.

Her gaze slips to me as the color leaves her face. She swallows as she meets his eye. "Don't."

"So there's more to it." His jaw bulges as he turns on me. He knows I'm involved in this. Not the details, but that there is something. He was worried from the beginning that I'd be a problem.

He storms back the way we came in. The front door slams.

"Oh, Indy." Sharon wraps her arms around her daughter and cradles her head on her shoulder while Indy sobs. The older woman's eyes fill too. "What happened?"

Mr. Jones engulfs them both.

My chest tightens and pain runs through my jaw and my arm. I grasp at my heart, because the ache is almost intolerable. There's so much pain here and I can't do anything to help. I can't take Indy in my arms and support her the way I want to. I should probably leave before Gray arrives and everything gets a thousand times more explosive.

Yet I know I won't take off. Not unless she tells me too.

"It's hard. I love Gray." Indy sniffles.

I can't stand here while she explains how complicated her feelings for Gray and me are to her parents, so I go to find EJ. Maybe he'll want to thump me, but there are things we should probably talk about.

He's sitting on the second step down from the porch with his head between his hands. I shut the door behind me and take a seat next to him.

"I knew something was going on between you two." He doesn't look up. "That morning I found you on her couch. But I let her convince me I was being unreasonable."

"Neither of us meant for things to progress like this." And before that day I didn't think there was anything more than friendship between us. Neither did she. "We tried to fight it."

"It's why she's been practically comatose for weeks, isn't it? Because she tried to cut you out once she realized."

I close my eyes and take a breath. "Yes."

"I want to tell you that you've fucked everything up." He cracks his knuckles. "That I was right in my initial assessment and that you're a parasite. I want to get my golf club and put it through your skull. I could build a legal defense that would keep me out of jail."

"I'm sure you could." I'm almost certain that I can think of a couple of cases from my time in my father's office with a defense that would work for him.

"Gray is my best friend." He drags his head up and rubs at his brow. "She's my sister. And they were happy."

"I know." I grip the rim of the step and squeeze. The night we met she was happy and looking forward to an entire future with him.

"You know, I didn't like the idea when they first started dating. I was worried that one or both of them would get hurt and that I'd have to pick sides. But they were so good together." He looks at me. "You couldn't just let them be happy? You couldn't leave her the fuck alone?"

"You can blame me." What does it matter? When she's gone there's almost no chance we'll cross paths again. "But we both know I'm not the reason. Your friend was holding onto her so tight, she couldn't breathe. He's the one that pushed her away. She's a shooting star. She's so bright and beautiful and alive in the present. Everything a guy could wish to be so lucky to find. Gray doesn't see it."

"You don't know that."

"Yes, I do. I've been where he is. Fixated on the future and not appreciating what I had." And as much as I don't like Gray—especially with Indy's emotions so torn—I feel sorry for him. Because it's going to hurt when he realizes it. "He's so busy trying to hold onto the fading tail of who she was that he's completely missing who she is. He'll still be holding onto that tail when she's gone. He'll still be trying to work out how he could have fixed it. That's not what Indy wants for him."

"But you're fine with there being no future here? You're fine with her dying?"

"Not by a long shot. But I know what I'm getting myself into." It's going to hurt like hell when it comes time to say goodbye.

A blue Tesla turns down the street.

"That's Gray," EJ says.

I climb to my feet. This is going to become an incredibly uncomfortable situation. "When he tells you that Indy slept with me before they broke up…it never fucking happened."

"Why are you telling me that?"

I squeeze his shoulder. "Because you don't have enough time to waste on doubting whether she could do something like that. But she wants him to believe it because she thinks it will be easier for him to let go if he hates her."

He snorts loudly. "If you think Gray could ever hate her—"

"I didn't say I believed it." If she were to wake up tomorrow with no tumor and a change of heart about being with him, he would take her back without another thought. I'm one-hundred percent sure of that. It's why he didn't tell her family. And why he's parking his Tesla in the driveway even though his gaze is glued to my truck. "I'm going to let her know that he's here."

Chapter Twenty-Six

Theo

"Does it really matter if she cheated on Gray?" Mr. Jones is asking his wife as I re-enter the house. Sounds like they're still in the kitchen. "Our little girl is going to die, Sharon. She's going to leave us. Does it really matter if she wants to have a fling with some...death coach...or whatever the hell he really is?"

"It's not like her." Indy's mom wipes at her face with both hands as I turn the corner. "They said this could happen. That the tumor could make her act out of character. It feels like we're losing her more and more each day. I'm not ready, Oz. I'm not ready for this."

"Neither am I, baby." He engulfs the smaller woman, stroking her hair and crooning private words that are so low I can't possibly make them out.

I glance around; Indy isn't in the room with them.

"Poor Gray." Sharon continues to cry in her husband's arms as she holds onto him tighter. "This must be hurting him so much."

A bitterness coats the back of my throat and turns my stomach. I knew what I was getting myself into, coming here tonight, but it's still awkward as hell. From everything Indy has said Gray has always been more than Indy's boyfriend and fiancé. I remember being accepted like that. Cooper's parents treated me the same way. Walking away from that...it was the second worst pain I've ever experienced.

Indy's dad lifts his head, his gaze catching on me. His eyes, so much like Indy's, aren't as cold as I'd expected.

I clear my throat. "Where's Indy?"

"Outside." One word and then he buries his face in his wife's hair again.

I leave them to it. Through the huge panoramic windows that overview the garden, I spot Indy taking a quiet moment to herself. She's sitting on a Cape Cod lounge chair, focused on her phone.

I step out onto the veranda and close the door behind me before striding across the lawn to join her. Glowing embers in the middle of a brick lined pit let out a little heat as the sun drives lower on the horizon. There's enough room on the seat for two so I straddle it behind her and sit. "How are you doing?"

"That was the roughest thing I've ever had to do." She leans against my chest and flops both legs over one of mine so that we're more face-to-face than chest-to-back. "If Gray weren't like family this would be so much easier. We'd break up and never talk or see each other again. But he belongs in this family almost as much as I do. I don't want to change that. When I'm gone they'll need each other."

When she's gone…I don't know how I'm going to recover from that. Which is not what I need to focus on right now. "They'll be okay, Indy. Your family is tight. Your brother isn't going to pick sides. Your parents will work out how to balance this situation. You haven't destroyed them by choosing you."

"I chose you a little bit too." She smiles softly, wrapping her arms around my neck.

"You did, huh?" I tease her, but it means the world to have this period with her. In such a short amount of time she's changed me for the better. Given me purpose. Helped me come to terms with my grief and my guilt.

I lower my head and press my lips to hers.

"Theo." She shakes her head as she presses her palms into my chest and moves away an inch.

It's for the best. I forgot for a moment why I came to find her. "Gray's here—"

A door slams. Gray's words are strangled with emotion. "You're kissing him? At your parents' house? In our spot?"

"Gray? No." Indy looks past me and the color leeches from her face. She starts to tremble. Her eyes glisten as she climbs from the Adirondack. "Gray, I am so sorry. I didn't mean—"

"I can't believe you." He sounds tortured.

"Gray." EJ clamps a hand on his friend's shoulder while he fires a warning glance at me as I rise to my full height. "Maybe we should—"

I step in front of her. "This isn't on Indy. I kissed her."

"You don't get to come here and kiss my fiancée in our fucking spot. These are my friends," Gray roars, the sinew in his neck standing out. "Our family."

Indy edges around me. "I'm not your fiancée."

He opens and closes his mouth several times, his Adam's apple working like the words are stuck in his throat. "You're right."

"Gray?" Indy chases after him when he storms back into the house.

It takes gritting my teeth to keep my feet planted where I am. To not go after her and make sure that he doesn't convince her to give in to keep him happy.

EJ stays too. We have our own weird stare off across the yard. Finally he grimaces. "Well, this is a shit show. I suggested he leave, but…"

"I'm the intruder."

"So I'm going to suggest the same to you."

Indy wants me here. "I can't do that." I won't. Unless she tells me to.

"I figured you'd say that." He lets out a long and slow sigh.

"What did he mean, our spot?"

"As far as I could guess, and I really don't want to, a lot of firsts happened in that particular chair." He opens the door. "Want to have a beer while you wait? Dinner won't be long, but I'm pretty sure it will be awkward as hell."

I glance at the innocent Adirondack as I follow him. If he's right…

We take our beers into the small den at the front of the house. There's a pool table and we play while we drink. In another life we might have become friends, but in this one, he's keeping me amused while his best mate and his sister talk in private.

He's not bad at the game, but I'm better and the first round is over before we're done with the beer. Indy still isn't back. I glance at the time on the clock on the wall. It's been almost fifteen minutes. "Where's your bathroom?"

EJ gives me directions, and I find myself on the second level. Apparently there's something wrong with the downstairs plumbing. I bypass open bedroom doors until I hear Indy and Gray talking. He walks out of the room before I can make out a word they were saying.

His gaze narrows and he marches toward me. "You're just a blip in our relationship because Indy's not herself at the moment. But when she gets better, and she's done with that heartbreak list, she'll come back to me. Do you want to know why?"

"You're deluding yourself," I say, quiet and firm. About Indy's health. About what she would do if she got a reprieve on this death sentence she's living with. I don't need to hear him rant about why he thinks he's better for her. Because if she were to get that reprieve I would take full advantage of it. I wouldn't give him a shot to get between us.

"Well, I guess we'll see how long you last." He shoves his shoulder into mine as he passes me. "I'm not going anywhere. I'm not going to stop loving her. What we have is far stronger than a fling. She's only with you because she doesn't know how to handle what's happening to her. She'll never love you."

He walks away and I uncurl my fist. My nails have cut into my palm while he spewed his opinion. Thoughts that have crossed my mind already in one form or another.

Indy walks out of the bedroom and startles when she notices me. "What are you doing up here?"

"Looking for the bathroom." I examine the half-moon cuts in my palm. "Ran into Gray on the way."

"What happened to your hand?" She tugs it down from my face so she can see the small flecks of blood seeping from the crescents.

I got angry, and I chose not to act on it. "I didn't think hitting him would be appropriate."

"Dinner time," Indy's mom calls from below.

"Be right down," Indy yells back, then tugs me further down the hall. "This way."

We enter an alcove that turns out to be a small powder room. She turns on the tap and wets a cloth. "Give me your hand."

I lean against the counter and rest my hand in hers, letting her dab away the bits of blood even though it would have been so easy for her to stand aside while I washed my hands in the running water. "He's not going to let go, you know."

"He's upset. What happened…" She stills with the cloth in my palm.

"Firsts?"

"All of them." She inspects her work under the ambient light from the hallway. Satisfied, she leaves the cloth on the side of the sink and shuts off the tap. "I didn't think. I should have, but I didn't."

"The timing was bad."

"It seems I have the worst timing in the world. With him. And with you."

"And by that you mean?" I pretend my heart isn't thumping on my tongue. Our timing is shit, but it is what it is. Unless she thinks it's better if we aren't together.

"I'm not a bad person, but I feel like I am," she whispers as she tucks smokey blue hair behind her ear.

"You're not." I lift her so that she's sitting on the counter. Take her cheek in my hand. Press my forehead to hers. "You have a big heart, sweetheart. That's why you feel bad."

"But it's just…it's so quick. I hate that he probably feels like I didn't care at all." A fat tear leaks from the corner of her eye.

I brush it away with my thumb. I kiss the salt from her skin. It seems like Gray has left a mark on every inch of her life—but I'll be damned if I pussyfoot around the past and let it overwhelm our time together. I want her focus to be on the present. On living. With me. "With enough time he'll realize it."

"But not today." She sighs.

There's the rap of knuckles on the arch that is the entry to the powder room and Indy startles. We both glance in the direction of the sound to find EJ standing there.

He raises one eyebrow. "While I appreciate the need for a moment away from all the tension downstairs the awkwardness is not being made better by y'all taking your sweet time up here. Let's get this over with."

He walks away while Indy slips from the counter. "And on that note, we better join everyone for another Indy-makes-it-awkward dinner."

"It's a theme night?" I smile with one side of my mouth as we follow EJ down the stairs. "You didn't tell me it was theme night."

He chuckles.

It's the most uncomfortable dinner I've ever been to. Gray scowls at me through the entire meal. EJ doesn't say a word to me because he's trying to play peacekeeper. He also doesn't talk to Indy or Gray either. Maybe it's genetics because Indy's dad said more words to his wife when I accidentally eavesdropped than he says at the table. Sharon, bless her, tries to make up for the whole family by piling extra servings of macaroni on my plate.

Indy slides the food around with her fork and occasionally lifts it to her lips, the tines barely covered.

"So you'll be moving home then." Mr. Jones finally breaks the silence.

"No." Indy glances to me for support.

"No?" Indy's mom reaches for her daughter across the table. "Are you going to keep living with Gray?"

Gray puts his knife and fork down. "We can make it work at the condo. I can sleep in my office."

"No, Gray. That's not going to happen. But I'm not moving in here either. At least not yet." Indy meets each of their confused gazes. "I know that I'm going to get sicker at some point and then I'll need all of you to look after me. But right now I want to focus on living. I have all these things that I want to do. And Theo is helping me with them."

"You're moving in with him?" Gray's chair scrapes on the floor as he shoves back from the table. "Is that what you're saying?"

"I know it doesn't seem ideal to any of you," she continues. "I can't imagine what you're feeling, Gray."

"Like I'm going to need a good lawyer." He starts unlatching the buttons on his shirt cuffs.

Under the table, I grip my knee so hard I'll have bruises. "You don't want to start a fight with me."

"You don't scare me." His lips form a white slash.

"Gray, sit down." Indy's voice shakes.

"Let's all just take a breath." EJ shoots Gray a warning look before turning to his sister. "Do you really think that moving in with your death coach is the best decision, Indy?"

"I'm not a death coach," I grumble under my breath. I don't care if he's sticking with it in an effort to keep Gray calm. I'm not some guy who made it his profession to help people come to grips with dying. I'm here only for Indy.

Indy's shoulders lift and straighten. "It's my choice. My decision."

"Christ, Indy." Gray drops into the seat. He seems to swing between wanting to kill me and wanting to beg Indy to come home. "You don't just throw everything away for a guy you barely know. You don't move in with him."

"Enough." Mr. Jones brings his hand down sharply on the table, making the dishes rattle. He lumbers to his feet until he's standing over all of us. "Indy, baby, you've always been a good girl. Unlike these two, I used to worry that you didn't get into enough trouble. But now isn't the time for you to be a good girl. These past few weeks I've watched you turn into a shell of yourself. Watched you struggle. It kills me that I can't make it better for you. I can't kiss your boo-boo or yell at that kid who pushed you over in the sandpit like when you were little. I can't Super Dad this situation."

"It's okay, Daddy."

He pinches the bridge of his nose and bows his head for a moment. His shoulders shudder and his wife reaches for the hand hanging limply at his side. He lifts his head and continues, "Before these last two weeks, you were optimistic. And happy. There was a light about you I haven't seen for a while. So if you need to stay with this…" He points at me, his fist unsteady with everything he's trying to keep in.

"Theo." Indy finds my knee under the table and holds onto it. I don't give a damn if anyone notices, I put my hand under the table and cover hers.

"Theo," he says. "If that's what is going to keep my baby girl in her best spirits, then that is what is going to happen. End of discussion."

"He has an angle. He has to," Gray snarls.

Indy turns her hand over in mine and holds on tight. I think she's worried that I might get up from this table and drag Gray outside for a heart-to-heart he won't like. As much as I would love to do that, it will only give her another reason to feel bad about hurting him.

"Dad," EJ starts.

Mr. Jones raises a hand to shut his son up as he turns to Gray. "Indy has made it very clear to me and Sharon that you're always to be welcome in this house. Just like you were before you two dated. You're family, and that hasn't changed. We know you're hurting and we'd do just about anything to make it hurt less for you. But…it might be best if we call time on this dinner and you go home. You're a grown man and my daughter is dying. If you push me, I will kick you out. If you make me choose between her happiness and you…or make it so she doesn't want to come home to her momma and me…I've got bad news for you, son."

Gray blanches.

"It's okay." Indy stands and moves around the table to hug her dad. "It's been a long night. And I'm tired. So I'm gonna get Theo to take me home."

"I'll get your purse." I step away from the table as she hugs her mom. Take a few cleansing breaths and force the tension from my muscles as much as I can. But I won't be at ease until we're on the road.

She meets me in the foyer. Takes her purse from my hand. She's run an emotional marathon tonight. With Gray. With her parents. And her brother. As we go outside she yawns widely and walks slow and carefully, like there's a drop and she could fall into it at any step. "Thank you."

I hold her elbow on the stairs and help her into the truck only to realize that we're stuck in front of Gray's Tesla. "Fucking fuck."

"I've got the keys." EJ jogs over with an overnight bag. "Figured it would be better if I came out instead."

"I appreciate it."

"Yeah, well, I'm not saying that I don't like you. Even though I probably should for what you're putting my best friend through. I'm actually sure you'd be a great guy to hang with. But any goodwill I show you is for Indy."

"Understood."

"Personally I think it would be a hell of a lot easier if you hadn't come into our lives."

"Unfortunately we are past the point where that was possible. I'm here for as long as your sister wants me around."

"Then you better look after her." He thrusts the heavy bag at my chest. "That's Indy's meds and some of her clothes. Give it a few days and I'll collect the rest."

"You have my word." I toss it in the backseat of the truck as he opens the Tesla's door. My phone starts to ring. I pull it out as he climbs into the vehicle. I'm not scheduled tonight. Why the hell is the bar calling me?

I discard the call and get into the truck. Indy is exhausted and I want to get her home. My phone vibrates to life a second time.

"Take it." Indy rests her head on my shoulder.

Her warmth is what finally makes my jaw unclench. Worst dinner ever and I'll do it again as many times as she needs me to. I decline the call. "I'll just text and see what they want."

"Okay." She closes her eyes.

A message comes back to me almost immediately.

Work: Hey man, we need you to come in. There's someone here asking for you. It seems important.

I put my phone away and shift the truck into reverse. "Do you mind if we stop by the bar on the way home?"

Chapter Twenty-Seven

Indy

"Indy, wake up."

My eyes flutter open as Theo pulls the truck into a parking space outside the bar.

I shift my head from his shoulder and cover my mouth as I yawn. I must have passed out before we hit the end of the driveway.

The leather seat groans as he moves. Cold air replaces the warmth of being pressed up against him. His lips graze my temple. "I've left the heater on for you. Go back to sleep. I won't be long."

"Okay." But I'm awake now so I rub the sleep from my eyes and watch him jog up to the bar. He disappears inside before I press my fingers to my aching skull. My stomach churns. Tonight has been a lot, and I need painkillers. The vial in my purse is empty. But there's a bag of my stuff on the back seat. Gray might be angry but he will still have packed my meds in there.

I climb over the seat into the back. As predicted they're all inside. He also packed clothes. My favorite pajamas and robe. Toiletries. The box my engagement ring came in.

I clutch the pink leather box to my chest as pain pierces my heart. Prying the two sides of the shell apart, I stare at the ring I had worn with so much affection this past year. Why would he put this in here? I hope it's because he can't stand to have it in his possession. Not because he's trying to leave that door open between us. The only thing I hope is that we can recover some of the friendship we once had before I die. It seems so impossible.

I toss the shell back in the bag and dig around for the painkillers. Uncapping the bottle, I pour two into my palm and then return to the front seat for my water bottle.

After swallowing them, I collapse against the leather. Am I crazy for walking away from Gray at the eleventh hour? For bringing Theo into the disaster that is my life? Definitely. I'm destined to hurt them both. I don't have a future. But they do. Acting like this...it's selfish. Wild. Completely unlike me.

Theo exits the club with a woman. Their heads angle toward each other they head for a jet black BMW. She seems happy to see him. Animated and friendly. She touches his arm more than once in that short walk. He keeps his hands stuffed in his pockets, his expression tight.

They talk for a few minutes next to the vehicle and he softens. Even laughs.

Here I am drawing him into my mess. Acting like we're starting something new. Like we could be happy. When every fiber of my being screams it's not true. The bucket list. My time with Theo. Everything. At some point this all ends in heartbreak.

She moves in to hug him, and he wraps both arms around her and holds on tight. A bitter taste fills the back of my throat. I don't know who she is to him, other than they must have history to act like this with each other. But maybe he could be happy long term with her. Or someone like her. And I wouldn't blame him for choosing that over this temporary thing we have.

They step apart and he kisses her cheek. Reaching for the handle, he opens her door. When she climbs in, he closes it for her. The BMW leaves the curb before he trudges toward me and the truck.

I slither down in the seat when our gazes lock. Stare at my knees and try to ignore the heat in my face that accompanies the burning desire to know who that woman is. I should want him to be with someone like her, right? Instead of counting down the hours with me.

He opens the door and climbs in beside me. His hand rests on the bottom of the steering wheel as he takes a labored breath. He doesn't say a word.

Like that night we ran into Nelson, I can tell he needs the time to compose his thoughts. We leave the bar in the rearview mirror. It kills me to bite my tongue. To not ask who she is. Or why she was looking for him. What does she want from him? Should I be letting him go?

Of course I should be. But that's not really the question. How long do we have before this all becomes too painful for either of us? Or perhaps it's just me that it will be painful for, and I'm projecting that there's far more here than there really is. He likes me, sure. He's also well aware that I'm dying. Perhaps that's even what makes this easy for him. It will never get any more complicated.

"That was Cooper's sister." He bites his thumb as we sit at a red light. Rests his elbow on the door and presses his knuckles into his temple. "Brooke."

"Oh." I crawl across the seat and curl up against him. Place my hand over his heart. My insecurities and doubts got the better of me, but they have no place between us. He needs me, I'm here.

"I haven't seen her since the hospital." He's deep into those memories, the aching of them washing off him in waves. But then he drapes his arm around my shoulders and holds on like I'm the balm that makes it all better.

"What's she doing here? Why now?"

"Looking for Nelson." The light turns green and he accelerates. His gaze is clouded with worry, his jaw chewing through his thoughts as he switches lanes. "He was at least checking in with her before…"

It hits me hard. What he'll say. "Before we ran into him?"

"We were the last people to see him. The cops haven't found him." He darts a worried glance my way. "And now they have no idea where he is. She asked me to talk to the police tomorrow. Tell them everything I know. I told her it isn't much. I told her he needs help. She's really worried about him."

Is he scared that Nelson will show up to finish what he started that night? The back of my neck prickles and my heart starts to pound. Or is he afraid the man will harm himself? Most likely it's both.

"I'll go with you." Whether I have anything useful to add is another matter. But I want Nelson to be found. He needs help dealing with his anger and pain. And I need Theo in one piece. Without any bullet holes in his stunning body and beautiful face. With all that life pumping in his veins.

We make it back to his apartment and I find myself glancing over my shoulder as we enter the building and climb the stairs. He dumps my bag on his bed and cleans out his top drawer so I have somewhere to store my clothes, while I line up my meds on his kitchen counter.

I come back in time to catch his dirty smile as he unloads a fistful of my panties into the drawer. My insides clench. Tonight was a lot, but it's over now.

He frowns as he pulls the ring box out of the bag.

Okay, so I was wrong. It seems I've bought a one-way ticket to constant emotional upheaval.

Theo holds it in his palm to show me. "He gave it back to you."

Gray isn't the ghost of boyfriends past so much as a living, breathing entity that, it seems, will always find his way between us. But I can't just cut him out of my heart. Or shut that part of my life off. "He did."

"What do you want to do with it?"

"I don't know." I take it out of his hand and push it to the back of the drawer before closing it. I guide his hands to my hips. "But I don't want to think about it now. I want to focus on this. You and me."

When I press up on tiptoe to kiss him and move his hand toward the small of my back, he gets the message and smooths it down to grab my ass. His lips graze mine then nibble.

Sparks light up inside me as he lifts me onto the old dresser. My knees part for him to step between. They grip his hips to hold him near as his palm covers my throat and tips my chin for his tongue to slide against mine.

Kissing him obliterates everything. All reasoning and doubts evaporate when he explores my mouth. I want more of him. Of us. So much more.

I memorize every inch of him when he takes his shirt and pants off. Watching him take off his boxer briefs is better than watching any Zac Efron movie. His golden skin is almost flawless except for the subtle bruising. All of it is hot under my fingertips. The muscles and sinew that make him look like a god jump and quiver with my touch.

I hold onto the details of the way we kiss. The tempered roughness and neediness that only takes a second to ignite.

I note the sparks that his fingertips tickle from my skin as he pushes my dress up until I have to wiggle to help release it from under my butt. The tremor in my belly when his knuckles brush my flesh. The way my arms go up like a ballerina for him to remove my dress. His huge palms wrap around the back of my thighs as he lifts me and carries me to the bed.

"What do you want, Indy?" He peels my panties back an inch and kisses the top of my mound. My belly tremors. "Do you want my fingers?" He eases the silk down another inch. "Or my tongue?"

I whimper when he kisses me right over my clit and then chases it with the tip of his tongue.

He drags my panties up to my bent knees and then down over my ankles. "Do you want my cock deep inside you? Or should I bring out that toy we bought last night and fill you with it?"

My clit is tingling and so are my thighs. He's the pussy whisperer, and my god, does she know it. I clamp around nothing so hard that my back arches from the mattress.

He kisses the inside of my thigh and waits.

"Not the alien cock." As hot as it was when we were in the store and he was telling me what he wanted to do to me with it, I'm not sure I'm ready to bring that into the bedroom. The damn thing is huge. Like a can of Pringles. "It's scary big."

"You don't want to be stretched? Or just not that much?" He laps at my clit. "Was I too much last night?"

"No." I dig my fingers into his curls. "That's...no..." Everything about last night was perfect. "I loved the feeling of you inside me. The way we fit." Every sensitive nerve ending he dragged his thick, pierced cock against. A wicked need awakens inside me. I do want to be stretched. Filled full of him. "The other thing on the bucket list." I press my hand to the headboard as he starts to fuck me with his tongue, his saliva coating my pussy. "From this morning in the shower."

"Your ass?" He stares at me with wonder as he slides a finger inside me and hits that spot that makes me dizzy with pleasure. "That's what you want? You sure?"

We've been together for such a short period, but time doesn't matter when everything else between us is so right. "I want it."

He picks up the bottle of lube from the bedside table and squirts some on his hand. Warming it, he trails his fingers up and down my pussy. He doesn't touch my ass at all, but the anticipation makes me whimper. Instead he returns to fucking me slowly with his fingers while his thumb finds my clit and adds enough pressure to make me want to combust. "Then you have to say it, sweetheart. Exactly what you want."

An orgasm is building in my peripheral. The heat in my clit is almost too much. "I want to do anal."

"You want me to fill your ass?" His gaze is dark and molten under those heavy lids. His chest rises and falls that bit faster.

"Yes," I cry out as I climb so quickly toward the peak of an intense orgasm, only for him to take his thumb off my clit. It recedes into a softer, insistent throb. I climb up and straddle his lap. "That's what I want, Theo. I've never done it before, and I want to experience it with you."

"You're not scared that it might hurt to take me? Especially with my piercings?"

"A little, but I trust you to make it so good. Whatever this is between us..." emotionally, physically, "I don't want to hold back on any of it."

He grows harder between my thighs and it makes me want to soar. He never once tells me that I can't do the scary things; he only makes sure that the experience will be everything I crave.

It's one of his traits I found myself attracted to in the first place. "And it's a bucket list item. You said so."

"My bucket list. Not yours." His voice is low and velvety-rough.

"Theo?" I catch his face between my hands and stare into his eyes. "I want it. I want you to fuck my ass. I want to feel you. I want to live with you...right now."

I rise up and kiss him, reveling in the way he makes me feel like I can conquer the world. Or at the very least, anal. He's my man of contradictions with his dangerous fuck boy exterior and his gentle and focused heart. His callous disregard for plans and his ability to make me feel secure without them.

I find myself on my belly on the bed. He lays on his side next to me so that we're face-to-face. His hand wanders between my thighs to tease my clit and when my hips buck, he slides a finger inside me. I'm slick from the lube and it takes nothing for him to push a second finger inside, building the banked embers of that lost orgasm into a new fire.

He watches me like he's picking out the detail. The exact angle of my hip as it rises from the bed. The first whimper that escapes me when he uses his thumb to press against my asshole. "Does it feel good?"

"Mmhmm." I lick my lips. It feels amazing. So many nerve endings fire to life under his touch. My insides clench around the fingers he's still thrusting in and out of my pussy at a languorous speed.

He uses his other hand to squirt lube between my cheeks. It's cold as it dribbles around his thumb but it warms quickly as he gathers it up and rubs it in so freaking slow.

Breath caught and body pulsing, I'm desperate for more by the time he wiggles the tip of his thumb into my ass. I fist the sheets as my head swims. "Oh...that's...holy shit."

It's something else entirely. It's this deep pleasure that I can't even find the words for. There's pain too. The tiniest sting to the stretch. And this urge. This need to take it. To move back on it so I can feel him deeper.

"You're so fucking sexy." He encourages me as he eases it in and out just that little bit. "You take my fingers everywhere so beautifully."

I mewl, my pussy clamping around his fingers. I'm so close to the edge and I'm pretty sure the only reason I don't go over is because he's keeping me on that razor's edge on purpose.

"A little more, sweetheart?"

"Oh God." I nod into the mattress as he replaces his fingers in my pussy with his cock.

He exchanges thumb for finger, fucking me just enough to keep me on that edge while he stretches my asshole. Adds more lube. Stretches me a bit more. Until he's satisfied that I can take him without it hurting. "Does it feel good? Should I keep stretching this gorgeous ass? Or do you think you're ready to take me? Because I want to fill you so fucking bad, Indy. I'm pretty sure I'm going to go straight to Heaven when I'm deep inside you."

"Oh fuck…" I close my eyes. His words alone have me needing it desperately. "I'm ready."

I'm empty without his fingers and cock inside me. That would be another first. Feeling that full and then that hollow. The achiness of it has me fighting for breath.

He rolls onto his side then pulls me into his arms so that my back is to his chest. His hot breath flutters on my nape while he spreads more lube on his cock. His lips burn on my neck as he notches the head of it at my asshole. "I want this to be so good for you. We'll go as slow as you need. You set the pace."

I push back on him slowly. Accepting the invasion of that place I've never had anyone or anything before. It hurts a little, but that's nothing to the dirty pleasure on the horizon. The urge to take his whole cock is more like a craving. Sinful. Delicious.

"Fuck, you feel so good." He groans as I take him. Praises me every step of the way. Until he's seated deep inside me. An arm over my hip, he pushes two fingers back into my pussy. He pulses them in and out while he drags out and pushes back in with his cock, hissing between his teeth. Pressing in deeper. "You were just made to take me, weren't you?"

Stars dance in my vision as the orgasm comes on far stronger than anything I've experienced before. It spills from some place deep inside me. Pounds through my whole body in waves as I spasm around his cock and his fingers.

"Fuck, Indy, sweetheart." He bands me to his chest with his lips pressed to my ear as he fucks his way to his own climax. "Fuck."

Neither of us moves for a few minutes while we catch our breath. He eases out of me so tenderly. "Let's get cleaned up."

"Okay."

He scoops me up and carries me into the bathroom. Turning on the shower, he holds me and kisses me while we wait for the water to heat up. "How are you feeling?"

"Good. So good." The connection between us has been strong since the first night we met, but tonight it's stronger than ever.

He puts me on my feet under the spray. Hands covered in bodywash, we explore each other in slow motion. The suds rinse away and still we linger. His fingers tease between my legs. My palm wraps around his hard length. Our mouths entwine in between soft groans and needy whimpers.

Tension coils in my core again. His lips find my nipple. His teeth graze it. My body responds like it's been deprived my whole life. Heat floods me.

"Indy…" His mouth is against my ear as he shuts off the water. There's quiet desperation in his voice as he slides one digit inside me then swirls it around my clit.

It matches what I feel inside. Everything with him is always more than I bargained for. So much more than I ever wanted. "I need you."

He grabs one of the towels on the rack and quickly wraps it around me before picking me up and carrying me into the bedroom. Water drips everywhere. The towel barely dries the flesh it covers before he strips me of it.

"Lube?" He crawls over me to kiss me.

I shake my head and smile. "Just you."

Eyes locked, he hikes my knee up at his hip as he fills me. He takes my face between his hands and stares at me with so much raw emotion. "You okay?"

"Yeah." I'm falling hard, and even though it can't last, this connection with Theo feels like the kind of spark you make big wishes on. I smooth my hands up and down his back. Holding him close. Pressing him deeper.

I don't know which one of us moves first, but the sensation is as intense as the emotion inside me. Kisses linger while our hands wander each other's body. Slowly they become more determined, desperate in the way they press and cling and pull.

Our bodies are in sync as the orgasm steals through me. It's sweet and intense and it sets off his climax. I see stars as he pulses inside me. This feeling in my chest expands. I care about him so much. It blows my mind that I found him, now, when it's all too late.

We stay pressed together, his weight supported by his elbows while he holds me close, his cock slowly losing its hardness before he pulls out.

Eventually he moves to his side and pulls me into him, so that my back is to his chest. "That was…you are so much more than I ever expected."

Maybe it's wishful thinking. Perhaps it's the fact that time is running out that makes it all the more intense. "Do you think if we met in another life that we could have been so much more?"

For a little while we lay there. His arms around me and his breath on my shoulder. Perhaps it's not a question I should have asked. It brings up big feelings for me. Gray was supposed to be my forever, but we never had a connection like this.

But Theo...he had that big love. The one that breaks you when you lose it. And asking him if he thinks we could have had a love like that isn't fair. "I'm sorry. I shouldn't have asked."

He scrapes the blue hair from my neck and touches his lips to my pulse point. "When I lost Cooper...I lost my self. I didn't want to be here anymore. I tried to end it...more than once."

Tears bite behind my eyes. My hold on his arm tightens. I hate that he's suffered so much. And I'm only going to add to it.

"Eventually I came to the realization that I could live in this world without her. But I could never live in it the same as I would have with her. You, Indy, brought me back to life in a way I didn't think was possible. So... if we'd met in a world where I'm not jaded and you're not dying, I have no doubt you would have been my heart and my home."

"But that's not the world we live in." And it hurts so much to think about our ending.

"We only have now." He turns me in his arms so that I'm looking into his eyes. "Let's concentrate on that. Find happiness in each moment we do have. Yeah?"

"Yes." I kiss him back when he lowers his mouth to mine. It's all I can really ask for. But I close my eyes anyway and wish there could be more.

Chapter Twenty-Eight

Theo

"The stars are so clear tonight." Indy pours hot chocolate into plastic cups from the flask we packed in the back of the truck, while I put together a small fire on the shore. The lake water ripples with the slight breeze coming in.

I glance up at the navy sky before my gaze drifts to her. The stars are bright, but she's brighter. She seems to glow when she's happy. Even with how hard every day is for her, she doesn't let it dull her enthusiasm or make her bitter. Being with her this past week... falling asleep with her in my arms every night...

My chest expands. My heart beats strong. Her warmth has brought me back to life. "Yeah, they are."

The flames spark and grow.

She purses her lips like she has more to say. I'm sure she does after Brooke stopped by the bar on her way out of town earlier. But tonight's bucket list mission is to stay up until the sun rises, so we have plenty of time.

I put down the seats and lay out a thin foam mattress in the back of the truck. We sit side-by-side on the tailgate while we drink our warm cocoa. She has her notebook and a pen in her lap. We've crossed off some things and added others.

Tiny embers shoot up into the sky like fireflies.

They found Nelson at a motel on the outskirts of town. Brooke's taking him home with her, and he's agreed to start therapy. That's why she came to the bar tonight. To let me know I didn't need to be watching my shadow. Luckily I happened to be on shift when she showed up this time.

It was a bittersweet visit. We both miss Cooper. But while I wandered aimlessly from one fight or drink or pill to another, Brooke went to therapy. She worked through her grief and set up a foundation in her sister's name. She went to college. She made a life that she's happy in. Even got married.

She told me she forgave me a long time ago for my part in Cooper's death. Wants me to forgive myself. And to look her up if I'm ever back home.

Her last words to me before she left were, "If you ever visit, let's have dinner. Mom would love to see you."

Perhaps it's time to consider counseling. Plan ahead for what's to come when Indy's gone. I got the name and number for a therapist from Pez before we left the bar tonight. One he and Ramzi see. It's on a card in my back pocket.

Tomorrow might be the day that I finally make a call that should have been made years ago. Back then I pushed everyone away. I could only focus on what I'd lost. This time with Indy has brought me a different perspective. Every day that I get to share with her is a gift. It's not guaranteed. But that only makes the time we have more precious.

She rests her back against the side of the truck. Tucks her toes under my thigh. "Do you ever think about going back home?"

And there it is. The question I've been waiting all night for her to ask. I wrap my hand around her ankle and lift her foot into my lap.

She spent the evening with me at the bar. Joked with Pez and talked to Lucas. Took a spin on the dance floor with Heath. And learned how to make a mocktail with Wade while I talked to Brooke.

I'm not surprised that she overheard some of our conversation. My stomach turns. "Sometimes. I miss Shae. Miss my parents. But it's difficult when you've run as hard as I have. When you do what I did…sometimes there's nothing to run back to."

"I can't believe they wouldn't want to see you."

I massage her foot. Press my fingers into the muscles. Smile at her pink toes. "Smiley faces?"

"Uh-uh. You're not getting out of this so easily." She leans over to shove my shoulder.

I capture her elbow. The kitten in the teacup temporary tattoo has faded. It feels like a measure of our time. The more it fades, the less we have. It's not enough. I want more time. I wish I could show her all the things that she wants to see in this world. "Give me that pen."

"Why wouldn't your family want to see you?" She offers me the pen.

I take it from her. Uncap it. Start by drawing a dot on the top of her foot. One dark spiral that I wish alluded to more time. Slowly, I add to it. "My parents tried to reach out to me for a while."

In the early days they still had hope. They thought they could reach me if they tried hard enough.

"After I did time, I went home. My dad gave me a job. My mom tried to love me enough that we could pretend that everything would be okay. But nothing could ease the pain. Or stop it from being my fault. I started drinking heavily. Heavier than I do these days. Started taking pills. They helped for a little while." I concentrate on the way the nib glides across her skin. On the dark lines and loops that I'm inking on top of her skin. "I stopped going to work. I started pushing everyone away. I moved on to harder stuff. I overdosed for the first time."

She reaches out and wraps her fingers around my wrist. Her gaze is full of compassion.

Sometimes you have to let your past out in pieces. Slowly, so you don't scare the person you care about away. Other times you have to tear open your heart and feel the agony in order to let it go.

Telling Indy about my past hurts like hell. But there's this sense of hope that it won't be quite so bad on the other side. The drawing becomes more concrete as I move up her leg. More swirls and lines become roses mid-calf. "I told my parents I'd get help. I'd quit. A month later I overdosed a second time. A week after that a third."

She covers her mouth with her hand. "Oh, Theo. I'm so sorry."

"It's okay." I shrug and let out a heavy breath. "It was years ago. I don't…I'm not like that now. But I hurt people while I was. Especially my family. I blew through any money I had access to. Mine and theirs. I even emptied Shae's piggy bank."

That wasn't the worst of it. But there's something about ripping off my little sister to get my next fix that makes me, still to this day, feel like absolute scum.

"It was killing them to watch me try to take myself out. And they didn't know if I'd be responsible enough not to try around Shae. They wanted to get me in treatment. They had this undying need to save me. I didn't want to be saved."

She plays with my hair while I fill in the spaces between the roses with blue skies over fields. Ripped pages that look like they came from her notebook. Clocks without the hands to tick tock away this time we have.

She doesn't say a word. Just waits for me to decide how much I want to tell her.

Her quiet touch soothes the tension from my muscles and makes it easy to open up to her about the worst parts of my life. "I took my mom's jewelry, whatever electronics were easy to carry, anything I could offload quickly to buy my next one way trip to join Cooper, and I left. I didn't look back. Somehow I couldn't manage to take myself out, though. I ended up making my way to the city. Ran out of money. Started sleeping on park benches."

"Your parents never tried to contact you?"

"They did." I smooth the ruffles of her black dress up her thigh to expose more creamy canvas for me to work on. The roses extend up over her knee at this point. "They came out here a few times. Tracked me down on the street. Got me a hot meal and a shower and a clean hotel room to sleep in for a night. Tried to talk me into coming home and getting help."

Mom would cry and Dad was so tense, holding in all his emotions. He had experience. Had seen clients go down the path. Didn't hold the same hope as my mom.

"I'd agree and then skip out with whatever I could sell before they woke the next morning. Be high by lunchtime. They got the message. Stopped trying. Left me to do what I was going to do. And that was right about the time I met Harlan.

"He was looking for his brother, who'd gotten himself into some pretty heavy trouble. He found me instead. I honestly don't remember what we said to each other in that first conversation. But he kept coming to see me. Brought me an old jacket and gloves to help me get through winter. Brought me hot meals a few times a week. And we'd just have these conversations about how fucked up our lives were. And it turns out Harlan's life is pretty damn fucked up, but unlike me, he was finding ways to deal with it."

"He's a good man. Compassionate." Indy smiles at the drawing that covers her leg from foot to panty line.

"Yeah, he is. He let me sleep on his couch and gave me a job." I work on improving the shading.

"Wait…" She touches my arm. "Did you work as a tattooist? But now you're a bartender?"

"And before that I was a law intern." I finish up and put the pen down. "Just because you can do something, doesn't mean that's what you should do."

"You didn't enjoy it?" Curiosity and sympathy color her voice.

I lean back and admire my artwork on her skin. "Actually, I did."

"So what happened?"

"As much as I was doing better on a day-to-day basis, I was struggling." It was all too easy to find another hit if I wanted one. Too easy to give in when it was offered. And way too hard to deal with my emotions. "And then I met Sigh. He came in for a shoulder piece. We got to talking about MMA. The next thing I know I'm fighting for him three nights a week to numb the ache the drugs used to dull."

Until I started falling back into bad habits and telling myself I had it under control because I'd constructed rules around my behavior. Never two days in a row. Never get so wasted I missed work.

"I started topping up with booze and then pills." Losing myself in willing pussy. I was on a dangerous and destructive path. Until Indy.

"Harlan's shop is his pride and joy. He built it from nothing. People know he's the best. Even though I was in a much better place, my choices were bringing me too close to being a liability."

Two lines form between her brows. She straddles my lap. "He fired you?"

"No, but he told me that it was a problem for him. And I respected him enough to quit and find another job." I don't begrudge that he was honest with me. He did so much for me, but I needed the fight and the things that came with it. Sort of a pick your poison kind of deal. "Besides I didn't want to lose his friendship. And I would have if I kept working with him."

"So now you're a bartender."

"And I actually love it. Getting to know people's stories. Being that person who listens. Dancing on the bar." I chuckle as I slip my hands under her dress to palm her ass. She's wearing this tiny bit of floss she calls panties. There's a whole lot of warm, bare skin for me to touch and knead.

She twines her hands behind my head. "It sounds like you're right where you need to be."

"It feels like it." With her on my lap and the crackle of the fire outside the truck.

She bites her lip and tucks her blue hair behind her ear. "So maybe your family would be happy to see you."

"I don't think so." I don't think my family will ever get past the irreparable damage that I caused. "I'm still drinking. Still taking pills."

Though that night we met in the bathroom was the last time I was high, actually. How long ago was that now?

"You haven't had a drink since I moved in with you." She stares into my eyes. "I don't believe you're that guy anymore. You're changing. Getting a handle on your issues. I see it."

"It's too soon." And I still need to deal with my emotions. See a therapist. I'm not ready to face them. They're older and my sister is grown—twenty-one this year—and I'm aware of how finite time is. But I'm not ready.

"Okay." She moves to her knees and sucks my bottom lip between her teeth.

My cock responds like we've been talking about sexual positions and not my past. Kissing her is the perfect ending to this conversation. Her whisky eyes don't judge me. Just being with her makes me feel at peace in a way I didn't believe was possible. When she grinds down on me, that's the kind of distraction that makes everything else fade away. Leaving only our need to get as close as two people possibly can.

I skate my arms up her sides as I help her shed her dress in the confines of the truck. "Those roses look so sexy on you."

"You're talented." She works my belt loose and pulls the leather from the loops on my jeans. "If it weren't for the chemo I'd want them tattooed on my skin for real."

"I'd love to see that." I peel my shirt over my head and toss it over my shoulder. "So much so that it makes me want to take photos so I can remember every exact detail to replicate it later."

"Let's pretend that we have all the time in the world." She reaches for her phone and lights up the screen. She holds it out to me with the camera app open. "Take the photo."

"Are you going to pose for me?" I raise an eyebrow.

She crawls off my lap and I climb out of the truck so she can arrange herself side-on to me. Legs bent at the knee and toes pointed, she presses her hands into the mattress and lifts her chest before pouting at me. She's fucking gorgeous. I literally can't take my eyes off her.

I take a dozen photos before she giggles and pats the mattress. "That's enough. Get up here."

I flip through before I send all those photos to my own phone. One of them will be my screensaver for longer than this thing between us will last.

I'm not going to read into why that hits me so hard, so I shed my jeans and crawl back into the truck to lay beside her. When she reaches for me, I bring her nearer. I memorize every detail of her face in the fire and moonlight while I help her out of her panties and touch her the way she loves to be touched.

Her leg hooks over my hip when she's ready. I trail my fingers up and down her spine as she wraps her hand around me so she can line us up. We take it slow until we can't anymore. Until her toes curl and she tightens on my cock so beautifully that I can only follow her lead.

THE HEARTBREAK LIST

When we're done we curl up in a blanket. The inky darkness gives way to charcoal and then to gray.

"Do you regret that you're not going to get married?" I pour the rest of the cocoa from the flask into our cups.

It's been on my mind since she chose me over him. And our conversation earlier about my past got me thinking about that girl I met in a club bathroom who knew who she was and what she wanted. Who would never have given me the time of day because she had it all planned out.

"I haven't really thought about it." She holds her cup with both hands as she sips at her drink. "I don't regret breaking things off with Gray. Even if you and I hadn't met, and I wasn't dying, he and I weren't right together. Eventually some stressor or event would have come along to show us that. But getting married... having my dad walk me down the aisle. Seeing my mom's eyes well up while we get me into my wedding dress. Having EJ and America standing up with us... those are the things that I'll regret missing out on."

The gray becomes warm orange and pink as we sit in our own thoughts.

"Would you rather get married or go to a waterpark?" Would she marry me if I offered? Would I be able to handle it knowing that she'll be gone soon? Would her family hate the idea? Of course they would. I'm not even sure why I'm thinking about it.

She rolls her gaze at me and giggles. "Waterpark, definitely."

"Way more fun." I turn my attention to the horizon. Her answer leaves me vaguely disappointed.

We watch the sunrise with my arm around her waist and her head on my shoulder and then we mark it off the list.

I drive us home, and she falls asleep on my shoulder. I come to a decision that I didn't think I would. But it's not about me. It's for Indy. And her list. I'd do anything for her.

Chapter Twenty-Nine

Indy

I bounce up and down in the seat next to Theo as he pulls the truck into the express pickup lane outside the airport. America's plane is already on the tarmac. She sent me a message two seconds ago to tell me that they're disembarking.

"You good to go?" Theo squeezes my knee below the hem of my shorts. His gaze drinks me in. "I can always park and we can go together."

"Nope." I already have the door open and I jump out. "I can't have you slowing me down."

He chuckles. "I'll do a couple of laps and meet you here."

"Can't wait." I shut the door and dash into the building. It takes me a few seconds to get orientated and work out where to meet America.

I didn't realize how much I needed her to come home until it became a reality. We've always been each other's support and encouragement, and going through the illness and the treatments without her...it's been hard. But now she's home.

I can see her up ahead at baggage claim. And in a few minutes we'll be on our way to the waterpark capitol of the world. A trip Theo surprised me with last night when he told me he arranged for America and his sister both to join us on this unexpected vacation. He'd been nervous when he admitted his parents only live six minutes away from where we'll be staying for the next few days.

America drops her bag, and we engulf each other.

"I can't believe you're here." I'm just so excited that she is.

"Oh my God, I love the hair. It's so vibrant up close." America holds me at arm's length. She smiles softly and her eyes glisten but she manages to keep it in check. "You look…"

"Like I should eat a meatball sometime." I laugh. I don't care that my hip bones jut out too much and that my cheekbones are more prominent than I'd like. I don't care that my head hurts all the time, and that I'm permanently exhausted these days. My bestie is home and we're about to cross something major off the list. "So are you ready for the biggest waterslide ever?"

"Uh, I've been ready all my life." She blinks a couple times and breaks out in a huge grin. "I can't believe you're finally ready to do it with me, girl. I've been trying to talk you into this forever."

"All it took was a brain tumor. And meeting Theo. Without him I might never have started my bucket list." I take the handle of her luggage. "We should hurry. He's waiting for us."

"Let me do that." She steals it from me and we make our way toward the exit. She keeps side-eying me. "I love that bikini top. And the leg. Is that another one of those temporary tattoos?"

"Theo drew it, actually." As it fades he retraces it. I think it's his way of trying to make it feel like we have more time. And I don't mind. I love the design. I want more time too. Maybe it's delusional, but when he draws on me, it feels like we have all the time in the world.

She bumps my shoulder gently. "You know I didn't mean it when I said you should replace me with him."

"I know. And I didn't." But I still feel bad. Like I've let her down because she's come home and everything is a mess.

"No, you replaced our boy Gray," she says drily.

It sounds so callous when she puts it like that, though she doesn't mean it to be. We speak our mind around each other. Always have. Still, I hate that Gray is hurting because of me. It was never my intention.

"Theo and I...we just...happened. I didn't mean to fall for him. Didn't plan for how much he'd mean to me. Friendship turned to more so quickly and out of the blue. But he's not who you think he is. Not the guy you met that night. He's so much more than a dirty mouth and a pretty smolder. He's my world in a way Gray never could be. I couldn't ignore that."

She stares at me thoughtfully. "You're content."

"I am." With everything. With every day that I have with Theo. With my family. And America. The next minute is all I can count on and somewhere along the way I learned that it's okay not to have a plan and to let life take me wherever it will. To experience life with both eyes on the now and arms open. I've been blessed with a point of view that not everyone gets to experience.

"You have this calmness about you that I didn't expect. I mean...I didn't know what to expect. Other than that I'm going to cry a lot. Because I'm not okay with the idea of you not being here. And I am going to miss you so fucking much." She punctuates that by wiping away the tears that are falling down her cheeks. "But you've made your peace with the situation, haven't you?"

"As much as one can." I lift my shoulder and let it fall. Does anyone ever really come to terms with their own mortality and leaving their loved ones behind? Because I'm still wishing that I didn't have to leave Theo. Or my family. Or her. "We should go. I can't wait to get to the Dells."

"We're going to have so much fun." America rolls her suitcase as we hurry toward the exit. "An unforgettable trip. It killed me not to tell you what he had in store when he called to organize it. But trust, it's going to be so—"

The world spins and I reach out to steady myself as the people disappear from my line of sight and the roof takes their place. I swallow convulsively as my vision darkens. My heart seems to slow as my thoughts grow sluggish.

Is this it then? Is this the moment where it ends? I thought I'd have more time.

"Indy?" America screams my name as she grabs at me frantically. "Indy? Oh God? Someone call 9-1-1."

Chapter Thirty

Theo

In another minute I'm going to have to move from express pickup, because the girls are taking a while coming out of the airport. I text Indy to see if there's a problem and whether I should find a parking spot so I can go inside with them.

No response.

Nerves flutter in my belly and I chew the inside of my bottom lip while I watch the screen until it goes dark. Light it up and watch it go dark again.

Still nothing.

I pick her number from my contacts. Put the device to my ear. It connects, and my breath stalls as I listen to it ring and ring.

I stare at the building entrance as her voicemail gives me the option to leave a message. I don't like this, but it's probably nothing.

I pull away from the curb to do another loop. No doubt they'll be out by the time I roll back around. My chest has grown tight and I rub at the flesh over my heart. This is nothing to worry about, right? Indy is fine. She was excited and happy this morning. She didn't even take pain killers because she said she felt good.

I was worried these past few days that we'd have to cancel the trip, so when she woke up in high spirits this morning, I was so relieved. But now...there's that feeling...that pins and needles feeling that tells me something is wrong.

An ambulance speeds past me, lights flashing. My heart moves to my throat. I can feel it thudding below my tonsils.

"It's not for Indy," I mutter to myself between breaths, even as my head spins. She's fine. Just fine. "Why is this traffic moving so fucking slow?"

It takes forever to get back to where I started. Throwing the truck into park, I jump out and run inside. I spot the paramedics before I spot America. I remember her from that night at the club. She stands beside them with her fingers pressed against her mouth while she stares down at the cluster of bodies.

I shove through people to get closer. I can't see Indy and I can't breathe until I do. Pain grows in my left side. In my jaw and my shoulder. Down my arm.

"Indy?" The paramedics have her blocked off. But those are her boots and those are my roses on her leg. My world comes to a screaming, shuddering halt.

"You need to keep back." A man in an airport security uniform thrusts his arms out in front of me, blocking me from getting to Indy.

I go through him anyway. He barely slows me down. And then she's in front of me. So pale and quiet. Eyes shut. Her expression as peaceful as it was this morning while I watched her sleep. Two men in paramedic uniforms are on the ground with her, working to stabilize her so they can transfer her to the hospital.

"Is she going to be okay?"

"You need to back up and let us work," one of the men says as they prepare to lift her onto a stretcher.

"Theo?" America approaches me. Wraps both hands around my elbow. "You're Theo, right?"

"Yeah, I..." grab at my hair as I glance at the woman beside me. "What happened?"

"One minute we were walking and then..." She presses her fingers to her mouth. "She lost consciousness. I watched her fall..."

The two men move Indy onto the rolling bed and then raise it to height. The people loitering wander away now that there's nothing interesting to see.

Indy's eyes flutter open. Her voice is a whisper. "America?"

"I'm here." I take her hand as the paramedics roll her past us. "I'm right here, sweetheart."

"Theo." She squeezes my hand weakly.

"I'm here too." America walks with me beside the stretcher as we make our way outside. "You scared the hell out of me."

She scared the shit out of me too. I'm still shaking.

"I'm sorry." Water dribbles from the corner of her eye. "I'm so sorry I'm ruining our trip."

"Don't even worry about it." America starts to cry too.

I'm numb though. Completely and utterly numb. Seeing her like that... "Let's just concentrate on getting some rest, huh?"

She nods as her eyes drift closed. "Okay."

The paramedics move the stretcher into the ambulance. One of them climbs up with her. The other moves to the front.

"We'll meet you there," I tell her.

They close the doors and the ambulance departs. I carry America's luggage to my truck and toss it on the backseat. She climbs up beside me in the front. "Has that happened before?"

"No." I really thought she was gone for a minute there. And I'm not ready. I'm not prepared for any of this. It takes me a moment to control the emotions threatening to choke me. To push them down enough to start the engine and pull into traffic.

America tries to distract me...or perhaps both of us, with small talk in between phone calls to Indy's parents and EJ. I don't know what she asks or what I say. I doubt she does either. When she calls Gray, I don't say a damn word. I don't take it personal. He's important to Indy. He should know.

America finishes that call and clutches her phone with both hands. "They'll meet us there."

I have no clue how we drove to the hospital as I find a parking space. What route we took or if I ran any red lights or had any near misses. That numbness has spread to my fingers and toes.

"She's going to be fine. She has to be." America is pep-talking the both of us as we jump out and hurry toward the entrance.

"I don't know." When Cooper died, I didn't have any warning and it was devastating. But with Indy...she's been warning me the whole time that this only ends one way. There is no happy ending here. And I don't know how I'm supposed to walk away and be okay. Not after today.

The doors are right in front of us when I stop.

America manages a couple of steps before she notices that I'm not keeping up with her. "Theo?"

What the hell was I thinking...getting involved with a woman who is going to die? Falling for her. It's so damn stupid. Plain fucking crazy. I can't do this anymore.

I can't do this again.

"Theo?" America is in my face, her dark eyes searching mine, but it's all trumped by Indy lying there so motionless in the middle of the airport.

"I really thought she was dead," I croak.

"It's okay." She grasps my forearm. Squeezes. "She's still with us. We have time."

She's still with us for now, but that doesn't mean it's going to stay that way. The next time could be the last time. I break out in a cold sweat. My heart seems to turn to stone. "I can't do it. I can't get any more attached to her. I can't say goodbye to her."

I shake my head as I start to back up. "I can't."

"Theo, she needs you." America tugs on my arm. "I understand how much you're hurting. I'm terrified that my best friend might not come out of this hospital. But she needs us both to be here for her. She needs you to walk your ass into this hospital and be there for her."

"I can't." I bring my hands up, palms facing out. It's going to hurt too damn much if I stick around any longer. I drag my keys out of my pocket. "I've got to go."

"What am I supposed to tell Indy?" America sobs. "This will break her. You understand that, don't you? It will crush her."

"Tell her…" I need to contact Sigh and get him to set up a fight. Put all this emotion into something that makes sense. I pull out my phone and start typing out that text. Hopefully he can find me an opponent who won't back down until one of is unconscious. "That it was nice knowing her. But we both know I'm not the kind of guy who was going to stick around while they put on the toe tag."

America gasps. "What the fuck?"

I turn my back on her. "It was nice seeing you again."

"You're seriously going to do this?" she calls out to me as I start to walk away from the building while hitting send on that message. "You're going to leave?"

I pause and glance back at her. "I already watched the woman I loved die once. If I stick around…"

Do I need to say it? That I can't go through it again? That I can't fall deeper in with Indy, knowing she's going to die. I thought I could handle the fact that I like her, but I can't. And if we keep going the way we are... it'll hurt far more than I thought it would. It already does.

She plants her hands on her hips. "You're afraid."

"Or just not stupid enough to be willing to put myself through it." I turn my back on her again and make a beeline for my truck. No, it's better I get out now. With fond memories and my heart still intact. Better to remember the way Indy was with so much life in her eyes, than to watch it all fade away.

By the time I climb in the truck, America has vanished through those big doors. I watch them for a while with my elbow on the window and my head resting on my fist. Gray arrives first. Then Indy's parents and EJ. She'll be okay now. With everyone she loves by her side. She doesn't need me.

My knee jiggles. It doesn't stop when I hold it down. Sigh's message takes forever to come through. I don't know how many times I have to light up my screen before it does.

Tossing my phone on the seat, I start up the truck. There's no fight tonight. Fuck.

Chapter Thirty-One

Indy

I rub at the skin around the port they installed in the crook of my elbow when I got to the hospital. I've been poked and prodded a hundred times since they brought me in. They've taken so much blood I could use a cookie. I'm currently waiting for the nurse to come back and collect me for a CT scan.

Out in the waiting room, Theo and America must be going out of their minds with worry. My parents and EJ are probably here too. Or they will be soon.

"Hey." America slips into the room quietly. She comes over and carefully hugs me. "They said I could only visit for a few minutes. How are you feeling?"

"I've been better." I rest against the pillows when she steps back. My head hurts and I am so tired, but that's nothing new. "I hate that I fainted and ruined what was supposed to be an amazing trip to the waterparks. You came all the way home for it."

"Don't worry about that now." She presses her lips together and sniffs. "I came home for you. You're here. So I am too. I can ask EJ to pick us up a pack of cards and we can play Go Fish or Gin Rummy."

A weak laugh escapes me. We've whiled away so many bored afternoons with card games.

"Where's Theo?" I glance at the doorway as though he will appear there, conjured only by how much I need to see his face.

She flinches and shifts uncomfortably. Finally she shakes her head. "He left."

"Oh." I'm suddenly bone weary. All I want to do is close my eyes. "Is he coming back?"

"I don't think so, Indy. He was pretty adamant..." She swallows on a sympathetic smile. "He's not coming back."

So that's it then? Our time is over. I wasn't prepared. I'm not ready.

"It must have scared him so much to see me like that." It breaks my heart to imagine what he must be feeling and thinking after having reality shoved in his face. The fact that I'm dying, up until now, has been an abstract idea. But the way I collapsed... "It must have made it all too real."

Stirred up memories of losing Cooper. Brought all that pain to the surface for him.

"You're not upset?" America questions me with a lift of her on fleek brows.

"How can I be?" How can I begrudge him wanting to end this now while our story is still vibrant and full of life. I'd rather he remember me like that, than watch me grow sicker. Even if it feels like my heart is being shattered into a million tiny pieces from which I'll never recover. "We don't have a future. We never did. And we both understood that going into this arrangement. Even when we complicated it with feelings, we still knew that it would end."

"But—"

"I'm tired." I turn my head to stare at the wall. I don't want to talk about him leaving. There's no point to doing so. A tear drips over the bridge of my nose. My heart is shrinking and all my sadness is overflowing. *I'm going to miss you so much, Theo. God, I hope you get everything you want and deserve in this life. I hope you find happiness. I hope you remember me as I was before today.*

America pats my arm as she stands. "I'll be in the waiting room, okay?"

When she leaves, I crumble. I cry so hard and for so long it feels like I'll never stop.

Gray enters the room and comes to the bed. His pale gaze is full of worry as he wraps his arms around my shaking form and holds me tight. "My poor Indy."

His hug is comforting like a fuzzy blanket. He smells as familiar as home. I cling to him as I cry into the button down shirt he's wearing.

He takes a seat on the bed and lifts me onto his lap. He rocks me the whole time that I cry for Theo. His lips press to the top of my bald head. "I've got you, babe. It's okay. I'm here. I'm not going anywhere."

I wear myself out in his arms. Doze there with the strong, steady beat of his heart in my ear, until the nurse comes back with a wheelchair.

"I need to take you for a CT scan now," she tells me.

I nod, prepared to scramble off Gray's lap, but he lifts me and places me in the chair instead.

"You're welcome to walk with us." The nurse starts to wheel me out of the room.

Gray follows us into the hallway. He pushes both hands into his pockets and shoots me an uncertain glance.

"Please, Gray." I don't want to be alone right now. Not until they work out what happened today and what my next step is.

He nods as he falls into step with us. When he offers me his hand, I take it and lean on his support.

He leaves me at the door to the CT room. "I'll go check in with your family. Tell them what's happening."

"Thank you." The door closes between us.

The nurse helps me onto the bed and I'm left alone with my thoughts while the machine runs. All I can think about is Theo. The way he smiles and the way those beautiful eyes of his crinkle in the corners.

The way he made me laugh.

Every sexy and sweet moment we've shared plays like a montage in my head.

Dancing on the bar.

Our first kiss as the rain grew heavy.

All those blue alien vibrators falling down around us.

Breaking glasses in the alley.

Making love in the back of his truck under the stars.

Being with Theo was the highlight of my life. And even if our time is over, every second we shared is worth this heartbreak. I would do it over and over again exactly the same. All of it. From crossing things off my bucket list to falling in love with him to this ache that feels like I'm being hollowed out.

The nurse takes me back to the room when the scans are finished. She helps me onto the bed and leaves when my parents come in.

They sit with me for a while. Worried and quiet. Barely able to take their eyes off me. EJ comes in a bit later. He sits on the bed beside me. "America told me Theo left. Do you want me to go find him?"

Hearing his name makes me tear up.

"He's not up to dealing with this part." I gesture at the hospital bed and the port in my arm and all of the scared faces of my family. This is probably only the first of many times I'll end up in the hospital during the time I have left. "I won't force him to watch me decline. It's for the best that we call it quits now. Really."

"You don't know—"

"I have a few months. Maybe, if I'm lucky, a little longer." I press my lips together. "We both knew where this was heading. He didn't do this to hurt me, EJ."

"I know." He wraps an arm around my shoulder and squeezes gently.

Gray and America brings snacks and coffee. America sits with my mother and holds her hands as they check in with each other.

Gray sits next to me on the bed. "How are you doing?"

"Okay." What else is there to say? I've missed him like a friend, but we're not friends like we were before we were lovers. And we might never get there. He doesn't want to hear about how much it hurts for me to lose Theo. He doesn't want to know that it hurts more after a few months with Theo than it did when I broke up with him after years together.

What we had was real. But with Theo...the way I feel about him is all-encompassing. I'm so grateful that I got to experience it.

"We have your results," the doctor announces as he walks into the room. He scans through something on the tablet in his hand before glancing at each of my family members. When his focus settles on me he gives me a friendly smile. "You're anemic. Your red blood count is severely compromised. It's a fairly normal side effect of the medications you're on."

"So it's treatable?" EJ straightens.

The gloom that has settled over the room lifts a little. My mom bursts into tears. My dad sits forward while he squeezes her shoulder.

"With these numbers we'd like to give you a transfusion," the doctor says. "And then we can look at supplements to help for as long as you're on the medications."

"It's not the tumor?" Gray's voice turns hopeful.

"Not directly, no. She fainted because of the anemia, which is a result of the meds." The doctor does something on his tablet. "That said, we don't have an update on the tumor's progress yet. I'm still waiting on the results from the CT scan. When I have them I'll be able to give you more information. In the meantime, we're going to get you set up for a transfusion."

"Thank you, doctor." I yawn as he leaves.

A few minutes later the nurse comes back. She orders everyone out of the room while she fusses around me. A second orderly enters as my family start to depart. Until it's only Gray and EJ left.

EJ gently rubs the top of my head with his fist before he climbs off the bed. "Glad you're still here, sis."

"Me too." I smile at him. Every minute I have with my family means the world to me.

"Indy..." Gray clears his throat when they're all gone. "Your friend...he isn't here..."

"Don't say it," I whisper as I turn away so he won't see me cry.

"Whatever happened with him...whatever it was he gave you that you needed...I just want you to know that I'm sorry I couldn't do that for you."

"You should hate me." I sniffle. God, I tried to make him hate me.

He grasps my chin carefully until our gazes lock. "I was hurt when you told me...I was so fucking angry. But hate you? I could never hate you, Indy. I'm here, aren't I? I'll always be here for you. I love you."

"Gray," I whisper through the tears that won't stop falling. Because in some ways I will always love him, but never in the way that he wants or deserves.

He stands and presses his lips to my cheek. "Get some rest and feel better. We'll talk later."

Chapter Thirty-Two

Theo

A couple of the guys look up from the tattoos they're working on as I storm into Harlan's shop. I press the heel of my palm into my forehead, scanning the room. My head feels like it's going to explode. "Where's Harlan?"

"Out back." Kian lifts his chin and points with that peacock blue mohawk of his. "You want me to get him?"

I march around the front counter and between the workstations. I'm not in a waiting mood. There are too many thoughts raging in my head. "I'll find him."

"Theo?" Harlan's eyes widen when I find him smoking a cigarette, leaning against the back wall of the shop. "Everything all right?"

"I feel like I'm dying. Or having a heart attack." I grasp a fistful of hair on the top of my head as I pace a stiff square. My jaw is as wound up as a steel trap. "Indy is in the hospital. We went to pick her friend up from the airport and something happened. She collapsed. They transferred her by ambulance."

"But you're not at the hospital?" Harlan pushes away from the wall as he puts the butt of his smoke to his lips and inhales. "You're here."

"She has a fucking brain tumor," I snarl at him as I punch the brick wall. It barely hurts though it tears the skin from my knuckles. "She's dying.

It could be today. It could be tomorrow. Or next week. But it's going to happen soon and I'm going to lose her. And I can't."

"You can't?" He stares at me thoughtfully.

"I can't." The pang in my chest brings me to tears. "I can't breathe. I can't think. Indy is going to die and there's nothing I can do to stop it. There's nothing I can do to make it hurt less. I can't be in love with her and I can't go through this pain again."

Harlan takes another drag of his cigarette. Lets the smoke billow from his nostrils. "What's the alternative?"

"What's the alternative?" My words come out strangled.

"Yes." He watches me patiently. Like he has all of this worked out while I'm losing my fucking mind. "You've just told me you're in love with her. So tell me how you see things playing out from here."

"I stay away. I don't let my emotions get any more twisted." I have some chance of coming out of this in one piece.

He grinds out the butt. Shakes another cigarette loose from his pack and holds it between his lips while he lights the paper. "Going to chain smoke, if you don't mind."

"Whatever." He knows I don't care about his bad vices. And I really don't care now because the only thing that I can focus on is that Indy is in the hospital. I have no idea if she's okay. And I have an entire future stretching out in front of me without her.

"You're already twisted up over this girl. Have been since before you brought her to my shop for that kitten tattoo."

"That's not true."

"Isn't it?" He raises an eyebrow. "Want me to recount every woman you brought to the shop before Indy?"

"Fuck you."

"Come on then, tell me you're going to be just fine walking away. That you're not in the middle of a panic attack because you're all up in your emotions over this girl."

"Fuck." I stumble until my back hits the wall. My knees give and I crumple. I'm having a panic attack. That's what this is. Because I'm losing her when I've only just realized what she means to me. I grasp at my heart. "The minute I saw those hospital doors I couldn't go in."

"You saw your first love go in doors similar and never come out." He crouches in front of me. "Are you really surprised that you would have anxiety about it? Especially when Indy is so sick."

"She's dying." I bury my face in my hands. Just because we don't want that to happen doesn't change her diagnosis.

"So am I." He coughs into his fist. "So are you. But we get to be thankful for every day that we have. We fight for it, don't we? Isn't that why you're still here? Because you fought to be? Isn't that what that whole bucket list you two were doing was about?"

"I don't know how I'm supposed to do this knowing I'm going to have to say goodbye." I wipe at my wet eyes. "When all I can think about when I look at her is how much I wish we could have a future. I want to love her for the rest of her life and mine, Harlan. Not just for a few months. Damn it. I think about marrying her."

"You're in far deeper than I thought then." He stares at me with so much sympathy as he straightens. "But you're the only one who can decide how strong you are. Whether you can handle living the entirety of your love while you can, or whether you walk away from that girl to protect yourself is your decision."

He butts out his second cigarette after only a few drags and goes back inside.

I rest my head against the wall while my heart rate slows and my lungs start to work properly again. For so long I've numbed my grief and my guilt over losing Cooper. But Indy…she made me remember what it's like to feel alive. To be happy and to love. To want more out of every day.

But I can wish for a future with Indy all I want; she doesn't have that kind of time. So the question is… if my future with Indy has to be lived in hours or days or weeks, will I regret that I didn't have the balls to live it? To be there for every single moment of our life together? Through the good moments and those ones that will shatter me? Can I give her the best of me in the darkest of her hours?

My phone pings with a new message. Someone pulled out and there's a fight if I want it. I can put Indy behind me and go back to the way I was in just a few hours. Standing up, I text Sigh back and then delete the message.

God, I hope America didn't tell her what I said.

Chapter Thirty-Three

Indy

"Hey." Gray raps on the door quietly before he enters. He takes a seat in the chair by my bed before he reaches out and clasps my hand. "How are you feeling?"

"Tired." It's been a few hours since the paramedics brought me in. The transfusion has pumped new blood into my veins that should make me feel better quickly. But so far it can't push back this fog I'm under. The only thing that could make me feel better is Theo. "Did he...?"

His jaw sharpens and a nerve in his cheek jumps. "America told me what he said. I don't think he's going to change his mind, Indy."

"What did he say?" It mustn't be good if neither America nor Gray will tell me, but then, perhaps that's exactly what I need. For his last words to sever this bond between us.

He shakes his head.

"Please." I hate that I'm begging him to tell me about Theo.

He rubs his temples as his chest deflates. "It's nothing that you need to hear."

I close my eyes against the burn in them. What could he say that would make me feel differently than I do? We both knew this is how it ends. With me in the hospital and him going back to a life that doesn't include me.

"Don't waste your time on him, Indy." Gray moves to sit on the bed. He pulls me into his arms and holds me tight. His shoulders shake. "You need to concentrate on being positive."

"Gray." I push weakly at his shoulders.

"I think you should move back in with me," he says. "I know how much living with your mom will drive you crazy. You can stay with me. I'll take care of you."

"Gray." I shake my head. "That isn't fair to you."

"We don't have to be together." His ice blue eyes blaze with emotion. "Or we can pretend he never existed and go back to how it was. As long as you're in my life."

"Gray." I clasp his face between both of my hands and stare into his eyes. I'm crying for him too now. For how much he loves me, and the pain that I've caused him. That I'll continue to bring him. Because I could never love him the way that I love Theo.

When Gray asked me to marry him it was easy to say yes because he was warm and safe and familiar. And because all of my plans included marrying my first love. It wasn't until Theo asked me if I regretted not getting married that I realized that my answer to Gray should have been no all along.

And then Theo asked me if I would rather get married or go to a waterpark. Offhanded, like it was a joke. I wanted to choose get married—to him—so badly.

I sniffle. "I love you, Gray. I have loved you since we were children. And I will love you until there's no more breath in my body. You're my family. My home. You're in every version of the future that I have ever imagined."

"I love you too." He smiles at me softly as he leans in to kiss me.

"You're in there as my family." I shake my head as I evade his lips. "Not as the man I'm in love with."

"You're in love with him, aren't you? Do you really think he feels the same way about you?" Gray looks sick to his stomach. "He's not even here, Indy."

"I know." And it's breaking me, but at this point all I can do is accept his decision. "And that's okay. I don't blame him for needing to walk away."

"Actually." Theo's gruff voice draws my attention to where he hovers just outside the door. "I'm right here."

Gray jumps up from the bed and faces him. "I heard what you said, asshole."

He barely flicks a glance to Gray before his gaze is on me. "It's true that I said some things that I deeply regret, sweetheart. I told America I didn't want to see them give you a toe tag. I still don't. If I could, I would fight death himself to make sure that never happened."

I chuckle as an image of him punching a hooded skeleton with a scythe pops into my head.

He sits on the bed. Reaches out and uses his thumb to brush away some of my tears. "I freaked out when we got to the hospital. It brought up a lot of emotions for me and I flipped out and I left."

"I figured." I cover his hand with mine. Press my lips to his palm. "I didn't blame you for leaving. Things aren't going to get better for us."

Gray scowls at Theo's back. "Indy, please—"

"They're probably not." Theo presses his forehead against mine. "Though these days I do believe in big miracles. And you, my sweetheart, are one hell of a miracle. You showed me what it is to live again. Gave me purpose. Made me want a future. I'm so in love with you."

"I love you too." I'm sobbing. "You gave me the freedom to discover who I could be. And somehow you still managed to keep me safe. You gave me the future I wanted. Even if only for a little while."

"We've had an adventure, haven't we?" He smiles through his tears.

"Such a great adventure." I smile back.

"I want to keep it going." He stares into my eyes, his gaze determined and warm. "For however long we have. Whether that's days or weeks. I don't want to miss one moment with you. I want to kiss you every time it rains and make love to you every night. I want to take you on the biggest waterslide in the world. And I want you to meet my family. Even if it's awkward and stilted because there's no time to fix things with them first."

"I want those things too."

"And I want to call you my wife, Indy. I want to marry you. I want to be the man you can depend on when the days aren't so great. I don't want you to move in with your parents when things get worse and our time is almost up. Not unless I'm there too."

"Is that so?" I giggle. He's so sexy-cute in his earnestness. It makes my heart swell.

He tips my chin up. "I want you to be my wife, and I want to be the last face you see before you close your eyes for the very last time. I want to love you for the rest of my life. But if I can only have the rest of yours to do it in, then I'll take each and every day that you can give me."

"All of my days are yours. My heart is yours." I press my lips to his. "Until we run out of time."

"I'll love you long after that, sweetheart." He angles my head to capture my mouth. Pours his love into a lingering kiss. Then kisses away my tears.

"Sorry to interrupt." The doctor enters the room as we break apart.

At some point Gray left, and I don't blame him. This time I've probably broken his heart beyond all repair. But I can't focus on the hurt now... can't waste a single precious moment as Theo moves next to me and wraps his arm around me. Our love is what I want to pour myself into. Our happiness. The time that we have left together.

"I have the results of your scans." The doctor flips through the information on his tablet. Smiles.

My breath catches.

Theo's fingers tighten on my hip.

"The chemo is working and the tumor has shrunk."

Theo's chest stills and then rises and falls deeply. "That's good news, isn't it?"

"It's positive," the doctor says. "It looks like surgery might be a viable option now."

"Oh my God." I cover my heart with my hand. It's started to race. A future with Theo might actually be a possibility.

"We're going to want to run more scans since the previous one showed no improvement. And we're going to have to get your anemia under control before we schedule you. There are risks with the surgery that we'll need to consider."

"But I could have a future?"

The doctor smiles at me. "This is good news, Indy."

"I need to tell my parents."

"I'll get them." Theo kisses my cheek and then leaves to find them. He's back a few minutes later with them and EJ and America all in tow.

I make eye contact with EJ. "Will Gray be okay?"

He shakes his head. "I don't know. It's going to take time."

The doctor tells them the same news he told me. That the tumor could be operable. That my risks have changed.

We've all broken down by the time he's finished. Mom and America wipe at their eyes multiple times. Dad and EJ ask the hard questions like what risks come with surgery and what my chances of a full recovery are.

The odds are still a little terrifying. It might not be enough. But there's a chance that Theo and I could have an entire life in front of us, and I want it more than anything. We could continue the bucket list. Add things like travel and having a family to it.

When the doctor leaves my family takes turns hugging me and whispering encouraging words before they file out too. Until I'm alone with Theo.

He leans in and takes my hand in his. Runs his thumb over my ring finger. "Do you feel like marrying me tomorrow? Or do you want to wait until after the surgery?"

"Tomorrow." I take a handful of his shirt and pull his lips to mine. I don't want to wait to marry him. I don't want to waste a minute. "Although I don't know if that's even possible. Can we get a marriage license that fast?"

He smiles at me, his gaze warm and soft. "As soon as we can then?"

"As soon as we can."

Chapter Thirty-Four

Theo

Indy's parents' backyard is packed with people. Some of them I know, like Harlan and the guys from the tattoo parlor, and Pez and the rest of the crew from the bar. They file into the huge yard and greet each other before finding seats.

Some of them I've never met before, but they're Indy's friends and family, so that makes them mine too. A few of them stare at me like they're at the wrong wedding. It probably came as a shock when they found out Indy was marrying a stranger instead of Gray.

Some of them probably think we're doing the wrong thing and that she should still be marrying him. He certainly did.

No one has seen him since he walked out of the hospital. He didn't answer EJ's calls or respond to his text messages about the change in Indy's prognosis. I don't fault him for taking off. And honestly, it's easier that he isn't here because I don't know if we could ever work out how to coexist peacefully.

He'll always see me as the man who stole Indy from him. He'll always be the guy who is in love with my wife. Well, she'll be my wife in a few minutes anyway.

She's upstairs with her mom and America. Getting ready. Sadie is with them too, helping with hair and makeup. Making sure my wife will be her most stunning self. Not that she needs any help.

An older version of how I remember my father is talking to Indy's dad. He has more gray than black in his hair these days and far more lines on his face. I'm pretty sure I put them there over the years. Mom is with him; she smiles nervously when our gazes meet.

We're a long way from fixing the relationships that I broke, but Indy asked me if I would regret it if I didn't invite them and the answer was yes. So I called them and told them about Indy and the wedding and needing them to be here, and they drove down the next day.

Shae came with them. She's around here somewhere. Probably taking a breather from all the people crowding around.

My heart stops as Indy steps through the doors from inside the house. She's the most beautiful woman I have ever seen in a simple white dress that floats around her knees as she walks toward me. Her blue hair is adorned with a garland of roses. "You're so beautiful."

The chatter hushes. The last stragglers make their way to their seats.

America carries a bunch of simple cream roses in each hand. She forgave me pretty quickly once I told her my story. Helped me pick out a ring while we waited for Indy to be allowed to leave the hospital. The white gold ring is shaped like a leaf that will curl around her finger once I slide it on. A small diamond sits between the two points.

It's a symbol of life. And of growth. Before her I was stagnant. I wasn't living. I was stuck in the past. But she made me feel alive. She helped me move forward. I will be eternally grateful for that. Cherish each day we have.

America holds one of the bouquets out to Indy. "You forgot these."

"Thanks." Indy doesn't take her gaze from mine as I lift her hand that will soon have my ring on it to my lips. Her eyes shine.

We have a drawer at home now where we keep the important pieces of our past. I showed her the engagement ring I bought Cooper so many years ago. Told her I understood that though our roads have branched into a new road together, it doesn't mean we don't hold a special place in our heart for the people we've loved before. Gray was and will always be important to her, just like Cooper will always be important to me.

But that's the past, and while it's okay to hold onto the memories, I'm not going to live in it. Right now is our time. Tomorrow isn't guaranteed. In fact tomorrow is going to be hell while we all wait for her to come out of surgery. I'm sick to my stomach just thinking about it. So for now I push it aside. Concentrate on my love for Indy. "Are you ready?"

"I'm ready." She smiles at me.

"Shall we?" her dad asks, as he comes up behind her. He offers the crook of his elbow and she starts to cry.

I leave them to have a moment while I make my way to where EJ and Harlan are waiting. I asked EJ to be my best man. Told him that it was something Indy had mentioned was important to her. Because she is what matters to both of us at the end of the day.

Oz walks his daughter up the makeshift aisle. Eyes glittering, he kisses her cheek. "You are loved, baby girl. Be happy."

He turns to me. "Be good to our daughter. She is so precious. Don't forget that."

I nod as Indy hands over her roses to America again. I swallow down the wetness that fills my throat. She is my home and I am hers.

We say our vows as the sun sets in front of the people who matter most, but for the entire time all I see is Indy. When EJ hands me the ring I slide it onto her finger. When the officiant tells me I can kiss my wife I kiss her with all the love that I have.

We celebrate well into the night. Until Indy grows tired. She fights it because she's nervous about tomorrow. The idea of surgery scares her. She tells everyone that she's fine, but she looks at me like it might be the last time she sees my face.

It scares me too.

When Indy can't keep her eyes open anymore, I take my wife home. She falls asleep in the truck. Only wakes as I carry her into our apartment at two in the morning.

"I love you so much." She wraps her arms around my neck as I lay her on the bed. "I can't believe that we got married. I'm your wife."

"You are my life." I kiss her as I take the garland from her head. "My heart. And my soul. Sometimes I think you are the very air that I breathe."

"I feel the same way, husband." She brings my mouth back to hers in a slow kiss. "Show me what it feels like to make love to a married man."

"You need to rest." God, it takes everything in me to turn her down. "We have to be at the hospital in just a few hours."

"What if we only have tonight?" She holds onto me. "What if this is the only chance that we get to make love as husband and wife?"

"That's not going to happen." But yeah, that fear is there, taking up space in the back of my mind. It makes my chest hurt like hell and my lungs seize every time I think about it.

"Theo?" She begs with those pretty whisky eyes as she sits up. "I'll get up and write it on the bucket list if I have to."

I can't say no to her and her bucket list. I never could. "Let me help you out of that dress."

With lingering touches and quiet words, we take off each other's clothes. I explore every inch of her bare flesh with my hands and my mouth. Until she's whimpering and quivering so beautifully for me. Then I make love to her like I never want it to end.

Her nails dig into my ass as she gets close and I taste the needy little noises she makes in each kiss while we stare into each other's eyes. I see the moment she hits her peak. The way her neck arches and her eyelids flutter.

I follow her with my own climax. My heart is so big it doesn't feel like it fits in my chest.

Afterward I hold her until the sun rises. Neither of us sleeps a wink. When the alarm goes off we get up and share a shower. I hold her close and we make love again. Then I load her bag into the truck while she climbs into the passenger seat, and I drive us to the hospital.

EJ meets us at the entrance. Indy didn't want anyone else at the hospital. Bleary eyed and wearing yesterday's suit, he thrusts a coffee at me. "Sorry, sis. But we're going to need the caffeine. You're the one who gets to have a nap."

Indy holds a hand to her belly. "Even if I didn't have to fast, I don't think I could keep anything down."

"It's going to go perfectly," he says once we've checked in at the neurosurgery office for pre-op. "They'll go in and remove all that gray matter you don't need. Leave the tumor."

Indy rolls her gaze at him. "Oh, he's got jokes..."

"It's going to be fine," he says more somberly.

I have no clue if he's trying to convince her or himself. Or if it helps at all.

Eventually they call her name and we wait while they take her through pre-op and get her situated in a room. She sits on the bed and I sit next to her and wrap her up in my arms. I don't know what to say to make waiting easier. So I think about the bucket list and the things we haven't put on it because we didn't have a future to look forward to. Things like family and travel. "If you could pick anywhere in the world, where would you want to go?"

She squeezes my knee. "As long as you're there it doesn't matter."

"Of course I'm there." I press my lips to her temple.

"Well, then. I have a whole list of places I'd like to go."

"But surely there's somewhere you want to go more than all the other places. A place we can start."

"Japan," she whispers. "I don't know why. I've always been fascinated with the culture."

"Okay. When the surgery is behind us, when you've recovered enough to travel, that's what we'll do."

"We'll go to Japan?" Her eyes light up as she lifts her hand to touch my face.

"Just to start." I take it in mine and kiss her knuckles.

"If we don't get to go..." She starts to cry silently. "If something goes wrong, or the surgery isn't successful, I want you to go without me. Take EJ. Experience it for me."

EJ rises and walks away to a corner of the room. Taking a moment to gain some composure. I don't try to bury or hide my emotions from her. "If that's what you want."

She takes my face in her hands. "I want you to keep crossing things off our bucket list. And I want you to not be alone."

"I'm not alone. You'll always be with me. Right here in my heart." I place her palm on my chest. "I'll carry you everywhere I go."

Eventually they come to collect her.

I kiss my wife like it might be our last kiss. Every fiber of my being holds onto the hope that it won't be. That we actually have a future to look forward to. The odds are in our favor now.

But if we don't...if this were to be it...the time I've had with her is truly worth it.

"I'll see you on the other side." She smiles at me over her shoulder as they take her away.

I smile back. "I'll be right here waiting, sweetheart."

Epilogue

Theo

I stare out the small portal window at the cotton candy clouds below. It's blue skies for as far as the eye can see.

"Japan, here we come." EJ drags his fists down his quads. He swallows hard as he glances down the aisle. "Where is that flight attendant?"

He's scared of flying. If I'd been aware of that fact I would never have agreed to take him on this trip. But I never could say no to Indy. Not even about this.

The flight attendant appears a few minutes later. She wheels her refreshments trolley, stopping at each row, until she gets to ours. "Can I get you anything?"

"Wh…" EJ clears his throat. "Whisky."

"Sir?" Our gazes connect and she does that double take girls do when they first notice the eyes.

"I'm fine, thanks."

"You so are," she murmurs.

EJ snorts into the rim of his drink.

Flustered, she moves on.

I take off my seatbelt and scooch past him into the aisle, following the attendant until she hits the galley.

My lips turn up as one of the toilet doors opens and a hand shoots out to grab my bicep.

The second Indy drags me inside the tiny cubicle I'm kissing her. "There's my girl."

"I can't believe we're doing this," she whispers in between kisses while she unzips my pants.

"You're the one who put it on the bucket list." I reach under her skirt and help her out of her panties. "Not that I'm complaining. I totally would have put it there if you hadn't."

"You know where you should put it." She yanks my mouth back to hers.

I lift her up and press her into the wall. "You ready for me?"

"Yes."

She whimpers as I slam home. Clings to me as I start to move inside her. Now that she's off most of the meds we're not having the same problem we were having. It makes things like joining the mile high club easier to put on the bucket list.

"Theo." She's already close.

I cover her mouth with my hand when she hits that edge. Keep her sounds just for me.

She pulses around me and it's all I can bear. I grunt into her neck as I come. My vision blurs. I see stars. My wife is a damn goddess.

We relinquish our hold on each other slowly. I put her back on her feet. With giddy smiles we fix each other's clothes.

I straighten a few strands of blue hair that are out of place. "I love you so much."

"I love you too." She draws me in for another kiss before she slips out of the cubicle.

I take a moment to give her a head start back to the window seat. A moment to reminisce on how fucking lucky I am that she's still here. Three months ago she went into surgery and I waited all day with my heart in my mouth. We didn't know if she would make it through. We didn't know whether it would make enough of a difference.

Until the doctor came to tell us that the surgery had gone as well as possible. And that while Indy's recovery time could be long, everything looked extremely positive.

The next few days were spent going back and forth to the hospital. She was doped up on some pretty harsh painkillers and anti-nausea meds. She slept constantly. They ran more scans.

It took a week for the doctor to clear her to come home.

Everyone chipped in to help. Her parents and brother. America was constantly coming and going. Gray called once and asked for her. Wanted to know that she was okay. Told me to look after her like she was the very center of my world. I could promise him that.

For another week after that she could barely walk from the recliner to the bathroom. She couldn't shower on her own. It was six weeks before she could lift more than a half-gallon of milk. By that point she was going out of her mind, needing to do something.

We started adding more things to the bucket list as a way to circumvent the boredom. Booked our trip to Japan when the doctors said it would be okay for her to fly. I begged EJ to come with us on the off chance it was too soon for her and we needed a helping hand. Indy wasn't against it since it was her idea in the first place.

Now we're on our way to cross Japan off the bucket list.

I leave the cubicle and make my way down the aisle. She glances up at me as I push past EJ and drop into my seat. Her smile takes my breath away as she slips her hand in mine. I press my lips to her temple as she stares out at all that blue.

But I'm staring at her. When I'm with her I feel content and alive and free. She is my blue sky. She is my home.

When I lost Cooper I thought I would never find my way. I am so fucking blessed to have found a love like Indy's.

Theo

I squeeze Indy's waist as we walk into Harlan's shop. Eyes lit up, she practically vibrates with anticipation. It took a long time to get here. And I don't mean to the tattoo parlor.

It's been six months since the surgery. We went to all the follow up appointments and finished the chemo.

Her hair has started coming back in. She's putting on weight; curvy in a way that makes me hard just thinking about.

She got the all clear to get inked the last time we saw her doctor. I sent Harlan one of the photos I took of my drawing on her leg.

Harlan greets us; smiling at her affectionately. "You're finally ready to get that tattoo?"

"So ready." Indy beams at him. "Did Theo show you the piece?"

"He showed me some gorgeous pin up girl. Very sexy."

I growl. "That's my wife you're talking about."

Harlan winks at her. "Some things don't change, do they?"

"What's that supposed to mean?" I ask as we follow him through to the station that he has set up for us.

"You growled at me for flirting with her the first time you brought her here too." He pats the leather seat. "Pants off and up you get."

Indy shimmies out of her pants. She's wearing cute black panties that give decent coverage since he's going to be working on her entire leg.

He rests his back against the locker and crosses his arms over his chest. "Still remember what you're doing?"

"What I'm doing?" I start. I brought her in for him to work his magic.

"You drew it. You know how to use the tools." He cocks a brow. "Indy, you want me to copy your husband's masterpiece? Or do you want him to ink his own damn emotions on your skin?"

"But I haven't tattooed anyone in so long. I'm out of practice." I squeeze the back of my neck. I could mess it up. And it needs to be perfect. Indy deserves perfect.

"Do it." Indy reaches out to me. "Flaws and all. The tattoo is special to me because you drew it. It'll mean even more when you ink it too."

"If that's what you want." God, I love the way she makes me feel ten feet tall.

"It is."

I take a few deep breaths while I get set up. While I get the ink ready for the outline, which is what we're doing tonight. Harlan takes a seat to watch us for a while. The three of us chat and laugh about anything and everything while I start to outline. First, the petals on her foot, then the roses and vines on her calf.

Eventually Harlan tosses me a spare set of keys and tells me to lock up once we're done.

"It's so good, Theo," Indy tells me with bright eyes while I outline the roses on her hip. "I love that I'll wear something you made just for me forever."

"I love that you're wearing my mark." Seeing her with my design on her skin; it makes me so hard. Knowing that she's all mine. I put the gun down and bring her onto my lap on this little stool I'm sitting on. "My love. My wife. It's sexy as fuck."

"Ever do it in a tattoo shop?" She grinds down on my erection.

I rub my thumb along my bottom lip. "No."

Her eyes are dark and wanton. She rolls her lips between her teeth to moisten them. "Can I put it on the bucket list?"

"Scoot back." I inch her back so I can undo my pants. Grasping my cock I stroke it a couple of times. "It's all for you, sweetheart. Sit on it."

She wraps her hand around mine on my shaft and lines up the head of my cock to her entrance. I grit my teeth as she lowers herself onto me.

"Having you ink me…it feels incredibly intimate." She starts to move. "I'm really turned on."

"You're dripping." I run my lips over her throat. "And I love it."

She shivers as my piercings scrape against sensitive spot after sensitive spot. She starts to moan. We stare into each other's eyes as I fuck her slowly. Every movement is drenched in our love. And when she closes her eyes and holds on to me as her orgasm takes her, I watch, starstruck by my beautiful wife.

"I love you," I say against her ear. "I'm so happy that my life is with you. That you're here with me. And that we have an entire lifetime to spend together."

Indy

I sneak up on Theo in the kitchen of our new apartment—one with all modern fixtures and none of those hideous oranges or browns—while he stands in front of the open refrigerator. He's gorgeously clean shaven and wearing a tailored suit. Apparently there isn't a dress code that doesn't suit my husband. He gives me tingles every time I look at him.

A casserole dish in one hand and a fork in the other, he scoops up big mouthfuls of my mom's loaded macaroni and shovels it between his teeth. Even his enthusiasm for my mom's cooking is appealing to me.

She spoils him often. I swear Mom loves Theo more than me and EJ combined. She certainly makes his favorites for family dinner more than she makes mine. At first I think it was because she was trying to fill the space Gray left when he took off.

He sold his condo and quit his job. The last I heard, he was living in some beachside bungalow halfway around the world. He's still close with EJ and he checks in with my parents now and then, but he hasn't spoken to me since that day at the hospital.

I miss the Gray that I grew up with. He was a brother figure to me. A best friend long before he was a boyfriend.

But my heart belongs solely to Theo. I'm so glad that my family accepted him the way they did. It's been a year since we got married in an intimate ceremony in my parents' backyard. "Happy anniversary, husband."

"Oh fuck." His eyes turn round as he power chews. "Don't sneak up on a guy like that, sweetheart."

"Put the casserole down and step away from the fridge." I giggle.

He seals the foil around the edges and slides the dish back in the fridge before he turns around.

"You know how fond I..." his jaw slackens as he drinks me in. From the cowgirl boots and the roses on my leg, to the teacup kitten on my forearm, which is now permanent. There are leaves floating on the side of my nape and a small ouroboros on my wrist too. I might be a little addicted to letting my husband ink my skin. It always ends with him deep inside me. Though not always at the shop, because sometimes Harlan sticks around to talk.

The last time we were there, Harlan finished Cooper's wings on Theo's back. It took several sessions over the last few months. There was so much shading involved in bringing the feathers to life. And then Theo had Harlan ink *serás mi corazón siempre* on his left arm, which Theo told me translates to *you'll always be my heart*. Because I will always be the woman who brought his heart back to life.

He tosses the fork into the sink and crowds me back against the island. "Have I told you today how beautiful you are?"

I smile. "You tell me every day."

"Well, it needs repeating…" His gaze narrows on my hair, which is short on the sides and long on the top. He reaches out to touch one of the tendrils that Sadie dyed blue and curled this morning. "This looks amazing."

"Thank you."

He grips my side where a sliver of skin peeks through between the white lace of my dress as he leans in and kisses me. I part to the sweet thrust of his tongue before I pull away. "We better go. Or we'll be late."

"You're right." He exhales softly. "Part of me would rather stay home and bang your head against our headboard. God, wife, you're gorgeous."

"Later." I push him away because his words make me needy. "I'm starving."

"Did you remember to pack your swimsuit?" He holds the truck door open for me to climb in.

"I did." I press my lips together to fight my smile as he closes the door. Along with my bikinis, I may have packed something big and blue for when we're alone. Double checked the batteries. Made sure we had lube.

He climbs in the other side. "Do we need to confirm when America's flight gets in?"

"She said that she had some last minute things to wrap up, so she won't be flying in until the day after tomorrow."

"Perfect." He smiles at me softly as he starts the engine.

I haven't seen my bestie in six months. She's still living in the UK and life has been hectic. She's made new friends. She even started dating some guy. Fell in love. She's been pretty cryptic about him these last couple of months, so I was looking forward to finally meeting him when they joined us at the waterpark. Even if I was nervous because she has a wild streak and a type that isn't always what's best for her.

But then he changed his mind about dating her or something. I'm not sure what the details are, only that he broke my bestie's heart. And that she couldn't get a refund on his ticket. So now she's bringing her friend Dove.

I bite the inside of my cheek. EJ acted so weird when I told him that earlier.

Whatever. When we asked EJ and my parents and Theo's to join us in the Wisconsin Dells to celebrate the anniversary of the surgery that saved my life, I knew it wouldn't be perfect without my best friend. And I already like Dove from the times we've chatted via video when I've called America.

"It's going to be great." Theo parks outside the diner.

"I'm so excited." My gaze automatically goes to the clock on the dash. "Two o'clock."

He smiles as he takes his seatbelt off and leans over to clasp my cheek. "Want to get pancakes? I know a place."

"I love you." I wrap my arms around his neck and press my lips against his. "So much."

Every day. In a million little ways. For as long as we have.

Indy

Theo and EJ are at the bar talking, while I sit with my parents at the table after dinner. It's been a long but awesome day.

We drove up to the Dells early this morning, leaving our luggage in the vehicles while we spent time at the waterpark. Then we had lunch and checked into our rooms before we spent the rest of the afternoon swimming.

We followed that up with a nice family dinner. Of course Theo made Mom's day by telling her that nothing is as good as her macaroni. I swear, if I offered me up alongside a dish of her loaded macaroni and cheese he wouldn't be able to choose.

"We're going to go back to the hotel." Dad stands and offers Mom his hand. "It's been a long day and I'm ready to hit the hay. We'll leave you young ones to continue the party."

Mom exchanges a glance with Dad and yawns into her hand. "I'm worn out."

I stand and kiss each of them on the cheek. "Get some sleep. We'll see you for breakfast."

They leave, and I join my husband and brother at the bar. They're talking in legalese. I have no idea what the subject is and they both drop it when they notice me.

"Mom and Dad went back to the hotel." I wrap my arms around Theo's waist.

"It's going to be a huge day tomorrow. What with your family coming." EJ points at Theo's chest.

"And America and her friend too." Theo presses his lips to the top of my head. He knows how excited I am.

"Dove." I remind them.

EJ's jaw tightens and he scowls at the drink in his hand. "You and I are going to be outnumbered, Theo. When these girls get together...all hell will break loose."

"Pity she isn't still bringing the boyfriend instead." Theo chuckles.

"You know, I don't think she ever told me his name." It makes me uncomfortable for reasons I can't put my finger on. Other than my diagnosis, which I put off telling her for far too long, we've always shared everything.

EJ tugs the collar of his shirt away from his neck. "Well, it doesn't matter now, does it?"

"I suppose not."

A new song plays through the speakers and my husband smiles. "Want to dance?"

"Sure." I let him lead me onto the small dance floor.

We dance chest-to-chest and smile-to-smile until the song is almost over. My arms are wrapped around his neck as I press my lips to his ear. "Meet me in the room in ten minutes?"

"Five." He squeezes my ass.

"Five." I step back, bite my lip and nod. I have a little bucket list surprise for him.

I tap my fingers against my thigh as I ride the elevator up to our floor. Swiping the keycard, I enter our hotel room and make a beeline for my suitcase. The blue alien vibrator is right where I put it, along with a tube of lube.

My insides tingle. Butterflies fill my belly. I still remember the first time Theo admitted that he imagined filling me with it. Back then there was no chance that I could have taken it. I wasn't well enough to even consider it, but now…

The door opens. My gorgeous husband walks up behind me. "I couldn't wait any longer to get you alone."

I turn my face for his kiss. My whole body follows. Until I'm holding the vibrator between us. "That's good, because I have a surprise for you."

"You do." His eyes darken as they land on the vibrator. "Indy?"

"I was thinking it's been on the bucket list for a while."

"You want me to fuck you with it?" His voice turns into a growl as he takes it out of my hands.

A shiver chases down my spine. "Please."

"Then strip for me, sweetheart. Get on the bed."

I tug at the knot in the fabric behind my neck. It comes undone, and I shimmy the black dress down my body until it's a puddle on the floor. My bra and panties follow. I climb up in the middle of the bed, my head elevated by the pillows so that I can see him through the angle of my spread knees.

He lays the toy and the lube on the comforter while he strips out of his own clothes. Then he climbs onto the bed and smooths his hands up my thighs, from my knees to my core. His thumb rolls across my clit and little lightning strikes go off inside me. I arch to his touch, my body already eager from hours of imagining him using the vibrator on me.

He takes his time. He always does. Teasing one of my nipples with his teeth, he palms the weight of the other while his fingers work their magic inside me. They open me up slowly, leave me breathless and aching and desperate. "Theo."

"You're going to take this whole thing so beautifully." His heavily-hooded eyes smolder as they drink me in.

The way he looks at me...is a strong aphrodisiac. It makes me feel powerful. Like I can accomplish anything. "I'm ready. I want it."

Picking up that thick blue cock, he covers it in lube. "I'm going to love watching you take it."

I inhale a sharp breath as he sits the head at my entrance.

He eases it in nice and slow. As prepared as I am...it's so thick that it takes a few moments to get used to the feeling. And then he turns it on.

"Argh." My hands fist the sheets as my eyes flutter closed. It's *holy shit* good. Even at its softest setting.

"Ready to take more, sweetheart?" Theo asks with a devilish growl.

I nod.

He fiddles with the buttons and a shockwave of high power vibrations have my body on the edge in a matter of seconds. "Oh God...I'm so..."

He turns it down and the orgasm recedes before it can take over. Over the next few minutes we play a game of cat and mouse. Him changing the vibrations and bringing me to the edge before giving me a breather. Until the next time when he doesn't change the setting and I tumble headlong into an orgasm that melts my synapses and turns my body to jelly.

When I'm done and I can't handle anymore he pulls the vibrator from between my legs and tosses it aside. Covering me with his body, he rests his weight on his elbows while he slowly enters me. "You are so sexy. Watching you come apart like that...God, I love you."

"I love you." I hold him close as we start to move, and even though I've just come harder than I've ever come in my life, those embers stir into sparks. And when he hits that spot inside me just right a new orgasm floods every cell of my body. His climax follows closely.

Afterward, he holds me in his arms like every second we get to spend this close is precious. I love that neither of us ever take the other for granted. That we both know what it's like to not have a future to be scared or excited about.

"There's something else I want to put on the list." His lips tickle my ear.

"What is it?"

He places his hand on my belly. "I want to put a family of our own on the bucket list. Not for right now. Or even the next couple of years. But I've been thinking about all the things that I would want to do with you in this life that we share. And a family is definitely on the list for me."

I press my lips together as I grow teary-eyed. Family has always been important to me. I imagine a little dark haired girl with my eyes. A boy with my copper locks and his daddy's eyes. "I want that too."

Indy

"Are you okay to go in and get America and her friend without me?" Theo squeezes my knee as he stares squarely at the road. He won't say it but he still has PTSD from the last time we picked America up from the airport.

I lean over and kiss his cheek. "I've got this. I promise."

"Okay. I'll do the usual." He draws a loop with his finger in the air.

"Be back as quick as I can." I grin as I jump out of the cab and head into the terminal.

I walk toward the carousel where luggage from the flight America and Dove were on is going 'round, but I can't spot either of them among the waiting passengers.

I don't notice the man until I walk right into him.

"I'm sorry. I should have been looking where I was going." Stepping back to give him space, I lift my gaze...my God, does he look good. My pulse starts to race. It's like staring at a ghost. "Gray?"

"Indy." His jaw is rock hard as he stares down at me, those icy blue eyes so much cooler than they used to be.

My palms start to sweat and my heart lifts into the back of my throat. It's been over a year and it still pains me that I hurt him so badly. I find myself wanting to reach out to him. Wanting to hug him. It would be as familiar as putting on an old, comfy sweater. But that's not who we are anymore. We're not friends. We are not family.

"Gray..." My voice comes out far too tiny. "What are you doing here?"

Acknowledgements

Thank you so much for reading The Heartbreak List. I hope you loved it.

I guess I should probably start with apologizing if this book caused you pain or distress. I know personally, I cried for about 70% of it because it hit close to home in some ways. I'm not sure I'll ever be able to read it without tearing up, but to me, that just makes this book that much more special. My heart still physically aches when I think about it.

To my writing coach, Chasity Moody Oleson. There is no amount of thanks that will ever be enough to sum up my appreciation for the hard work you put into talking me through this book.

To Chelle Pimblott, you have been my rock these last couple of years while my brain has been all topsy turvy. Thank you for your input.

To Kimberly Millhouse Holmgren, thank you for your yellow highlighter efforts!! It can be so hard to see the roses for the trees sometimes. You made it easy.

Natasha Joanne, literally the best PA ever. Sorry, I am such a disorganized mess. Thank you for your graphics and constant reminders to get things done. Love you, woman!

Tami Lund, thank you for polishing all the edges off my mess. I couldn't do this without you xx

And again, thank you to everyone who picked up this book and gave it a chance!!! I am so thankful that I get to share my stories with you.

Play List

Single You Up: Jordan Davis.
You Proof: Morgan Wallen
Marry Me: Thomas Rhett
The Fighter: Keith Urban ft Carrie Underwood
Alive: Adelita's Way
Shut up and Dance: Walk The Moon
Can I Shower At Your Place: Amy Shark
Treat You Better: Shawn Mendes

Also By Misti Murphy

Misti Murphy's other titles:
https://www.mistimurphy.com/readingorder.html

Printed in Great Britain
by Amazon